A notice to every nervous bride—consider this:

For me, being a wedding director is a little like substituting for Cinderella's fairy godmother sans a magic wand. As a bridal consultant I routinely deal with bad hair days, grooms having third thoughts and hors d'oeuvres that won't stretch far enough to feed a horde of unexpected cousins. On the up side, the career benefits include a constant diet of romance and an aisle seat.

So if you want your wedding to go off without a hitch, call me.

Andrea Kirkland

Please address questions and book requests to: Harlequin Reader Service
U.S.: 3010 Walden Ave., P.O. Box 1325, Buffalo, NY 14269
Canadian: P.O. Box 609, Fort Erie, Ont. L2A 5X3

Marriage, Inc.

ELIZABETH MORRIS
THIS DAY FORWARD

Harlequin Books

TORONTO • NEW YORK • LONDON
AMSTERDAM • PARIS • SYDNEY • HAMBURG
STOCKHOLM • ATHENS • TOKYO • MILAN
MADRID • WARSAW • BUDAPEST • AUCKLAND

HARLEQUIN BOOKS
225 Duncan Mill Road, Don Mills,
Ontario, Canada M3B 3K9

ISBN 0-373-30123-5

THIS DAY FORWARD

A Letter from the Author

Dear Reader,

This Day Forward was my first romantic novel and has always been my sentimental favorite, although I must admit there were times during the months of writing that I was tempted to abandon the project. As a beginner, I had no idea what power characters can exert. Who knew that Andrea Kirkland and Matt Donaldson would grow from sketchy paper people into opinionated individuals who invaded my head day and night? They argued with me over every line of dialogue, refusing to budge until I let them speak their own words in their own style. They ignored my attempts to help them overcome the problems that kept them apart and insisted on finding their own solutions. Although I never quite knew from scene to scene where they might lead me, I finally gave up and followed them—it was either that or miss my deadline.

Eventually I learned to trust their judgment, and even better, we came to like each other very much. I hope that you, too, will find them good friends.

Best,

Elizabeth Morris

To Eddie

Chapter One

Silk dress swirling in emerald folds against her legs and fingers curved lightly around the stem of a champagne flute, Andrea Kirkland moved through the crowded salon, every bit the cool professional. Not one of the several hundred wedding guests would have suspected that this was her debut as a bridal consultant.

"The crab puffs are divine! Who is your caterer, dear?" a city councilman's wife cooed, shagging her arm.

"We use Coronet, Mrs. Milford. It's a small firm, and just getting started, but their quality is impeccable. Have you tried the stuffed mushrooms?" she responded to another in a long string of glowing testimonials to the lavish buffet. Graciously providing the caterer's business card, Andrea resumed her circuit of the room.

But her serenity was only a pose; her insides felt like tepid aspic, and her arches were on the verge of collapse. *Another ten minutes of smiling and my face will crumble like a wet saltine,* she told herself wryly.

Pausing beside the French doors, she peeked surreptitiously at her watch. In one more hour the reception would be history; she could spend the rest of Christmas Eve in a steaming tub with nothing more pressing to think about than how to keep her five-foot, four-inch frame from slipping under the suds. The prospect was enticing, but she pushed it aside, compulsively rechecking every item on a mental list of "must dos."

Reassured that she hadn't forgotten anything crucial, she surveyed the room, mentally granting herself a well-deserved pat on the back. The decorations on which she had lavished so much time and attention were spectacular. Masses of creamy poinsettias provided a beautiful contrast to long-leaf pine and flickering red tapers, and a perfectly formed, twelve-foot spruce ladened with white velvet doves and hand-blown crystal bells graced the alcove beside the antebellum staircase.

Glancing through the leaded glass panes at the Currier and Ives confection outside, Andrea drew in a satisfied breath. The snow had been an unexpected bonus; a white Christmas in this part of Virginia was rare, but since late morning, fat, fluffy crystals had been falling at a gentle pace, draping the rolling landscape in a pristine veil. It wasn't deep enough yet to pose a serious inconvenience, and it provided just the right ambience.

The knot of tension in the pit of her stomach began to unravel. For most of December, a host of imaginary disasters had dragged their clanking chains through her dreams: what if the bride—not exactly a paragon of grace—tripped over her train and plunged headlong into the five-tiered cake? The ghastly vision of Clarissa Bellamy, the mayor's daughter, peering owlishly at the cream of Laurel Valley society through a mask of egg whites and sugar was far more terrifying than Ebenezer Scrooge's specters. But the ghosts proved nothing more than that—Clarissa was now safely Mrs. Albert Fairchild.

The only jarring note had been the mother of the bride. Opinionated and hopelessly bourgeois, the woman raised tackiness to an art form. In Andrea's former job in a New York fashion salon she'd learned how to handle difficult clients, but Mrs. Bellamy, the prototype of the breed, seemed hell-bent on making her life miserable.

Now, as she spotted Mrs. Bellamy charging toward her full tilt, exasperation darkened her luminous gray eyes to the color of wood smoke. The woman's ample figure was sausaged into bright red satin, and she sailed up on an overpowering tide of Shalimar.

"You're a magician, Andy—an absolute wizard! How you managed all this in four months is nothing less than miraculous! Doesn't my little Clarissa look regal? Clothes with simple tailored lines are so right for her," Winona said smugly, the orchid corsage on her bosom quivering with the excess of her maternal pride.

Andrea took a hasty sip of champagne to subdue the amusement welling up in her throat. If the dowager's original plans had not been scuttled, her daughter would have marched down the aisle of St. Paul's Presbyterian as a raw-boned replica of the Princess of Wales.

"She is lovely, Mrs. Bellamy, and I'm glad you're pleased with my work."

"So far, so good. But as they say, it isn't over till it's over," the mayor's wife warned.

Andy gritted her teeth; the woman's fondness for clichés was a constant annoyance.

"I must say I'm still disappointed about the ushers. I had my heart set on having them dressed as toy soldiers. I suppose you did the best you could, but I'm sure if you'd tried a bit harder, you'd have found someone to make the costumes," Winona said, pouting. Switching gears, she brightened and leaned closer, nodding toward a gathering at the punch bowl. "That woman in the hideous mauve suit is my best friend, Muriel Ellison. She's a dear person, but as the old saying goes, her taste is all in her mouth. Her Nancy got engaged last month, and if Muriel doesn't have professional help, the wedding will be a total mess. I'll have her call you after the holidays."

With a final proprietary pat on Andy's shoulder, Mrs. Bellamy steamed off again into the sea of guests, her corseted form parting the waves like a crimson-clad battleship.

"Can I have the autograph of Laurel Valley's latest social sensation, preferably on a nice fat bonus?" Jason Markham, her indispensable assistant, sauntered over, a tray of champagne flutes perched jauntily on fingertips that would've looked more at home balancing a football.

"Bonus, my foot! Stingy as that woman is, we'll be lucky to break even," Andy fumed. Belatedly remembering where she was, she looked around guiltily. Reverend and Mrs. Westphall were a few paces away, but their intense absorption in the crab puffs made it unlikely that they'd overheard her rash assessment of their hostess. Lowering her tone to an indignant whisper, she continued, "Yesterday she had the nerve to cancel the florist because she claimed he was padding the bill. I had to write a personal check before he'd deliver the arrangements to the church!"

"We'll make it up, and plenty more besides," Jason murmured, a jubilant grin lighting the tobacco brown expanse of his face. "W.B. has a lot of clout around here. If she says we're in, we're in."

Andy felt a flash of affection for the young man. Hiring Jason, a graduate student in hotel management at nearby Prescott College, was the smartest thing she'd done when she opened Weddings Unlimited, her consultant service, six months ago. He was born and raised in this small Southern town, and his knowledge of its social dos and don'ts had saved her a few embarrassing gaffs. But more importantly, the two of them shared an effortless camaraderie that was developing into bedrock friendship.

"Mrs. Bellamy's not going to give us a good recommendation. Every time she opens her mouth, a complaint comes out. I'm sick of hearing how badly I've goofed up her daughter's wedding."

"That's bull! Matt Donaldson told me this is one of the best-managed affairs he's ever seen, and he ought to know. When you get a chance, he'd like to talk to you." The undisguised eagerness on her assistant's long face gave him the air of a Great Dane hopeful of a scratch behind the ears.

Andrea looked blank. "Matt Donaldson?"

"I've only mentioned him a million times," he reminded her patiently. "He's on loan to the college from the Regent Hotel chain—holds seminars in customer relations and all that good stuff. If you'd like to meet him, I'll go cut him out of the herd."

"Whoa, cowboy. Have you forgotten we're running a reception here?" The last thing Andrea wanted was to be roped into a dusty discussion with some pompous academic. The straps of her high-heeled sandals were waffling her insteps, and her stomach made no secret of its displeasure at being ignored all day. She set her half-finished champagne on Jason's tray, her fingers trembling slightly with prolonged tension.

"Our newlyweds have to be at the airport by five. I know it's only three now, but we can't have them missing the plane. Has the limo arrived yet?"

He nodded. "The chauffeur is in the kitchen stuffing himself and complaining about the weather."

An internal alarm went off. "Are the roads bad?" she queried worriedly.

"Not yet, but the snow is changing to freezing rain. It could get messy later."

"Oh, Lord, the airport's sure to close! Ten to one, the only snow-removal equipment they have is a shovel and a push broom," Andrea groaned. "See if you can reserve the bridal suite at the Laurel Inn just in case."

"It's as good as done, boss."

"And check..."

Jason's amber eyes glinted with amusement. "Take it easy," he interrupted. "Everything's under control unless you collapse and we have to call the rescue squad. Find a quiet corner and park it, will you? I can handle things out here."

"I could use a breather," Andy sighed, thinking longingly of the secluded library off the entrance hall of the Bellamy mansion. "Be back in five minutes. Oh, and Jase..." She paused in her flight to refuge long enough to add, "Ask your Mr. Donaldson to drop by the shop next week. I'll bring in lunch, and the three of us can talk."

The broad smile with which her assistant rewarded her would have warmed the heart of the pickiest orthodontist.

A cursory once-over of the cozy book-lined retreat revealed no other fugitives from the gala—but then the dim light from the lamp on the desk did not reach the wing chair in the far corner. Breathing in the mixed, pleasant pungency of leather bindings and faintly fruity pipe tobacco, Andrea slipped off the offending sandals and massaged her strained calf muscles, wriggling her stockinged toes in the luxurious plush of the beige carpet. Respite from the noise outside improved the throbbing in her temples, but she was still annoyed by her latest encounter with her client.

"Take your toy soldiers and stuff them! If it weren't for me, this wedding would've been a Grand Ol' Oprey version of the

Nutcracker Suite,'' she muttered with a glare toward Winona's portrait over the mantel.

Retrieving a comb from her purse, she padded over to the gilt-framed mirror and attacked her chestnut hair with a vigor that sent it flying in a honey-dappled halo around her gamin face.

"Twenty-eight years old, and I don't have the backbone God gave an eggplant! Why have I been letting that pretentious penny-pincher walk all over me? Next time she opens her big mouth, I'm going to strangle her with her own tongue!" she promised, replacing the comb and pulling out a lipstick.

A discreet cough from the far side of the room so surprised Andy that the tube of soft pink cosmetic she was applying flew from her fingers. Swallowing the impulse to scream, she whirled to face the intruder.

"What're you doing here?" she blurted out, mentally cursing her penchant for holding solitary conversations. If this man repeated her embarrassing soliloquy, Weddings Unlimited would be dead in the water.

"I came in to nurse a headache, and I must've dozed off. Sorry if I startled you, Miss Kirkland." The muscles under the man's pin-striped suit were obviously trained to work as a team; he rose from the wing chair and stretched to a height of six feet without a single wasted motion. Stifling a yawn, he sauntered over and extended a hand that looked as if it could easily crush tin cans. "I've been trying to get close enough to introduce myself all afternoon. I'm Matthew Donaldson."

The planes of his face were too angular to deserve the label handsome—striking was a more accurate adjective. His aquiline nose and his high cheekbones gave him the look of a warrior, and the jutting chin hinted at obstinacy. But the power of his features was tempered by deep-set eyes the shade of polished mahogany, and small, upward-slanting lines at the corners of his full mouth could only have been etched in by humor.

Shaking his proffered hand perfunctorily, Andrea decided that her best move was a strategic retreat.

"Pleased to meet you, Mr. Donaldson. Now if you'll excuse me, I have to get back to the reception." She quickly recovered

the lipstick and was halfway to the door when his deep voice
brought her up short.

"You'll probably need these." Matthew's Lincolnesque face
was perfectly serious as he held out her shoes, but his eyes
danced with mischief.

Mouth open and her cheeks flushed a dusty rose, Andy
stared down at her unshod feet. Under the circumstances, there
was only one thing to do; she started to laugh. He added a
gravelly chuckle, and some mysterious alchemy between them
filled the library with pure gold.

"Mrs. Bellamy would've died a natural death if I'd come
charging out barefooted," she said, reaching for the sandals.

Instead of relinquishing them, Matt knelt down in front of
her.

"In college I had a part-time job as a shoe salesman. Let's see
if I've still got the touch." His hands dwarfed her slender foot
as he lifted it and slipped the flimsy straps in place.

She teetered uncertainly, searching for support, but her
choices were limited. The doorknob was out of reach, and the
nearest table was cluttered with fragile bric-a-brac; she could
either risk smashing Winona's twin Dresden shepherdesses, fall
on her rear or steady herself against him. The decision was
surprisingly easy.

I'll bet the man's allergic to kryptonite, she mused, her fingers gripping his shoulder a tad more tightly than the situation
called for. An interesting vision of Donaldson in a phone booth
switching his suit for tights and a cape flashed into her mind.

He grinned at her impishly, and arranging his face in a par-
ody of an earnest clerk, he continued, "I have to be honest,
miss. This style doesn't give you much leather for the money,
and it's hardly practical in a blizzard. Now we stock a lovely
army boot that comes in twelve stunning shades."

"I'd prefer sneakers. Something in red with a high heel,
perhaps," she joked in return.

"Sorry, my grandmother bought the last pair. Could I interest you in hand-embroidered Alaskan mukluks?"

Andrea's answering quip died in her throat as his fingers
cradled her heel; the humor of the moment metamorphosed
into subtle warmth. For the space of three heartbeats, she for-

got to breathe. She stared down at the nape of his neck, wondering at its vulnerability and liking the way his dark hair lay in curly-crisp commas against his olive skin.

"No, thank you. Whale fur makes me sneeze," she replied after her lungs started working again. The lightness she was trying for came out a husky murmur.

He rose to his feet and grinned down at her. "Glass slippers, then. Every princess should have some. Never know when you might run into an enchanted frog."

"You're mixing your fairy tales, Mr. Donaldson. Cinderella's prince was charming, not amphibious."

Winona Bellamy's abrupt entrance brought Andrea back from never-never land with a decisive thump.

"I've been looking all over for you," the mayor's wife complained, marching in with Jason in tow. "The airport runways are icing over. I doubt seriously that Clarissa and Albert will be able to connect with the flight to Aruba."

"I'll call the airline and reschedule them for tomorrow, Mrs. Bellamy. Not many people fly on Christmas Day, and it shouldn't be hard to get reservations."

"Mr. Markham's already taken care of that," the woman informed her coldly. "Thank God he has his mind on what he's doing."

Anger tightened Andrea's chest, but she held it at bay. "Then I don't understand the problem."

"What will Clary and Albert do tonight?"

What comes naturally, if they have any sense, Andy thought grimly. "Pardon?" she queried aloud.

"My daughter won't hear of spending her wedding night at home."

"I understand her feeling." Fatigue put an edge to Andrea's voice. Catching her assistant's pained grimace, she modified the tone. "I mean, naturally Clarissa wants everything to be perfect, and I promise you, it will be. The newlyweds will stay at the Laurel Inn tonight."

Jason shook his head dolefully. "There's not a vacant hotel room left in the valley. The Romance Writers' convention has them all booked up until after New Year's."

"Andrea, I'm very disappointed in the way you've handled this," Mrs. Bellamy snapped.

Andy's temper reached its flash point. "You're holding me responsible for the weather? I . . ."

"Miss Kirkland has been discussing the snowstorm with me, Winona, and I believe I have a solution. If the Presidential Suite at the Richmond Regent will be satisfactory, I'll see that it's made available," Donaldson cut in smoothly.

"That's most kind of you, Matthew—the Regent is the finest hotel in the area—but Richmond is nearly forty miles away. The roads . . ."

"We're prepared for most emergencies. I can have a four-wheel-drive vehicle here before the reception's over."

"I'm so grateful for your help." The woman shifted her bulk, a crafty gleam lighting her dishwater pale eyes. "The mayor and I hadn't counted on the extra expense. Does the Regent offer any type of discount?"

"Your daughter and her husband will be our guests, of course," Matthew said as he picked up the phone on the desk and dialed.

Andrea gaped in disbelief as he quickly completed the arrangements.

"Make sure there are fresh flowers in the suite, and, oh, yes, a champagne breakfast in the morning, Ben." Donaldson cradled the receiver, and taking the mollified dowager's arm, escorted her back to the salon.

"How'd he do that?" Andrea queried the beaming Jason as they followed.

"Being a Regent big shot didn't hurt," her assistant replied smugly. "When I grow up, I'm going to be just like him. The guy's only thirty-five and already district manager of a major corporation."

"If he hadn't stepped in, I'd be roasting on the open fire along with the chestnuts," Andy murmured, watching the attractive man ply the mother of the bride with punch. "I don't know how to thank him."

"You'll think of something." Jason gave her a nudge in Donaldson's direction.

She did not have far to go; Matt met her in the center of the room just as the orchestra began a waltz.

"I really appreciate what you did, Mr. Donaldson. Please have the bill sent to me, or if you prefer, I'll write you a check after the reception."

"That's not necessary. Southern hospitality is Regent's hallmark. Besides, it's just good business. Mr. Bellamy will think of us next time he hosts the regional mayors' conference."

"But I'm grateful for your help, and I'd really like to pay..."

"Oh, well, if you insist. Half the price is that you dance with me," he cut in, slipping an arm around her waist.

"I suppose I can squeeze that out of the budget. What's the other half?"

"The Regent staff has had problems with wedding management. I'd like you to give them some technical assistance."

Andy eyed him dubiously. "I'll do my best, but my experience is rather limited," she chattered, wary of the warmth his touch renewed. "What kinds of problems?"

He drew her close, steering her into the old-fashioned rhythm. "Mostly scheduling. And they're also rusty on the latest methods for strangling the bride's mother," he teased.

She ducked her head in embarrassment. "That wasn't meant for public consumption. My mouth sometimes gets ahead of my brain, Mr. Donaldson."

"Matt," he prompted. "Personally, I thought it was a damn good idea, and I promise I won't snitch on you. Now hush up and let me concentrate. Frogs can't waltz without counting."

Thanks to childhood ballet lessons and an innate sense of timing, Andrea automatically made the right moves—a fortunate reflex, since her mind was too busy with sensory overload to guide her feet.

He spun her through the stately cadence, the crystal chandelier, suspended from the high ceiling, showering them with fragmentary rainbows, at once brilliant and soft. The music blended snatches of conversation into an ebb and flow of sound as soothing as the whisper of a distant ocean.

Matthew was wearing a heathery cologne he did not really need; the clean male scent of his skin was fragrance enough. He moved against her with a lazy, sensual grace, mesmerizing her with the power of his body.

Andy could not remember ever having felt this way before, though admittedly her basis for comparison was limited. The pressures of paying her own expenses and maintaining good grades had put a severe crimp into her social life at Ohio State. Later in New York, dedication to the intricate details of launching spring and fall lines for Couturière Margo consumed most of her energy. Her only serious relationship had been with Patrick Harahan, a designer at Margo's.

In the middle of a particularly tricky series of steps, she caught herself wondering if Matthew Donaldson was as expert in other physical areas as he was at dancing. The thought made her stumble.

"Sorry." She dismissed the dizzying flood of perceptions, blushing furiously.

"Are you all right?"

Concern flickered in his eyes, and his arms tightened to steady her; the gesture only added to her vertigo.

"I just got overheated. Er, I mean, it's w-warm in here, isn't it?" she stammered. Her breathing was a trifle ragged, and she pulled back. "Let's sit the rest of this one out."

"Not a bad idea." Matt grinned wryly; she couldn't tell whether he was relieved or disappointed.

"Hang on; I'll get us out of traffic."

He steered her across the dance floor toward a quiet alcove, stopping under the holly-garlanded archway that led into the entrance hall. They stood facing each other, his hands resting lightly on her shoulders.

"Feeling better now?"

Andy's yes was hesitant. In all honesty, the way she was feeling before was not half bad.

Needing something to distract her attention, she fixed her eyes on the greenery above; a large bunch of mistletoe dangled enticingly above his head. She swallowed nervously, hoping he wouldn't notice it, then praying he would.

He did.

"I'm allergic to flies, croaking gives me a sore throat, and I hate lily pads," he complained softly, raising her chin with the tip of his finger. "There's only one way to get rid of this damned spell...."

His kiss lay gentle on her mouth, the fragile brush of a hummingbird darting, exploring, then, finding nectar, lingering to savor it. Much too quickly, it was gone.

Andy stifled an involuntary move to recapture it, willing her hands not to cradle his face. "You haven't changed a bit, Matt. I guess it didn't work." Her tone was joking but shaky.

He shrugged and twined his fingers with hers. "Then we'll have to try again."

Andrea loosened his grip, concerned that she was feeling too much, too fast; her three-month affair with Patrick Harahan had begun with the same dizzying rush of attraction. *You jumped without knowing where you were going to land and ended up scraping a mess off your feet. Don't make the same mistake this time,* she told herself.

"Too much Christmas Eve magic can be hazardous to the health, not to mention my career" came out more briskly than she intended. "I do have to get back to work now, but thanks again for your help. I'll check my schedule and let you know when I'll be available for a meeting at the hotel."

As they turned back to the salon, he smiled down at her; there was much more than humor in the depths of his eyes. "The last five minutes paid your debt in full. The fact is, I owe you a refund. Do you have plans for this evening?"

"Uh-huh—a hot tub, a hunk of brandied fruitcake, then I'll probably hibernate for a week."

"You're going to miss the Christmas concert? That's as close as you can come to treason in Laurel Valley."

"I didn't even know about it. What's the big deal?"

"The Oratorio Society performs, and there's a potluck supper afterward. This year it's being held at Prescott's chapel. Would you like to go with me?"

She shook her head. "That sounds nice, but I'm really bushed."

"My little sister, Jennifer, is singing with the choir. It's a first for her—she's never performed in public before." His face reflected love, pride, and something else Andrea couldn't quite read. "The kid's taking it all in stride; I'm the one who needs moral support."

The eagerness in his voice sorely tested her decision, but she stood firm. "I haven't put up my tree yet, and there are still a few presents that need wrapping. Thanks for asking, though."

"In case you change your mind, the concert starts at eight-thirty. I'll be in one of the front pews, wearing mistletoe."

As Matthew disappeared into the crowd, Andy felt a light touch on her shoulder.

"Way to go, boss. I knew you two were made for each other," Jason whispered.

THE BEDRAGGLED FIR Andrea had positioned in front of the living room window in her small apartment on Petunia Lane leaned at the precarious angle of a reveler after one too many trips to the wassail bowl, and the rope of plastic holly she had taped around the door frame was already sagging in the middle.

Arms akimbo, she surveyed her feeble attempts at yuletide cheer with little enthusiasm and wondered why she had bothered. "I don't even like Christmas!" she muttered, picking up an elaborate card from her parents that had come in yesterday's mail.

Duty demanded that she call Cincinnati to acknowledge its receipt, but she made no move toward the phone. Even if her parents were home, which was doubtful, they would be nearing the climax of an annual argument that had started the previous New Year's Eve, and the prospect of becoming a long-distance referee was even more depressing than the lopsided tree.

Andrea's jaundiced view was not a recent acquisition; she had to sift through a number of painful holidays before she uncovered the wonderful Christmases she had spent with the Mascari family, her next-door neighbors in Ohio. The thought made her scramble for a box of photographs she had stowed on the closet shelf.

The framed eight-by-ten she retrieved had been taken just before the pageant at Our Lady of Hope where the newest addition to the prolific family was to be the main attraction of the living crèche. "It wouldn't be Christmas without a Mascari in the manger" was Father Clanahan's favorite joke.

Although time had faded some of the picture's colors, the happiness radiating from the subjects' faces was as clear as it had been the night the picture was taken. Squeezed into the place of honor at Mama Rosa's feet, twelve-year-old Andrea grinned self-consciously at the camera, with her fair skin and gray eyes, as noticeable among the sturdy, dark-haired Mascaris as a lily in a tulip garden. But when she was with her neighbors, she never felt out of place or unwanted, as she sometimes did at home. Children were the heart of the Mascari family, and there was always room for one more.

Andrea was not going to settle for less than that; long ago she had decided that her future would contain at least six babies. Each little face was perfectly pictured in her mind now.

"And their father, of course," she reminded herself, nibbling on one of the lumpy, strange-tasting sugar cookies she had thrown together when she got home after the Bellamy reception. The features at the head of her fantasy table had always been hazy—Patrick certainly would not have filled the role— but to her surprise, and no little dismay, she found that they had suddenly taken on a new clarity. Matthew Donaldson was now smiling at her over his imaginary eggnog.

"Cut that out," she muttered. All the more leery of the instant magic he had woven, she tried to dispel it. "Champagne on an empty stomach does weird things to the brain—he's probably boring as hell."

Grimacing, she threw down the cookie, and the assesment of Matt's personality notwithstanding, decided to attend the the concert. "I'm not going to see him. I just need some fresh air," she told herself, rummaging through her closet for something to wear.

Ten minutes later she surveyed the growing pile of discards on her bed in disgust. Dressing wasn't usually such a major production, but somehow it seemed vitally important that she look just right tonight. "Enough, already! This is a Laurel Valley concert, not a New York fashion show," she said, slipping on tailored slacks and a matching cashmere sweater. A whisper of dove-gray eye shadow and a touch of lipstick completed the drill; her fine-grained skin required no help from a bottle, and blusher would have been redundant over the healthy rose of her cheeks.

"You're truly crazy, you know that?" she informed her reflection. The insistent buzzing of the door bell cut off further diagnosis of her mental state.

"That can't be anybody but Agnes Avant," she groaned, pulling on a pair of soft leather boots. Her nosy landlady had a penchant for popping in at inconvenient hours, and to prevent an endless siege of the latest Laurel Valley gossip, Andrea put on her down jacket and knit cap.

"I was just on my way out, Mrs. Avant," Andrea began as she answered the door. But the rest of the excuse died in her throat, and her mouth dropped in astonishment at the surprise waiting outside in the hallway.

Chapter Two

A gingerbread mansion topped with chocolate-frosted turrets and surrounded by a jelly-bean wall stood grandly on the foil-covered tray Matthew Donaldson was holding. His eyes clouded as they took in Andrea's apparel. "I should have called first, but you said you didn't have any plans for the evening. I won't keep you long," he said.

"I was on my way to the chapel. I changed my mind about the concert," she admitted sheepishly. "Do enchanted frogs always carry their castles around with them?"

He laughed, anticipation replacing disappointment on his face. "I snitched a couple of these from the Regent, and I'm trying to dispose of the evidence. If an irate chef with a Polish accent comes around, you don't know me," he instructed as Andrea ushered him into the living room.

"You have no idea how much I needed this. I was beginning to feel like a Grinch because my tree is so terrible," she said, making room on the coffee table for the sugary concoction.

"It's not quite as bad as Charlie Brown's," Matt said diplomatically.

They stood looking at each other awkwardly.

"I guess it's too early to go to the chapel," Andrea said finally, stripping off her hastily donned outerwear. "Would you care for eggnog?"

"No, thanks, I hate the stuff."

Remembering her earlier fantasy, Andrea worked hard to suppress a grin. "Me, too. Take off your coat and make yourself comfortable."

As Matthew followed her suggestion, Andrea studied him covertly through the thick fringe of her lashes. Her assessment at the reception hadn't been wrong; if anything, she had underestimated the man's attractiveness. His navy sweater made no attempt to hide the way his finely proportioned upper body tapered into the hard, flat planes of his stomach—power without bulk. And the way he fitted into the Levi's made the inseams cry for mercy.

When the tour was over, infatuation stretched out before her like a rosy, cloud-lined abyss. *Go on and jump,* an inner voice urged.

Shut up, fool, she ordered it, concentrating on his gift. She touched one of the diamond-paned windows with a careful finger. "No one ever gave me a castle before," she murmured.

"Tastes as good as it looks. Try a bite of shingle." Matt broke a small piece of chocolate from the roof and popped it into her mouth.

A tingle of electricity zipped down her spine as his fingers lightly brushed her lips, then moved on to trace the curve of her cheek.

"Would you like a cup of coffee? It won't take me a minute to make some. Or how about cognac? All I have to do is pour that," she chattered nervously, breaking the contact. She reached for the decanter beside the castle, knocking over the framed picture she had left on the table in the process.

Matt rescued it. "Is this your family?"

Andrea shook her head regretfully. "The Mascaris were our next-door neighbors. I stayed with them the year my parents spent the holidays in Greece, so I got in on the family portrait," she explained.

"There certainly were a lot of them," he mused aloud.

"Nineteen kids, if you counted all the cousins. I never had to take my dolls over to the Mascaris because there were always real babies to play with. I love big families, don't you?"

His glance was startled. "I never thought much about it," he said, reaching for his coat. "We really should get going. I promised Jenny I'd sit up front where she could see me."

The change in his manner was oddly abrupt, but Andrea dismissed it as anxiety over his sister's coming performance.

Outside, all that remained of the storm was an occasional flake drifting through the icy air; Petunia Lane was a white-gowned matron festooned with sparkling baubles. Residents of the neighborhood had spared neither expense nor imagination in celebration of the season. Plastic reindeer and camels vied for grazing space on the pocket handkerchief lawns, and strings of multicolored lights twinkled from every window, porch and bush in sight.

As Andrea and Matthew mushed along the snowy sidewalk, the crescent moon and a host of stars peered cautiously at them through a tear in the thinning clouds.

He reached over to tuck the end of her knitted scarf more snugly about her throat. "The closest cleared parking space I could find was near the chapel. I hope you don't mind walking."

"Not at all. I love being out in snow."

"Me, too." Matt balled up a handful of white crystals and aimed at the mailbox on the corner. "Jenny can't get enough of the stuff, either. She made me promise to build her an igloo tomorrow."

"It better be for midget Eskimos. There are barely four inches on the ground. Back home in Ohio, we wouldn't even have considered this a good sprinkle," Andrea replied with a laugh.

"You Buckeyes have privileged childhoods. In Baton Rouge, the closest I ever got to a white Christmas was playing with a paperweight my Aunt Luvenia gave me."

Andy's eyes widened in surprise. "You don't sound like you are from Louisiana."

"UCLA and a few years working in California did away with most of my accent, but it slips back occasionally. I notice it more when I'm with Jennifer. Her drawl is contagious."

"I have always been intrigued by Louisiana. Spanish moss, mysterious antebellum mansions, hoop skirts . . ."

"Swamps, mosquitoes, tornadoes," he added to the list with a wry grimace. "The place isn't all magnolias and moonlight, but it does get in your blood."

"Do you go back to visit your family often?"

The humor in Matt's gravelly voice vanished. "There's nobody left. My father's been gone since I was a teenager, and a year ago Mother died. That's when Jenny came to live with me."

"You're lucky to have each other. I was an only child," Andrea said softly.

"Are your parents still living?"

"Yes, but we pretty much go our separate ways." She shoved her mittened hands deeper into the pockets of her down jacket and suppressed a shiver of loneliness.

"Cold?" Matt's arm encircled her shoulders.

"A little." It wasn't exactly a lie—the tip of her nose was chilly—and it got the desired result. He pulled her closer, matching his stride to hers.

"Is that better?"

"Uh-huh." The casual affirmative was an understatement of how radically her situation had improved. She felt safe, and his nearness set her heart thumping against her rib cage like a claustrophobic canary.

"Laurel Valley must be quite a change for your sister. Does she like it here?" Andrea asked, less to elicit information than to take her mind off the shakiness in her knees.

"Not really. She hasn't learned to cope with Mom's death yet, and maybe she never will. I spend as much time with her as I can, but I'm a poor substitute. I can't seem to get the hang of talking girl-type stuff."

Matt's forehead furrowed in bewilderment, an expression that looked foreign to his face. Andrea guessed that he wasn't used to being unsure of his ground, and she felt a tug of sympathy.

"Maybe what you need is a full-time housekeeper," she reasoned.

"We've gone through two already. Mrs. Pickering's our latest, and sometimes I think she's about ready to throw in the towel."

Little Jennifer must be a real lulu, Andrea mused warily. "Doesn't want to do windows anymore, huh?" she joked aloud.

His chuckle was without mirth. "I wish it were that simple. Jenny's really a sweet kid, but sometimes she can be difficult."

Matt came to a stop, his grip tightening on her arm. "Whoa! You want to get us busted for jaywalking?" he asked, nodding toward the red traffic light blinking at the entrance to Prescott Square.

Andrea realized with surprise that their destination was only a short block away; other concertgoers were making their way across the quadrangle. She'd been so absorbed in their conversation that she'd lost track of distance. She backed self-consciously out of the circle of his arms; the staid citizens of Laurel Valley did not take kindly to public displays of affection.

Matthew's face grew pensive, almost distant, as they crossed the chapel's snow-blanketed lawn.

"Is anything wrong?" she asked, gingerly skirting an icy spot on the broad granite steps.

"Jenny was upset when I dropped her off. I hope it won't affect her performance," he answered absently. "I had to put my foot down when she wanted to bring her dolls. You know, the teenagers with all the accessories . . ."

"Barbie and Ken," she supplied with a chuckle. "My best friend and I used to stage the most elaborate weddings for them. We had everything but an irate father with a shotgun!"

"So that's how you got your start," he teased, ushering her through the arched oak doors. "Looks like a large crowd. I hope all the good seats aren't taken."

Although Andrea had passed the Gothic chapel frequently, this was the first time she had been in it and she was charmed by its Old World grace. Preceding Matt down the red-carpeted aisle to a pew in front, she glanced appreciatively at the polished beams arching to the ceiling. The windows were dark now, but she could imagine their glory when light streamed through the jeweled panes.

"I hope the choir sings 'Lo, How a Rose E'er Blooming.' That's my favorite carol," she murmured, stripping off her jacket and Fair Isle knit cap.

"You're out of luck. They're doing Handel's *Messiah* this year. Jenny's the soprano soloist."

She stared at him in disbelief; she'd assumed his sister was about ten, or twelve at the most. "But that's difficult even for the most mature voices. Jennifer must be exceptionally talented."

"She's amazing." There seemed to be no excess of brotherly pride in the statement; it was a simple declaration of truth. He folded Andrea's coat, tucking it beside him on the seat as he continued. "When she was eight, she sang the aria from *Madame Butterfly* in Italian after only hearing the recording once, and she had the accent and pacing down pat. Jenny learns by listening; she can't read a note of music."

Andrea scooted closer to him to make room for an elderly couple standing in the aisle. Taken aback by the unexpected revelation, she smiled at them distractedly and leaned back against the carved support of the pew.

She had always gotten along well with children, but she had never dealt with a prodigy before. No wonder the kid is high-strung, she thought uneasily as the organist appeared and began the muted strains of a Bach prelude.

The audience settled into program-rustling anticipation as the robed singers filed slowly into the loft. Andrea grinned as she recognized one of them.

"What on earth is Jason doing up there? He couldn't carry a tune if it were strapped to his back!" she whispered with a chuckle.

Matt shrugged. "Most folks in the Oratorio Society aren't ready for the Met, but they enjoy what they're doing." He leaned forward, the expression in his eyes a mixture of pride and anxiety. "There's Jenny now."

"Where?" She searched the choir for a child with features like Matt's.

"Second from the end on the front row."

The person occupying that position was a slender, beautiful girl who looked to be in her late teens. Long hair spilled in a sunny cascade around her shoulders, framing a face that seemed formed of porcelain. Spotting Matthew, she waved happily.

"T-that's your s-sister? But..." Andrea fought to regain her composure, finishing lamely, "Somehow I thought she would be much younger."

Matthew's eyes clouded. "In a way, she is. You see, Jenny is mentally retarded."

Andrea was at a loss. "I'm sorry" was the only response that came to mind, and that seemed patronizing. She lapsed into silence, stealing a sidewise glance at him as the concert began. He leaned forward, tension in every line of his body, but he relaxed as the timeless story unfolded, his lips soundlessly forming the words as his sister sang them.

Whatever Jennifer Donaldson's problems, they did not include her voice. Her rich soprano soared above the congregation like a joyous dove, serenity and an aching sweetness in every perfect note. Her example seemed to inspire her fellow choristers; the occasional missed cues and dissonance typical in amateur glee clubs were absent. That evening, the Laurel Valley Oratorio Society gave a performance worthy of Carnegie Hall.

When the echo of the last, triumphant "Hallelujah" faded into silence, Andrea found herself on her feet, her hand clutching Matthew's arm tightly and her cheeks wet with tears.

"Sorry, guess I got carried away." She glanced around in embarrassment, sure that everyone was watching. But she need not have worried; they were all too busy drying their own eyes to notice her. Fumbling vainly in her purse for a tissue, she added, "Jenny is an absolute miracle."

Wordlessly, Matt handed her a handkerchief, his face shining with tenderness as they waited for the choir to disband.

"How was I, Bubba?" Jennifer rushed up and enveloped her brother in a bear hug. "I thought I was gonna mess up the part about the shepherds, but I remembered just in time. Flocks, that's what they were watching! That means a whole bunch of sheep. Did I do all right?"

"Better than that. You were terrific, honey." Matt brushed aside a strand of her hair and kissed her forehead. "I want you to meet someone special. This is Andy Kirkland."

Matt's designation caught Andrea off guard. Flushing with pleasure, she extended her hand to his sister. "Hello, Jennifer. Your solos were really marvelous."

The young woman shook it hesitantly, her violet gaze bright with curiosity and a wariness that bordered on hostility. "Why have you got a boy's name? You don't look like a boy. You're pretty."

The compliment, almost an accusation really, was delivered in a Southern accent that was pronounced but charming. Recalling the earlier conversation with Matt, Andrea smiled inwardly. A few weeks around Jenny and she'd be flattening her vowels right along with them.

"Thank you. You're pretty, too."

"I know," she responded ingenuously. "I'm hungry, Bubba. Can we go get something to eat now?"

Matt laughed and guided the two women down the aisle, not an easy task with everyone stopping to congratulate the star of the moment. Jenny loved the attention, blooming with each well-deserved tribute. Her feet scarcely made contact with the red carpet.

It's hard to believe she's—that way. I wonder how it happened, Andrea thought, her mind edging around the grim label as the crush of people separated her from Matthew and his sister. Jenny did not fit the stereotypical image the term *retarded* conjured up. Though her behavior was admittedly immature, she was physically well-coordinated. And there certainly was nothing wrong with her musical memory or timing; she had not missed a single nuance of the complex cantata.

Caught up in the puzzle, Andrea forgot to watch where she was going and the heel of her boot nicked the instep of the person beside her. "I'm so sorry," she mumbled contritely.

"For someone who can't weigh more than a hundred and ten dripping wet, you sure walk heavy!" Jason groaned. He turned to the pretty girl on his left, pretending an injured limp. "The woman who just disabled me for life is the slave driver I'm always complaining about. Andy, this is Sara Paige.''

Andrea acknowledged Sara's murmured greeting with an approving smile; Jason's newest lady was a definite winner. Small and compact, she fairly bubbled with energy. Her tumble of midnight curls bounced around a face the color and smoothness of butterscotch pudding, and a sprinkling of cinnamon freckles graced the bridge of her upturned nose.

"Let's sit down and wait till the stampede's over," Sara proposed, leading the way into an empty pew.

"Impersonating a singer is usually a misdemeanor, but in Jason's case, it's a felony. How on earth did he get in the choir?" Andrea teased.

"He's got a strong back. We make him carry the music and clean up after rehearsals," Sara answered with an impish grin.

"What did you think of the performance, Andy? Wasn't little Moonshine something else?" Jason interjected.

"Moonshine?"

"My nickname for Matt's sister. There ought to be a law against being so beautiful and having that much talent at the same time. Don't you think Weddings Unlimited should sign her up before she gets away?"

"What do you mean?"

"We need a new soloist. Today Mrs. Flemming flatted thirteen notes—I counted them—and she looks like she should be driving a Mack truck. Jennifer Donaldson would add a lot of class to our act. The way she handles Handel, 'Oh, Promise Me' should be a snap."

"You've got a point. I'll run it by Matt and see what he thinks," Andrea responded, hesitant to commit herself before she knew what kinds of problems the scheme could entail.

Jason's face was knowing. "Good idea. He's kind of careful when it comes to Jenny."

She did not miss the subtle underlining of the adjective. Glancing toward the back of the chapel where the lovely soprano was now holding court, she noted Matthew's guarded posture. One arm about Jennifer's shoulders, he was standing slightly forward as though to interpose himself between her and the well-wishers. He met Andy's eyes, his craggy face relaxing into a grin as he beckoned for the trio to join them.

As they walked into the multipurpose room where the pot-luck supper was laid out, hunger riveted all of Andrea's attention on the festive tables. The spread was a gourmet tribute to the town's varied ethnicity; among other things, pans of lasagna, New England baked beans, arroz con pollo and crispy spring rolls mixed a bouquet of mouth-watering aromas. Off to the side was an array of every dessert known to mankind.

"I feel guilty eating when I didn't bring anything," Andrea said, spooning up a small helping of steaming chili.

"You can be an honorary Markham for the night. My mother made enough fried chicken to put the Colonel out of business." Jason grinned, spearing a crispy drumstick and adding it to the growing assortment on her plate.

"Ten zillion more calories," Andy groaned between bites of the succulent meat. "Why can't carrot sticks taste like this?"

"'Cause we'd all turn into rabbits," Sara answered as she tackled the potato salad with abandon.

Matthew stopped serving Jennifer's plate long enough to interject, "I don't see that you have to worry; your calories all seem to go to the right places." He grinned devilishly as his eyes traveled past Andrea's slender waist.

Jenny's face grew cautious as she watched. "Can I have some cake, Bubba?" she asked, tugging at his arm in a transparent attempt to refocus his attention.

"Sure, Princess. But first, eat a little of your salad," he coaxed, straightening the wide ribbon that held her Alice-in-Wonderland coiffure in place.

Andrea wondered if he had picked out his sister's clothes. Not that the outfit was unbecoming; the rich royal blue of the velvet A-line dress deepened the violet clarity of Jenny's eyes, and its exquisite, handmade lace collar emphasized her air of fragile innocence. But the style and her low-heeled pumps were meant for someone half her age.

"Do you like my brother?" the object of her covert appraisal piped up curiously.

"I think he's very nice," she responded.

"You aren't going to marry him, are you?"

The heat in the crowded room seemed to shoot up ten degrees as Andrea grappled mutely with the unexpected question.

"Take it easy, squirt. You're embarrassing Andy," Matt protested.

"I just wanted to know. You look at her they way you used to look at Kristin," Jenny said defensively.

Kristin? Andrea glanced speculatively at Matthew through the silken cover of her lashes.

He reddened. "That's ancient history, Jenny. I thought we agreed not to talk about home business in public." The warning was indulgent but reproving. Matt was plainly relieved when Mrs. Bellamy's arrival called a halt to the inquisition.

Ladened with an overflowing plate and a king-sized cup of eggnog, the mayor's wife shouldered Andrea out of the way and planted a loud kiss on Jennifer's cheek.

"I've never been so moved in my entire life! This little angel had me boo-hooing like a baby," the mayor's wife gushed. Turning to Matt, she continued in a loud aside, "You have a heavy burden, Matthew, and I must say I admire the way you carry it. So many families turn their backs on these unfortunate children."

Matt stared at her impassively, a slight tightening in his jaw the only sign that he was disturbed. "Your admiration is misplaced, Winona. I have no burden," he said, his tone quiet but deadly.

Shock at the woman's monumental insensitivity held Andrea momentarily speechless. Her initial dismay was quickly replaced by fury as the gratuitous outpouring continued.

"Retardation is one of my favorite causes. The mayor and I contribute quite heavily to the wonderful work of the Ark—that's Laurel Valley's local independent living program, you know." Beaming benevolently at Jason, she continued, "Isn't Rhoda Hall, the director there, your sister, Mr. Markham?"

"Rene Hill is my cousin, Mrs. Bellamy, and you can't imagine how thrilled she was with the bundle of cleaning rags you sent over last month." Sarcasm dropped Jason's tenor to baritone.

"The things I donated were previously owned clothing, not rags," she snapped indignantly. "But between you, me and the gatepost, sanitation supplies are not a bad idea. The last time I visited the Ark, I was appalled at how messy those people were."

Various methods of shutting Winona's mouth flashed through Andrea's mind. She was weighing the pros and cons of decapitation with a plastic fork when Matt's sister saved her the trouble.

"You're the messy one. You've gone and dribbled gravy all over your sleeve," Jennifer announced solemnly, offering Winona her napkin.

Piggy face quivering with malice, Mrs. Bellamy glared at her and huffed off.

"Donaldson by a knockout in the first round!" Andrea chortled.

Matt seemed more dismayed than delighted by his sister's victory. "That wasn't a very polite thing to say, Jenny. You have to be more careful about hurting people's feelings."

"Is that why the lady got mad at me?" Jenny queried sadly.

"She's not mad, Moonshine—her girdle's pinching her brain, and she can't stand the pain," Jason interjected. Bowing grandly, he offered one arm to Jennifer, the other to Sara. "Ladies, let's go raid the caramel cake."

"Being around my sister is never dull. She generally says the first thing that comes into her head, and it sometimes plays havoc with my social life," Matt remarked ruefully to Andrea while the other three busied themselves with dessert.

"She's honest, and that's more than you can say for ninety-nine percent of the population," Andrea responded. "Besides, Winona got exactly what she deserved. I sure could have used Jenny's help at the reception."

"Speaking of this afternoon . . ." He paused to rescue an olive that was about to roll off the edge of her Styrofoam plate. Popping the tidbit in his mouth, he continued hopefully, "When can we get to work on the spell again? The treatment must be doing some good, because the ribbing between my toes is gone. New Year's Eve, let's try for the warts on my . . ."

Jennifer moved quickly to his side before he could specify the site, her small face a cloud promising thunder. "I want to go home now, Bubba."

Matt bit his lip in obvious irritation. "In a little while, Jenny. You haven't finished your cake, yet."

"I don't want any more. My head hurts." Sudden moisture spiked her golden lashes.

"You must be very tired, Jenny. A fine performance like you gave tonight takes a lot of energy," Andrea murmured sympathetically.

For a moment, a glimmer of friendliness lightened the unreadable violet eyes to azure. "You really like my music?" she asked carefully.

"I sure do. I'd love to hear you sing *Madame Butterfly*. It's one of my favorites."

"Not now, though," Matthew interposed hastily. "Run and get your coat. Andy and I will wait for you at the front door."

The tempest threatened again. "Does she have to go with us?" Jennifer pouted.

"She sure does, and we will both be glad for the company. Now you mind your manners, young lady," Matthew warned with a stern frown.

"I think I'll hang around here a while longer, Matt. Dessert looks too scrumptious to miss. You two go ahead," Andrea interrupted in an effort to sidetrack the brewing storm.

"It isn't safe for you to be out alone," he protested.

Arms akimbo, Andrea put on a show of mock exasperation. "I think I can make it four blocks by myself, thank you very much," she said dryly. "This is Laurel Valley, not the Big Apple. I haven't heard of a single crime since I moved here, unless you want to count Mrs. Simpson's not curbing her dog!"

"Don't sweat it, Matt. Sara and I will walk Andy home," Jason offered quickly.

Matthew's face held both disappointment and relief. "Thanks for understanding, Andy. I'll call you to make plans for next week," he promised.

She nodded, extending her hand to Jennifer. "'Bye, Jenny. Have fun making your igloo tomorrow."

The expression on the young woman's face was stony. Ignoring Andy, she tugged at her brother's arm again. "Hurry up, Bubba. We didn't hang my stocking yet."

There was a coldness in the pit of Andrea's stomach as she watched them leave, and she glumly downgraded her chances for a relationship with Matthew. Was Jennifer Donaldson's antipathy for her personal, or did it cover anyone with an interest in her brother, like the mysterious Kristin, for example?

"What will it be, boss, pecan pie, carrot cake or double fudge brownies?" Jason asked.

"None of the above, thanks," Andy said with a sigh.

The dessert she really wanted was not on the table. The party was suddenly as flat as week-old ginger ale, the smell of the rich food was making her queasy, and the tinny insistence of piped-in carols started a dull throb in her temples.

"Merry Christmas, and the very best of the season to you," Mayor Bellamy boomed, capering up in a moth-eaten Santa suit.

"Bah humbug," Andrea muttered under her breath.

Chapter Three

It was Friday, a mean-spirited, drizzly January sixth that had no redeeming value, social or otherwise. Andrea sat in her minuscule office in the rear of the bridal boutique alternately fiddling with a pile of invoices and staring bleakly at the telephone.

New Year's Eve had been a major disappointment; she had toasted the birth of the infant with a solitary glass of diet cola and watched images of Times Square lunacy flickering from the television. Earlier in the day, Matthew Donaldson called with his apologies, explaining that Jennifer had developed a fever and did not want to be left with the housekeeper. The conversation ended with amorphous resolutions to "get together soon," but nothing had come of them. He had not called since, and she was damned if she would make the first move.

"Fever, my foot—more like a galloping case of sibling manipulation! Go ahead, ring all you want. I'm not going to answer," she addressed the silent instrument furiously, knowing that if it obeyed, her resolve would fold like a chocolate bar on a hot radiator.

"Why in the hell am I getting involved in this?" Disgusted by her preoccupation with the subject, she retrieved a ledger and doggedly examined the entries she'd made since the business opened; black-and-red ink were running a dead heat. And Jason had apparently misjudged the weight of Winona's recommendation; the few congratulatory calls and vague inquiries after the Bellamy affair hardly constituted an economic boom for Weddings Unlimited. Andrea had come to Laurel Valley on a shoestring and a few quick mental calculations told her she was about to reach the frayed end. Her checking account now had a balance of $349.67. Savings would carry her through February, but what then?

"Worry about it after lunch, Scarlett," she muttered, reaching for her coat and purse.

Andrea's depression was not cured by the shopping spree that followed, but the silk blouse and other goodies she bought on sale at the department store across the street did lift her mood from suicidal to merely gloomy. Three hours later, when she returned to the bridal boutique, the phone on the counter was finally ringing, but as luck would have it, she was on the wrong side of the locked front door juggling an umbrella, her unwieldy parcels and a pizza. The key was somewhere at the bottom of her large, very junky pocketbook.

"Suppose it's him," she muttered, frantically stacking the packages on top of the pizza box and trying to secure the handle of the umbrella between her chin and shoulder. The system wasn't working too well. "Please don't hang up. I'm coming as fast as I can!"

"Here, let me help you." The small woman who was standing under the shelter of the awning above the multipaned showcase window walked over through the drizzle to take the packages.

Andrea threw her a brief thanks, then burrowed into the purse like a frantic mole.

Two precious rings elapsed before she came up with the key, and another was wasted as she jammed the still-open umbrella in the doorway. By the time she reached the counter, the only sound coming from the phone was the petulant whine of the dial tone.

"Damn!" she said, cradling the receiver none too gently.

"What do you want me to do with these?" The question reminded Andrea that she was not alone.

"Here, let me take them. I do appreciate your help," she said, smiling at her rescuer.

"Think nothing of it. And dear—" the elderly lady removed the plastic rain scarf from her silver Gibson Girl coif, creased it carefully and tucked it into the pocket of her coat before she finished the sentence ''—I wouldn't worry if I were you. I'm sure he'll call back.''

Andrea glanced at her curiously. "How do you know it was a him?"

"If you would risk spreading your pizza all over the sidewalk for a her, you're in trouble."

The droll comment was delivered in an alto modulated by the hint of a tremor, Katharine Hepburn cast in the role of a Southern grande dame. And the resemblance did not end with the voice. Although time had changed the translucent skin from satin to crepe, the beauty of her face was preserved by classic bone structure.

"I'm Henrietta Hewitt, and I presume you're Andrea Kirkland."

The hand she offered was surprisingly strong, its grip firm, though the thin fingers felt chilled.

"I'm very pleased to meet you, Mrs. Hewitt," Andrea said, immediately liking the old woman. "Could I offer you a cup of tea? It won't take a minute."

"Black coffee if you have it. Tea makes me think of arthritis and crocheted afghans."

Behind luxuriant dark lashes Henrietta's emerald bright eyes were alive with wicked mischief. Moving with deliberate daintiness, she followed Andrea into the workroom, adding, "And it's *Miss* Hewitt. I haven't yet had the pleasure of matrimony, though I suppose there's still hope. I'm only sixty-seven."

While the coffeepot was perking, Miss Hewitt took off her coat and wandered over to the worktable to inspect a shipment of veils Andrea had unpacked earlier. She held up a seed-pearl mantilla.

"This is so lovely. Would you try it on for me?" she said wistfully.

The request was a surprise. "Sure," Andrea agreed, securing the comb in her chestnut curls and adjusting the heavy folds of Spanish lace into a cascade around her shoulders.

"It's perfect for you. You shouldn't sell it. Save it for your own wedding," Henrietta commented.

Andrea shook her head and removed the ornament. "It would probably dry-rot before I get around to using it."

"I doubt that. Matthew Donaldson doesn't strike me as the sort who wastes much time."

Andrea almost dropped the coffeepot. "How did you know about him?" she asked, setting a steaming mug in front of Miss Hewitt.

"Small towns are blessed with extremely efficient grapevines, my dear. Two days after the concert, our gossips had already named your firstborn."

A flush crept into Andrea's cheeks. "I'm afraid everyone is in for a big disappointment. Matthew and I are just casual acquaintances, and under the circumstances I doubt that we'll ever go beyond that stage," she said somberly.

Henrietta's eyes narrowed slightly but she made no comment. Turning back to the veils, she switched subjects. "All of these are nice, but they can't hold a candle to the one in the window. When I take my lunch break from the Ark I stop to look at it."

"The Ark? Isn't that the independent-living program for re—er, handicapped people?"

"Yes, I work there as a volunteer." Miss Hewitt's mind obviously was not on the Ark. Pushing away the untouched beverage, she fidgeted absently with her spoon. "You know, that headpiece is exactly the one I always dreamed of as a young girl."

"You can't really appreciate it through the window. I'll go get it," Andrea said, ignoring the elderly lady's protests. She returned with a garland of pale ivory rosebuds to which was sewn a transparent cloud of baby-soft silk organdy. Impulsively, she placed the circlet around the silvery topknot on the elderly woman's head and handed her a hand mirror. "It's gorgeous," she said.

As the thin fabric swirled gently around Henrietta Hewitt's face, an almost mystical transformation occurred. A rosy flush spread across her high cheekbones, and her eyes sparkled green fire. She was not young again, simply ageless. And she was beautiful. She sat quite still for a moment, staring at her image, then closed her eyes and laid the veil aside. "Thank you for indulging my whim, and I apologize for taking up so much of your time.''

"It was my pleasure," Andrea said. "Would you like to see something else?"

"No, I really must be going. My car is under the weather, and I'm afraid I have missed the bus. May I use your phone to call a cab?"

"No need for that; I can drive you home. As you can plainly see, I'm not swamped with customers. Where do you live?"

"On Greenhill Road, the other side of Laurel Valley. But it is a twenty-minute round trip, and..."

"I won't take no for an answer," Andy said firmly, gathering up her belongings.

As they hurried through the chill rain to Andrea's battered station wagon, she thought she heard the phone inside Weddings Unlimited ringing, but resolutely ignored it.

"You'll have to point me the right way. I haven't had time to learn Laurel Valley," she said, swabbing at the gathering vapor on the windshield with a tissue. The defroster was erratic at best.

"Straight down Main, left on Parkwood and six miles to Greenhill," Henrietta directed. Leaning back against the cracked upholstery, she continued, "It's very kind of you to go to all this trouble for me, especially when you're waiting for a call from someone as handsome as Matthew Donaldson. If I were forty years younger, you would have some real competition." The elderly woman's accompanying laugh was as smooth as warm clover honey.

Andrea decided a quick switch in subjects was in order. "I have to confess I don't have the foggiest notion what independent-living programs are all about. What do you do?" she queried.

"We try to help young adults who are mentally handicapped get along in the real world. Our clients have either been with their families or in institutions most of their lives, and things like handling their own finances, dealing with bureaucracies and building relationships are more than they can cope with alone."

"What happens after they graduate?"

A shadow passed over Miss Hewitt's expressive face. "Some do just fine by themselves, others need minimal supervision, and the rest don't make it. It's a long road when you have to take five steps to everybody else's one." She glanced at Andrea levelly, continuing, "But in spite of their limitations, they have so much to give. You'd be surprised at their capacity to love and accept others."

"I'm sure I would," Andy countered grimly, thinking of Jennifer's resistance to her. She was usually reticent about unloading her problems, particularly on someone she had just met, but this woman had worked with people like Matt's sister. What would be the harm in asking her advice?

She quickly outlined the situation.

"Remember, Matthew is all Jenny has left, and she can't risk losing him. Take it slowly and she will come around. She is a remarkable young woman," Miss Hewitt observed.

"Jason, my assistant, suggested that I hire her as a soloist. What do you think?"

Henrietta shrugged. "It's hard to predict how she would handle it, but given her tremendous talent, she'd probably do very well." Her face lost its guise of objectivity, and a note of excitement came into her voice. "It could be a wonderful opportunity for her, though. When Jenny first came to Laurel Valley, Matthew put her in our day program, but she was not ready. The experience left them both a little shaken. It took courage for him to let her perform at the concert. Your support could mean a lot for them both, and I suspect he'd be very grateful for your help."

A phantom sensation of Matt's arms encircling her made Andrea's insides quiver. "Gratitude isn't exactly what I had in mind," she said in a low voice.

The elderly woman smiled. "That, too. Slow down now or you'll miss my house. It's the brick one with the yellow shutters."

Andrea chugged to a stop in front of a small, comfortable-looking house set back in a grove of trees. Miss Hewitt started to get out, then hesitated. "Would you mind if I came back to visit from time to time?"

"I'd love it." Impulsively, Andrea reached over to touch the other woman's shoulder. "I hope this doesn't sound presumptuous, but I think we're going to be very good friends."

"It certainly has taken you a long time to reach such an obvious conclusion, Andrea," Miss Hewitt observed dryly. "I knew that right off."

LATER THAT AFTERNOON, as Andrea started up the stairs to her third-floor apartment, she felt better than she had all week. A smidgen of woman talk is food for the soul, she told herself happily. She had been so busy getting established that there had not been time to meet many people, and she had missed having another woman to confide in, even one thirty-nine years her senior. Henrietta Hewitt was going to be a welcome addition to her life in Laurel Valley.

But reality caught up with her before she reached the first landing. "What life? According to my bankbook, I'm terminal," she muttered, regarding the loot from her capricious shopping spree guiltily. "A hundred-fifty-dollar telephone bill due and I go out and buy a silk blouse—not a smart financial maneuver!"

What difference would it make if the phone were disconnected? No one wanted to talk to her, anyway, she decided, stewing once again over Matt Donaldson's inexplicable silence. She could have sworn there was something special growing between them, but maybe when the mistletoe magic had worn off, he discovered he was not so enchanted, after all.

"Why don't you call him, stupid? You're not some Victorian wimp who has to wait for him to make the first move. The worst that can happen is that he brushes you off!" she argued with herself as she marched past the second level.

Intent on her mission, she almost tripped on a pair of long legs draped in front of the top step.

"I knew it was you when I heard you talking to yourself," Matthew grumped, edging gingerly up from his seat on the floor. A quarter of the way, he slumped down again, a grimace of acute discomfort contorting his features.

"What is it, Matt?" she said with real alarm.

"Nothing," he snapped, then sheepishly added, "I screwed up my back helping to dig a car out of the snow on New Year's Day. So much for my good-neighbor policy."

He hadn't called because he'd been incapacitated! A wave of relief engulfed Andrea; then, ashamed that his accident was the cause of her sudden joy, she took his arm solicitously. "Let me help you up before your spine fuses into a pretzel."

As soon as he was in a standing position, he shook off her assistance and, walking as though he had been run over by an eighteen-wheeler, followed her through the apartment door.

"It's about time you got home! And while I'm at it, why don't you ever answer your phone at work? That's a hell of a way to run a business!" he growled, limping over to the couch.

"I don't need you to tell me how to handle my affairs," she said coolly. "And stop being surly, Kermit. It makes your warts more noticeable."

Matthew gaped at her, then threw back his head and laughed. "I'm sorry, but I don't handle the sickness bit well. Watching television game shows for a week has done weird things to my disposition."

She hung their coats in the closet and headed toward the kitchen to deposit the flat, square box that held her dinner. "Can I get you anything?"

"I would kill for a slice of that pizza. Mrs. Pickering's been force-feeding me chicken soup," he said wistfully. Then he added with a wink, "Hold the onions, though. I've got plans."

The look he sent along with the food order nearly melted Andrea's knees. Hurriedly shoving the pie into the oven, she turned the dial to low—the thermostat tended to be schizo-phrenic—and considered the options for an accompanying beverage. It was either diet soda or the expensive French wine she had stashed away for a special occasion. The decison was amazingly simple.

"Would you open it? I always squoosh in the cork," she said, returning to set two crystal goblets and the bottle of Montrachet on the coffee table.

"Nineteen seventy-eight? Whew!" Matthew's whistle was appreciative as he did the honors.

"You'll just have to make do. I'm all out of Ripple." She settled down at the other end of the couch and looked at him obliquely. "How's Jenny feeling?"

His lips tightened. "Fine. She really didn't have a fever at all. I caught her stirring her cocoa with the thermometer. I wanted to call back and explain, but I felt like such an idiot, falling for that old chestnut."

Miss Hewitt's assessment was right on target. *His sister is only trying to protect her turf,* Andrea mused sympathetically. "I'm sure she didn't intend to spoil your plans," she said aloud.

"Don't make book on it. That kid can be very wily when she puts her mind to it." He sipped at the wine as though it were hemlock. "I'd also like to apologize for her behavior last week."

"I hope you didn't haul your aching back all the way over here just for that. An apology isn't necessary," Andrea protested.

"Maybe not, but you're getting one, anyway. And there's another item on my agenda . . ." he started, straightening up with difficulty. The motion was apparently ill-advised; pain shadowed his eyes, and he winced, positioning his head at at an unnatural angle.

"Is it worse, Matt?"

"Only when I breathe," he admitted.

She was out of her seat in a flash. "Try to relax," she ordered, tucking a cushion between the couch and the small of his back. Unbuttoning the collar of his shirt, she knelt beside him and kneaded his tense muscles.

"That is a little better, but can you reach around back? It hurts most right between the shoulder blades."

At the angle she was positioned, the only way Andrea could get to the spot in question was to put her arms around his neck. The breadth of his upper torso and the chamois-soft smoothness of his skin nearly made her forget that the purpose of the exercise was first aid.

The man is in pain, she reminded herself, ruthlessly squelching a tendril of heat that had taken root in the vicinity of her navel.

Matt closed his eyes, the small rumbles of satisfaction emanating deep in his throat resembling purrs from a well-nourished leopard.

"You ought to have your head examined. Driving over here in your condition when you could have called wasn't very bright," she scolded, exasperation adding unnecessary vigor to the massage.

"Take it easy, will you? That stuff you're rubbing is skin, not Naugahyde," he grumbled. "I didn't drive; I walked. And you're probably going to have to give me a lift home."

"Okay, but it will cost you."

"Hey, that's my line!" He opened one eye and leered comically at her through his indecently long, silky lashes. "Are you about to take advantage of my innocence?"

"What innocence?" Andrea ignored the quickening pace of her pulse and tried to change the subject. "What's the other item on your agenda, Mr. Donaldson?"

Matt clasped his arms about her waist and drew her down in his lap. "The spell, of course. You certainly don't expect me to go through the rest of my life with webbed feet, do you?"

"Watch out, you're going to hurt your back again."

"No pain, no gain."

His fingers drifted through the chestnut satin of her hair, discovering the slender column of her neck in a slow-motion dream sequence. Gently, he lowered his mouth to hers, his taste the sweetness of summer mornings, the salty-clean satisfaction of ocean air.

The kiss was incredibly tender—neither hesitant nor demanding, both comforting and exhilarating—and it awoke an appetite Andrea had never realized she had. Like the fine wine they had shared, its impact was subtle but deceptive. Her pulse quickened perceptibly. The effect on Matt must have been similar, because she suddenly felt the measured beat of his heart take on a more insistent rhythm.

"Lord, you are lovely," he whispered, breaking the contact and caressing her upturned face with his eyes and fingertips.

"Thank you kindly, but you're not supposed to interrupt a sorceress at work," Andy admonished, brushing her mouth along the strong line of his jaw.

The embrace took on a new intensity, their needs coalescing in a rising imperative. His hands and the power of his body provoked a starburst of new feelings, and Andrea went beyond rational thought to a level where the only impetus was hunger.

Fortunately, reason and instinct didn't both desert her at the same time; a pungent warning of imminent disaster caused her to break the embrace.

"The pizza is burning!" she gasped.

"So am I."

"Yeah, but you won't set off the smoke detector," she quipped breathlessly, struggling to a sitting position.

"Wanna bet?" he groaned.

She laughed, planting a last quick kiss on the tip of his nose. "Well, at least the spell is broken. Welcome back, Your Royal Highness."

Rescuing the Italian pie from the oven gave her time to rein in her runaway hormones, but their dinner looked like the remains of the Chicago fire. And a rapid rummage through the refrigerator for a substitute produced only a wilted stalk of celery, a half can of tuna and one egg. She had not bothered to grocery shop lately; eating out seemed a lot simpler, particularly since her culinary skills were at best rudimentary.

"It's either a tuna sandwich sans bread or a midget omelet...." She cut the menu short as she watched Matt shift on the couch, trying to find a less painful position. "Forget the food; you need to be in bed."

"I thought you'd never ask. Please be gentle," he murmured, holding out his arms. His eyebrow quirked like the circumflex over a long vowel. He was obviously enjoying the flush that heated her cheeks.

"I'm taking you home," she said firmly.

"I won't go unless you promise to share a bowl of Mrs. Pickering's chicken soup with me."

Hesitancy to face Jennifer's hostility battled with the insistence of Andrea's empty stomach. Hunger won hands down. "I'll get our coats," she agreed.

A ten-minute drive brought them to the front of a charming two-story brick house at the end of Prescott's faculty row. As she stepped onto the columned front porch, Andrea fought off a flutter of nervousness. *I'm going to make Jenny like me if I have to stand on my head to do it, because I'm not letting her brother get away,* she told herself firmly.

Before Matthew got his key in the lock, the door was opened by a middle-aged woman whose dress, sensible shoes and tightly waved hair were all the same shade of gray. The pale eyes behind her wire-framed spectacles were snapping.

"Lord-a-mercy, where have you been? I was just about to call the police!" she huffed as they stepped into the lamp-lit hallway. "I could just see you all crumpled up on the side of the road...."

Matt stopped the stream of dire observations by hugging the woman's comfortably padded shoulders. "Andy Kirkland, say hello to Mrs. Pickering, the relentless jailer I've been telling you about. She makes the best peach pie north or south of the Mason-Dixon line."

The housekeeper smiled, pleasure at the compliment changing her plump face from nondescript to a faded prettiness. But the expression chilled as she extended her hand to Andrea.

"I've heard a lot about you," she said briefly.

"Don't believe a word of it."

The weak attempt at a joke lay dying between them. *Just what I needed, another dragon to conquer,* Andrea groaned to herself.

"Ida, I'm hungry enough to eat cardboard," Matthew interjected hastily. "If there's any roast beef left from yesterday, would you throw together a couple of sandwiches for us?"

"We waited dinner. I suppose I could set another plate."

"Please do." Matthew's tone held an edge that sent the housekeeper hurrying toward the kitchen. Ushering Andrea into the high-ceilinged living room, he helped her out of her coat. "I'll go upstairs and get Jenny. Make yourself comfortable; we'll just be a minute."

Andrea watched him curiously as he strode off. His body language had undergone a subtle change; his movements were somehow crisper and more impersonal than before. She shrugged away a slight feeling of discomfort and for want of something better to do, studied her surroundings.

Most of the furnishings were ordinary, supplied to visiting professors by the college, she supposed. But here and there were touches that made the room unique. A lush-piled Chinese rug softened the shine of the hardwood floor, and fitted in the alcove made by the bow window was an antique writing desk that could have graced Tara. She idly scanned the built-in bookshelves beside the fireplace; Shakespeare, Mark Twain and Proust shared space with Steven King and Isaac Asimov. All looked very well-used.

Delighted by its presence in Matt's library, she picked up a leather-bound edition of Kahlil Gibran's *Prophet*, one of her favorites. Rosa Mascari had given her a copy as a high school graduation present.

Andrea's throat tightened as she quoted fragments from the verse that had meant so much to her Italian friend: "Your children are not your children. They are the sons and daughters of Life's longing for itself.... You may house their bodies, but not their souls, for..."

"...for their souls dwell in the house of tomorrow, which you cannot visit, not even in your dreams," Matthew continued, reentering the room alone. His voice was curiously detached. "I see you're well acquainted with Gibran."

She nodded. "Mama Mascari said that poem saved her a lot of mistakes in raising her family. She made me memorize the lines so my kids would have the same advantage."

He moved to her side, and as he looked down at her his eyes were unreadable pools of darkness. "Are children important to you?" he asked quietly.

"Not really. I plan to stop after I have half a dozen," Andy said, reaching for, but falling far short of, flippancy. "What about you?"

"I haven't given it much thought," he answered briefly, the contours of his face taking on a rigid set.

"Do you like kids?" she persisted, aware that she might be backing him into a corner but unable to stop.

"I haven't had much experience with them," Matt said evasively.

The afternoon lost some of its shine. She doubted that she could ever have a serious relationship with a man who did not share her view on the importance of family, and that was certainly the signal Matthew was sending out now.

"Mrs. Pickering says the food is ready," Jennifer interrupted from the doorway. Her lips were fixed in a polite half smile, but her gaze was as penetrating as a sapphire-tipped drill.

"Hi, Jenny. It's nice to see you again," Andy said, hastily widening the distance between her and Matt.

Jennifer cut her eyes toward her brother, then, lowering her lashes, stared at the floor. "You, too," she mumbled. It was obviously a programmed response.

Conversation over dinner was awkward to say the least. Andrea tried the weather, Matthew's back trouble, and even Barbie, but no subject elicited more than a monosyllabic reply from his sister. Mrs. Pickering did not add much more, and Matthew's contributions seemed forced and anxious. If it had not been for the lure of an excellent roast and pearl onions in cream sauce, Andy would have been tempted to flee the table.

"I don't know where I'm going to find room for this," she protested as the housekeeper passed her a huge helping of fudge cake topped with homemade ice cream. "But I'm sure going to try. Chocolate is my most favorite in the whole world."

"Mine, too," Jennifer confided, the guarded set of her face relaxing somewhat.

Matt cleared his throat. "Jenny, don't you have something to tell Andrea?"

"I'm sorry I was so mean to you at the concert" came out with the enthusiasm of a well-rehearsed robot.

"And..." her brother prompted.

"And I want you to come to my birthday party next month."

Andrea did not know quite how to respond. It was clear that the invitation was tendered under duress, and she wished with all her heart that Matt had not interfered.

Getting up from the table, Jenny went over to the sideboard and retrieved a crumpled square of paper and a magic marker. "I'm making you an invitation. You can have it as soon as I put in one more thing." Adding a few lines, she laid it beside Andy's plate, explaining, "I drew all the hearts because I was born on Valentine's Day."

Andrea smoothed out the creases and studied the drawing: at one end of a long table, seated in front of a tiered cake, were three stick figures designated "Mrs. P.," "Bubba" and "A"; at the other end, well separated from the party, was a very small person labeled "Me." All four had straight-line mouths.

At a loss, Andrea was silent for a minute. It was a graphic illustration of the extent to which the young woman must feel threatened. How would Henrietta handle the situation? she wondered.

"Don't you like it?" Jennifer asked.

A light bulb flashed on in Andrea's head. "It's a beautiful invitation, honey, but if I may borrow your pen, there's something I'd like to change."

Jenny frowned. "What?"

With swift strokes, Andrea outlined another scenario at the bottom of the invitation. Her drawing had four figures all sitting together, their hands linked on the table. "This one is you, because you're the guest of honor," she said, pointing to the slightly larger person in the middle. "You're so lucky. Only very special people are born on Valentine's Day."

"I know." Jenny studied Andrea's version, then started to giggle. "You didn't finish their faces."

Andrea handed her the marker.

The teenager quickly added have-a-good-day smiles. "See, we're all having fun now. Will you come, Andy?"

"I wouldn't miss it for the world." Andrea glanced at the small gold watch on her wrist. "I'd better head for home. Thanks so much for the feast, Mrs. Pickering. Let me give you a hand with the dishes."

"No such thing," the housekeeper said, beaming as she bustled up from the table. She gave Matthew and Andrea a knowing wink and beckoned to Jennifer. "Come on, darlin'. We'll wrap up a piece of cake for Andy to snack on later."

"You don't have to walk me to the car. It's starting to rain again," Andrea murmured fifteen minutes later as she and Matthew stood on the porch in the bright glow from the light over the door.

"Is it? I hadn't noticed." He appeared to be struggling with a heavy internal decision.

"Was there something else you wanted to talk about?" she prompted.

"It will wait until Monday. I'll come by the shop around ten if it's convenient."

"Okay."

A chill breeze blew droplets from the gathering drizzle over them. As she started down the steps, he took her hand and drew her closer. "You were much better at handling Jenny than I was. You not only sensed that she was feeling excluded; you knew exactly the right thing to do about it. How did you get to be so wise?"

"The drawing was pure luck helped along by a little advice from a good friend."

"Those six babies are going to have one hell of a mother. I hope their father will realize what a lucky man he is." The steady warmth of his gaze grew into a barely controlled flame, and she raised her face expectantly. Instead of meeting her eager mouth, his lips grazed her forehead. "Good night, Andy."

What she heard beneath his words sounded more like goodbye.

Chapter Four

The Matthew Donaldson who appeared in the doorway of Weddings Unlimited's workroom at nine forty-five on Monday morning was not one Andrea had ever met before. From the tips of his gleaming oxfords to the crown of his immaculately groomed hair, he was the up-and-coming young businessman. But it was his manner rather than the gray flannel suit that made him unrecognizable. His eyes were distant, and his features were arranged in a coolly impersonal mask. Andrea found the metamorphosis unsettling.

She slid down from her perch beside the drafting table, where for lack of something more pressing to do she and her assistant were having a morning break. Hastily swallowing the bite of jelly doughnut she was munching, she smiled at Matthew. "I guess we were so busy talking we didn't hear the front bell."

Jason sauntered over to the coffee maker. "We saved you the blue mug because it's the only one without a chip. You want cream and sugar, Matt?"

"Nothing for me, thanks. I have had my quota of caffeine for the morning," he answered, glancing at his watch. "I have to be in Richmond by eleven, but I don't think this will take too long."

His crisp tone had an immediate effect: Jason straightened up and surreptitiously buttoned the collar of his sport shirt.

Not only did Andy find this captain-of-industry pose irritating; she had had a long, uninterrupted weekend to think over the events before and after dinner on Friday, and she had come to the conclusion that Matthew's last comment about her babies' potential father was his way of excluding himself from the competition. What she considered a polite brush-off stung more than a little. "We wouldn't want to keep you," she said sweetly, deliberately finishing another bite of doughnut before she continued. "What was it you wanted to discuss?"

Without further preliminaries, Matthew drew a slip of paper from the inner pocket of his jacket and handed it to her.

It was a check made out to Weddings Unlimited. At the bottom was written, "For consultant services." The amount made Andrea's eyes glaze over.

"What is this for?" she gulped, showing it to a very curious Jason.

Smiling, Matt reached over to whisk a smudge of jelly from her cheek, and for a few precious seconds her frog prince returned. "With your help I'm going to turn the hotel into the wedding capital of the entire free world."

She stared at him suspiciously. "Are you sure you fell on your back and not your head?"

The playfulness in his expression once again gave way to professionalism. "I'm dead serious. The Richmond Regent is the perfect place for honeymooning—picture-book setting, a damn good staff and a superb kitchen. And we have already landed the Whitney-Bowman reception for the first of March. If we handle it well, it could make our reputation."

"Whitney-Bowman?" Jason's amber eyes widened with excitement.

Andrea's reaction was sightly more subdued, although she was impressed. For months the society pages of every paper in the state had been plastered with news of the engagement of State Senator Whitney's daughter, Miranda, to Philbert Bowman, the youngest elected representative in the Virginia House of Delegates.

"That is terrific," she murmured, wondering exactly where she was to fit in the scheme of things.

"It would be if my assistant, Rena Stanford, hadn't quit the day after Christmas. As it is, there's no one to coordinate the arrangements. I'd like you to take her place, at least on a temporary basis."

Andrea balanced a growing exhilaration with a careful consideration of the pros and cons. No bridal consultant in her right mind would think of turning down such a plum, and for certain, Weddings Unlimited needed the money, but her experience with Patrick had taught her the pitfalls of working with a man to whom she was attracted. "Sounds interesting. Why did Miss Stanford leave?" she hedged.

"*Mrs.* Stanford. She's having a baby. Besides, we both felt it was time for her to move on," Matthew answered sourly. At her skeptical glance, he expanded the explanation. "Sometimes I'm not the easiest person in the world to get along with. I hate slipshod work, but I do give my staff and consultants free rein to express their own creativity. Could you live with that?" he challenged.

"You can't be too much worse than Winona Bellamy."

"Does that mean you'll do it?" He looked at her intently, seeming to weigh her hesitancy.

"Well . . ."

Jason's foot moved under the table to tap her ankle. "If you're worried about our other commitments, the calendar is fairly clear for the next few weeks, Andy," he said helpfully, the expression on his face adding a silent *Have you lost your mind?*

Putting aside her fears, Andrea nodded, her manner as brisk as Matthew's. "I don't think there'll be any problem."

"Will the amount I've offered by adequate?"

She looked at the check again and could not suppress a broad smile. "You could have hired an entire platoon of experienced consultants for this much. I feel like I'm robbing you blind!"

"The Regent puts out top dollar for the best. And by the way, that doesn't include your salary, Jason. You'll be paid directly by the hotel."

Jason frowned. "It's nice of you to include me in the deal, Matt, but I don't think I'll have the time. Since this is my last semester, my schedule is a real killer."

"Not to worry. I've already spoken with your adviser about a Regent internship for you. The work experience will count as academic credit toward graduation."

"You've got to be kidding.... This is the most fantastic thing that ever happened to me!" Jason's jubilant exclamation was punctuated by a heel-clicking leap. "If you all don't need me anymore, I've got to run over to the bank and tell Sara."

Andrea's dry "Knock yourself out" was superfluous; her assistant was already headed for the door.

The situation had gotten beyond her control, and she hated the feeling only slightly more than the smug self-assurance in Matthew's manner.

"So nice to know you've handled all the details. What would you have done if we hadn't accepted your offer?" she asked, not bothering to hold back the sarcasm.

"I was sure you would." He opened his briefcase and took out a sheaf of papers. "Here are some background details on the Bowman and Whitney families. You might have to do a little more digging, but most of the essentials are here. You pull together some ideas for a theme and day after tomorrow we'll drive to Richmond so you can meet the staff you'll be working with. Will that give you enough time?"

"I won't know until I check my schedule," she said irritably, feeling as though she were runner-up in a confrontation with a steamroller.

Her dismay at his preemptive tactics must have been evident on her face, because as he studied her, the set of his chin softened into uncertainty. "I tend to go off like a berserk bulldozer when I think I have a good idea. I didn't mean to back you into a corner."

She fingered the Whitney-Bowman papers nervously. "I could have said no if I had wanted to. I'm very grateful for your offer, and I'll try not to disappoint you," she said stiffly.

He started to leave, then turned back. "I'm free tonight if you'd like to toss around a few ideas about the reception over dinner," he offered.

She shook her head stubbornly. "Thanks, but I work better alone."

"Suit yourself."

"And I'll put together a presentation that knocks you right off your pompous ass," Andrea muttered as the front door closed. When Jason returned, she was already wading through the background material.

"Okay, Andy—where do we start?" He rubbed his hands together in anticipation.

She looked up absently. "I think I can handle it, Jase. Since there is nothing else to do, why don't you take some time off to celebrate with Sara?"

"You're the boss," he said quietly.

THE NEXT WEDNESDAY, it seemed that everyone in greater downtown Laurel Valley had suddenly discovered Weddings Unlimited. The phone started ringing the minute the shop opened, and a half hour later, a surprised and somewhat harried Andrea found herself riding the crest of a decidedly bullish upswing in the matrimony business.

She had spent the last two days closeted with her sketchbook, typewriter and the material Matthew had given her. The result was a polished presentation that was safely tucked inside the portfolio on the drafting table. Taking a sip of her now tepid coffee, she wandered over and fingered the neat blue cover absently. As hard as she had worked on each detail, an aggravating feeling that she might have forgotten something still persisted.

"Am I glad to see you," she said with relief as her lanky assistant wandered into the office. "Already we've got two new weddings and a retread, and it isn't even lunchtime yet, Jase!"

"Ain't love grand?" he observed. "By the way, what's a retread?"

"Mr. and Mrs. Wilfred MacDougal are celebrating their twenty-fifth anniversary and want to renew their vows," she supplied with a chuckle.

"Seems to me they ought to leave well enough alone. They already have six children."

Andrea absently rubbed the small of her back to relieve the nagging nibble of fatigue. "Last week we couldn't even buy a phone call. I wonder why we're so hot all of a sudden."

"Someone must've leaked word that we're working Whitney-Bowman," Jason mused aloud, a look of self-satisfaction settling across his blunt features. Folding his long frame into the swivel chair, he reached for a paper bag on the desk and pulled out a pastry.

"Wonder who could've done that?"

"Beats the hell out of me. When I mentioned it to Winona Bellamy, she swore she wouldn't breathe a word of it," he answered innocently between munches. "Want a Danish? The prune is kind of stale, but the apricot's not bad."

"Why didn't you just take out an ad in the *Laurel Valley Trumpeter*?"

"Winona's mouth is more reliable and a lot cheaper. You have to admit my method got results."

Andrea shook her head in exasperation. "But suppose Matt hates the proposal and we don't get the job?"

"He won't and we will. When is he picking you up for the Richmond meeting?"

"In an hour. How do I look?" She pirouetted slowly so that he could judge the effect of the gunmetal Pierre Balmain suit she was wearing. A lengthy struggle with hot rollers that morning had disciplined her curls into a shining cap that fell straight to her shoulders, then swung under in a soft curve.

"Mahh-vulous, dahling," he quipped, but there was not much humor in his eyes.

She opened the portfolio and thumbed through it hesitantly. "Can I practice the presentation on you?"

"Sure." Jason stared down at his half-eaten pastry as though he had discovered an alien substance embedded in its filling.

His feelings are hurt. The belated flash of insight took Andrea by surprise. *Of course they are, stupid,* she chided herself. *He wanted to help, but you cut him out of the whole process.*

"The reception will be a Hispanic festival," she began guiltily.

"Isn't that kind of exotic?" Jason interrupted.

"It was the only thing I could think of that wouldn't turn the reception into a Hatfield-McCoy reunion," she explained. "Miranda Whitney and Philbert Bowman don't seem to have a single thing in common. Her family is old money, staunchly Democrat and a little to the right of Attila the Hun."

"And his side of the aisle will be packed with self-made progressive Republicans," Jason supplied.

"Bingo! But I read in the clippings Matt gave me that the two of them met while they were on holiday in Puerto Vallarta. *Voilà*—instant reception theme." She showed him a sketch of a flower-decked plaza surrounded by adobe facades and flanked with terra-cotta pottery. "Piñatas suspended from the ceiling of the ballroom will be the main event. I know that they're traditionally used at Christmastime and for children's birthday parties, but they can be adapted to a wedding motif and filled with small gifts for the guests. And we'll serve classical Mexican fare, finger foods like miniature tacos to begin with, and later a sit-down buffet starring chicken mole and beef barbecue. What do you think?"

"Slick. Matt should be impressed." Her assistant gnawed his thumbnail thoughtfully. "Music by a strolling mariachi band, of course. There's a group in D.C. that's supposed to be super—played gigs at the Mexico City Hilton before they came to the States. Want me to see if they're available?"

It was the one touch she had not considered. "Book 'em, Danno," she said, flashing him a grateful smile as she slid the sketch back in the folder.

Her *Hawaii Five-O* imitation brought an answering grin to his long face.

Andrea sobered, realizing with a pang how much she had come to rely on this intelligent and sensitive man. When they had gone over the rest of the details, she said contritely, by way of apology, "This is a day late and dollar short, but from now on you're in on everything."

He grinned. "Appreciate your confidence. Is there anything special on tap for this afternoon?"

She shook her head. "Nothing urgent, but you could try and dig up more on Miranda and Philbert. I'm really twitchy about this one, and it won't hurt to cover every base twice. If something comes up, call me at the Regent. Matt's office number is on the Rolodex."

"I can take care of everything." His tone was slightly indignant.

She patted his shoulder in passing. "I wish you were giving this presentation. To tell you the truth, I'm scared witless."

As she started for the front of the shop, he called out after her, "If you talk as good as you look we don't have a thing to worry about. Break a leg, boss lady."

"Not too shabby on the outside," she confided to her sleek reflection in the glass of the door, adding with a wry grimace, "but the inside is a mess!"

She might have been this nervous before, but she couldn't remember when. It wasn't having to give the presentation, she decided; it was having the new Matthew Donaldson judge its worth.

The downhill slide of their fledgling relationship had started with Kahlil Gibran, she mused, wishing she had never picked up the book and blabbed on to him about her burning desire for six children. *Well, if he doesn't like kids, who needs him?*

I do.

Caught up in the internal argument, she did not notice the two-seater foreign sports car until its horn discreetly announced its arrival.

Andrea's impulse was to scramble, but she steadfastly resisted it. Slinging her black topcoat casually around her shoulders, she sauntered onto the sidewalk with the aplomb of a *Vogue* model.

Matthew's eyes reflected admiration as he opened the car door and helped her stow the portfolio in the small space behind the passenger's seat, but his greeting was flippant. "I don't know what to say. It isn't every day that a princess waltzes into my life."

"Good afternoon, Your Royal Highness is what I'm used to," she said tersely. "You're ten minutes late."

"Sorry to keep you waiting," he said stiffly, turning the key in the ignition. The car came to life with a guttural purr.

She racked her brain for something to say that would not sound hostile. "My compliments to your carriage maker. The elves in the Black Forest put in a lot of overtime on this baby."

"Actually, I prefer the Pumpkin GT, but it's in the shop for a transmission overhaul," he responded laconically.

Andrea was floundering in the quagmire of their breezy banter, so she shifted to what she hoped was more solid ground. "How's Jenny?"

"Fine." Matthew concentrated on missing a trash can that had rolled into the street before he continued. "I spotted a birthday present for her yesterday in McGruders toy shop: a dollhouse with electric lights that really work. Isn't that perfect?"

Or not, Andy answered silently, uncomfortable with the idea. Shouldn't he be encouraging Jennifer to relinquish Barbie and company in favor of more adult pursuits? *Butt out, this is none of your business,* she told herself firmly. Following that advice, her "Hmm" was carefully noncommittal, and it would have served the purpose if she had not added, "On my eighteenth birthday, Mama Mascari gave me a pair of pearl earrings. It was a rite of passage for me—I've never forgotten how grown-up they made me feel. I thought perhaps I would try to find some just like them for Jenny."

"Her ears aren't pierced."

"Hey, that's no problem. As part of my gift, I'll take her to the jewelry store to have it done. They have trained technicians right on the premises." Andy was warming to the prospect. "Listen, we could make a big deal of it—lunch, a little shopping—a real ladies' day out on the town."

She beamed at him, waiting for his confirmation of her brilliance. Instead, his forehead creased in disapproval. Belatedly, she noticed the tightening of the muscles in his jaw.

"Or I could get clip-ons, but they pinch...." Andrea trailed off. Not wanting to leave the issue dangling, she faced it squarely. "Did I just put my foot in my mouth?"

"Of course not. Pearl earrings for a typical eighteen-year-old are a lovely idea, Andy, but Jennifer is not typical. Rites of passage are only for those who grow up, and she never will," he commented sadly.

Particularly if you don't let her. The thought brought a rush of guilt. Who was she to judge the way this man dealt with his sister's problem? She wisely withheld her two cents' worth of analysis, murmuring instead, "I'll think of something more appropriate."

Matthew nodded in agreement, turning his attention to what passed for heavy traffic in downtown Laurel Valley: two station wagons and a battered Chevy pickup cruising at a snail's pace past City Hall.

Realizing that further discussion of the subject would be useless, to say nothing of potentially dangerous to their already shaky relationship, Andrea shut up and occupied herself with the scenery.

The hamlet's main street was a provincial sycamore-lined affair that some long-dead visionary had hopefully named Broadway. Halfway through the town it bifurcated to encircle a statue of a Confederate general to whom numerous decorations had been awarded over the years by weather and disrespectful sparrows on their way to Georgia. At the intersection of Broadway and Lee Avenue, polyester-draped mannequins in the window of Meyer's Department Store stared mournfully across the street at the casket-handle railings marching up the front steps of Pickett's funeral parlor. And at the end, Valley Baptist lifted its prayerful arms to heaven, promising a little something extra for the faithful. Altogether the effect was reassuring.

"Southern America is alive and doing well," she murmured with a chuckle.

"This is a pleasant little town, isn't it?" he commented as though reading her thoughts. His dark eyes warmed a few degrees. "It's not exactly the center of the social world, though. I understand that Willa Prichard, your predecessor, had a hard time making ends meet. How did you decide to come here?"

"With the help of a straight pin. The first ad I stabbed in a trade magazine was Mrs. Prichard's, and the rest is history."

"I'm surprised you don't find it dull after living in New York."

She grinned wryly. "I do miss the Met, and sometimes I would kill for a good pastrami sandwich, but dull has its advantages. You have to work real hard to get mugged in Laurel Valley."

He chuckled, heading the car onto the interchange that led to Route 60 east. "I'm curious. Why did you become a bridal consultant in the first place?"

She shrugged. "That is rather complicated. I never had the talent to be a top fashion designer, but I had to learn that the hard way—my career at Couturière Margo consisted of doing all the grubby work of scheduling and coordinating, and I found out I was pretty darn good at it. When you add that to the fact that I'm an incurable romantic who loves weddings, you have an instant bridal consultant."

He frowned. "Somehow I got the impression that you had been in the business all along."

"The Bellamy wedding was my first. I told you I didn't have much experience," she said a touch defensively.

Matt's face was apprehensive. "Have you ever made a presentation like the Whitney-Bowman package?"

She got very busy with an imaginary smudge on the sleeve of her suit. "Not exactly, but I used to coordinate Margo's spring and fall showings. There isn't really much difference."

He swallowed hard. "We could go over the details of your proposal right now if you like. A trial run before the meeting might not hurt."

"I would rather not." She laughed uneasily, joking, "Don't you know that bridal consultants are superstitious about premature unveilings?"

He did not seem amused.

"Seriously, I would prefer that you and your staff hear the presentation at the same time," she hedged.

"Why?"

Because I'm scared to death that you'll hate the whole thing; then I'd get mad, and we'd never speak to each other again ran through Andrea's head. Aloud, she said loftily, "It's better for the development of group dynamics. And anyway, you can't look at the sketches while you're driving."

"I'm perfectly capable of understanding a concept without visual aids. If you give me a synopsis of the main points, we can iron out any potential problems before the meeting." His foot pressed harder on the gas pedal, and the vehicle sped past an eighteen-wheeler.

"The only problem I foresee is being smeared all over the highway. In case you haven't heard, the speed limit is fifty-five," she offered sweetly.

Matt gritted his teeth, but he did slow down. "I don't usually like surprises, Andrea. I operate better when I know what's ahead."

"Thank you for sharing that with me. Maybe I should have asked you to help me write the proposal," she said coolly.

"It might not have been a bad idea."

Andy bristled. "If you don't trust my competence, I'll be more than happy to return your check. I certainly wouldn't want to embarrass you in front of your staff."

They glared at each other. She was sure the confrontation would end in an explosion when inexplicably his face softened.

"Of course I trust you, but I inherited a severe case of Donaldson Control Syndrome from my father, and sometimes it runs away with me. I warned you I'm not easy to work with," Matt reminded her ruefully, warmth once again filling his ebony eyes. "And you're nobody's pushover. We're in for some damned good fights, aren't we?"

"It looks like it," she said grimly, the image of her battling parents springing immediately to mind.

"We got off on the wrong track, sweet. Can we go back and start from the beginning?" He reached for her hand and held it until her fingers uncurled from their clenched position.

The small endearment was hard to miss and impossible to ignore. "You bet."

As the tension drained away, she felt foolish. It was not his lack of confidence she should be worried about; it was her own. "Okay, let's talk about Miranda Whitney and Philbert Bowman. The basic motif for the reception is—"

"Shh—no more business until we get to Richmond. You and I are going to be the major topic of this conversation," he interrupted. "Do you like brussels sprouts?"

She stared at him in puzzlement. "No, but—"

"Neither do I. What about spinach?"

"It's good in salads, but I hate it boiled. What do green vegetables have to do with us?"

His eyebrows peaked in amusement. "I want to learn everything there is to know about Andrea Kirkland. How do you feel about Bela Lugosi?"

"Lon Chaney was a better actor. Did you see *E.T.*?" she asked, getting into the spirit of the game.

"Yes."

"Did you cry when it seemed that he would die?"

"Blubbered like a baby," he admitted. He put his right arm around her shoulders and drew her as close as he could, considering the bucket seats and console.

"Let's try not to let this project get in the way of our personal relationship, Andy."

"And vice versa," she said quickly.

"I'd rather get another job than try to replace you."

At that moment, Andrea made an extremely important discovery. Take away the man's broad shoulders, the slightly off-center dimple that dented his strong chin, the eyes that could go from storm to sunshine in the space of a heartbeat, and what would be left?

A thoroughly nice, genuinely decent human being. Magic was fine, but there was going to be much more to this than wading knee-deep in stardust.

"I like you a hell of a lot, Matthew Donaldson," she told him softly.

Chapter Five

The Richmond Regent, a soaring tower of steel and amber glass, was set on a wooded bluff overlooking the James River. Its architect had achieved a perfect balance of high-tech functionalism and Southern hospitality; the hotel was modern and luxurious, yet at the same time warm and unpretentious. The land was carved in a series of gentle terraces banking down into a wide, horseshoe-shaped drive at the entrance level. Masses of azaleas and rhododendrons, brown and pinched in the thin sun of January, would in spring fill the air with a riot of color and scent.

"You were right. This is the perfect setting for romance," Andrea said as Matthew escorted her through the foliage-filled atrium to the elevator. She blushed as soon as the words were out of her mouth.

"I was hoping you'd notice," he teased.

The reception area of the fifteenth-floor office suite was carpeted in celadon green, a color repeated in the Oriental tile inlaid on the lacquer coffee table in front of the long sectional. Three of the chalk-white walls were unadorned, the fourth graced with a magnificent silk screen from the Sung Dynasty period.

"Thank God you finally got here, Matt." The woman hurrying through the doorway beside the screen was a tall redhead with a breathtaking face and a body to match. Relief was evident in her enormous blue eyes as she tossed aside the stack of printouts she was carrying and sat down at the computer on her desk. "We have one hell of a crisis on our hands!" she added, beginning a rapid tattoo on the keyboard.

"Par for the course on Wednesday. What's up, Lynn?" Matt strode over to her side to stare at the screen.

"A mix-up in conference scheduling. There are fifty-three irate Beavers in the lobby demanding their rooms!"

"That's impossible. The lodge convention doesn't start till tomorrow." He loosened his tie and leaned over the console, punching in entries of his own. "Where is Benson?"

"Downstairs trying to keep them from building a dam around the reservations desk."

Andrea could not suppress a laugh.

Matt grinned at her, gesturing for her to join them. "Andy Kirkland, my administrative assistant, Lynnette Mac-Namara." He handled the introduction quickly, relieving Andrea of her coat and portfolio.

"I'm glad to meet you, Ms MacNamara," she lied as a whiff of the seductive scent Matthew's girl Friday was wearing wafted past her nose. The generous dimensions of Lynn's upper torso did not make her the least bit glad. Feeling a touch defensive about her own, more modest proportions, Andrea unconsciously drew in a deep breath. She relaxed considerably, however, when she noticed the gold filigree band on the ring finger of the other woman's left hand.

"I'm afraid we'll have to postpone the Whitney-Bowman meeting until this Beaver mess is straightened out, Andy," Matthew apologized. "It could take quite a while. Would you like to wait in my office?"

"If there's time, I think I'll grab a sandwich. I missed lunch today," she answered.

"We can have room service bring something up," Lynn suggested.

She shook her head. "I've never been to the Regent, and I'd like to nose around."

"Try the Quarterdeck if you like seafood," Matthew called after her as she headed for the glass-enclosed elevator.

Descending into the main atrium was like drifting slowly through the heart of a rain forest. The glow from the massive skylight overhead was gradually dimmed by a profusion of philodendron, ferns, ficus and dozens of other plants Andrea could not identify. Originating at the mezzanine level, a waterfall splashed playfully over mossy rocks and down into an orchid-surrounded pool at the bottom.

"So this is the high-rent district," she murmured to herself, following a path that meandered through the foliage. The Quarterdeck was on the other side of an Oriental-style bridge under which fat, goggle-eyed fish swam in lazy circles.

Andrea wrinkled her nose in frustration at the line of people in front of the restaurant.

"It will be at least half an hour. Would you like to wait in the bar?" the hostess asked a couple at the head of the queue.

Turning to start for the newsstand and a quick candy fix, Andrea was stopped by a light touch on her elbow.

"Miss Kirkland? Right this way, please."

The man who guided her past the line and to a cozy window table with a splendid view of the river was a David Niven lookalike with graying temples and a charming accent.

He seated her, answering her unspoken question. "Mr. Donaldson gave an excellent description of you."

Andrea could not think of an appropriate response, so she smiled, hoping the light was too dim for him to notice her sudden blush.

"Would you care for a glass of wine?"

"N-no, thank you," she stammered, struggling to recover from the unexpectedness of the preferential treatment she was receiving. "Iced tea will be fine."

"May I suggest you try the specialty of the house? Our seafood sampler is quite good."

"I'd like that," she answered with what she hoped was a passable imitation of Grace Kelly's regal nod.

"Hot damn!" she murmured jubilantly as he glided away. She leaned back and closed her eyes, soothed by soft strains of a string quartet and inordinately pleased that even in the midst of a crisis, Matthew had taken time to arrange this for her.

"I hate to disturb a beautiful daydream, Andy, but we have a nightmare to deal with!"

Her eyes flew open to the sight of a breathless Jason standing beside the table. He set down his briefcase and slid onto the banquette opposite her.

"What are you doing here, and who's minding the shop?" she asked incredulously.

"Miss Henrietta Hewitt came in, and I shanghaied her," he said, puffing. "I couldn't catch you before you and Matt left, so I just took off after you. Andy, we can't use the Hispanic festival theme."

She straightened up quickly. "Why not?"

"I called Nancy Ellison—she went to school with Miranda Bowman, you know. Anyway, Nancy said that except for the fact that Bowman and Whitney found each other there, Puerto Vallarta was a total disaster. Philbert broke his leg falling off a horse, and Miranda came down with Montezuma's revenge. You even mention Mexico, and both of them turn the color of guacamole."

Andrea's jaw sagged in dismay. A cold hand closed around her throat at the thought of having to tell Matthew there would not be any presentation. "Oh, my God! What are we going to do?"

The waiter picked that moment to place a large orchid-garnished seafood platter in front of Andrea. She closed her eyes and turned her head away.

"Is ma'mselle displeased?" he queried anxiously.

"Everything is fine," she said, edging the plate toward the center of the table. At the moment, the last thing she wanted was food.

"May I bring the gentleman something?"

"I'll share hers," Jason said, spearing one of the plump pink shrimp on its bed of crisp lettuce.

"How can you eat at a time like this?" she hissed.

"I panic better on a full stomach." He leaned over to open the briefcase, retrieving a neatly bound folder, and handed it to her. "See what you think of this."

After scanning the first few paragraphs, Andrea did a double take and began again, this time poring over every word. "This is simply marvelous, Jason! When did you do it?"

He looked down, tracing hesitant squares on the tablecloth. "While you were doing your presentation. I was just goofing around, so I thought I'd try my hand at writing a proposal. I figured I could use it for a class project or something."

"What made you think of this particular theme?"

His voice took on an air of excitement. "You were right about Philbert and Miranda not having much in common, but what they *do* share is a deep love for the history of this state. He graduated from William and Mary, and her grandmother is a bigwig in Virginia's chapter of the Daughters of the American Revolution. The idea of setting the reception in Colonial Williamsburg sort of jumped out at me. You really think it's good?"

"Good? It's wonderful—magnificent—spectacular, all of the above!" She picked up her fork and attacked the crab Louis. "Okay, let's go over this baby from the beginning."

By the time the waiter appeared with a message that Matt was ready to start the meeting, the platter was empty, and Andrea had grasped every detail of the proposal. "Let's go knock 'em dead," she told her assistant triumphantly.

Besides Matthew, Lynn and Benson, the manager, the group around the impressive oak table in the conference room of the office suite included Sam Zaccaro, a design engineer, Patricia Blake, culinary liaison, and Fred Price, budget analyst. All looked expectantly at Andrea as she stood to begin the presentation.

She had no idea how Matthew would take what she was about to say, but she had to say it, anyway. Studiously avoiding his eyes, she patted the portfolio she had brought with her and began. "What I have here is two days of sweat. My proposal is comprehensive, highly detailed and extremely neat. It is also utterly useless."

A surprised murmur circled the room.

"In trying to do this all by myself, I overlooked one simple rule—it is impossible to produce good work in a vacuum." Andrea could feel a new confidence flowing through her. Regardless of the consequences, what she was doing was right; that knowledge steadied her shaking legs. She drew in a deep breath and met Matthew's intent gaze levelly. "I'm telling you this to make a very important point. I want us to start and finish this project as a team."

Andrea turned to Jason and smiled. "Now about the real proposal. Luckily for all of us, Weddings Unlimited has strong backup capability, so I'm going to shut up and let Jason Markham, the man who did the work, tell you about it."

Jason's jaw dropped almost to his chest. When he recovered his composure, his eyes were shining, and a million-watt grin lit his dusky face.

His Williamsburg theme was a smash. Two hours later the group was still excitedly hashing out the details.

"I'm dying of curiosity, Andy. What is the theme of your other proposal?" Lynnette asked as the meeting wound down.

"Yes, and why won't it work?" Patricia Blake seconded.

Andrea quickly outlined the plans for the Hispanic festival, ending with a droll account of the engaged couple's Mexican mishaps. "Next time I'll be more careful about doing my homework," she added, closing the portfolio.

"Folks, what we have here is a twofer," Matt said. He rubbed his hands together gleefully.

"Ain't it just?" Lynn agreed. "Andy, have you ever heard of Tio Tamale?"

"The Mexican fast-food chain?" she queried.

"Yep. It's based right here in Richmond. And Julio Sanchez, the owner, has twin daughters who are getting married in August. Every hotel and caterer in the commonwealth will be after a piece of the action," the redhead crowed.

"But Regent will get it, because we'll get in the first and best shot. Our preliminary work is already done," Sam Zaccaro finished.

"*Olé,*" Andrea responded weakly.

"But before we count our new chickens, let's finish hatching this egg, group," Matthew said with a chuckle. He made assignments and suggested they reconvene in a week. As the rest of the group was filing out, he turned to Jason. "This is as good a time as any for you to start at Regent. I'd like you to stay for the rest of the afternoon and brainstorm with Fred Price on the budget for the reception."

The young man's face was troubled, but it cleared as he glanced at Andrea; pride glistened in his eyes. "Matt, I appreciate what you've done for me, but I don't think I can accept the internship. Business at the shop is picking up, and I wouldn't want to leave Andy shorthanded."

"I can manage, Jase. You can't afford to turn down an opportunity like this," she protested.

Matt looked as though he were going to second her objection, then swallowed hard. "I understand. And really, you'll learn as much, if not more, with Andrea. Look, I'll talk to Dr. Richardson again. I'm sure I can convince him that you should earn academic credit for working at Weddings Unlimited."

"Thanks, man—you're something else." Jason shook his hand, then turned to Andrea. "I'd better get back now. See you at the shop, boss."

"Before it's all over, that kid is going to be in the Fortune Five Hundred," Matthew predicted after Jason left.

"At least," Andrea agreed, busying herself with the portfolio. She was unaccountably nervous.

"Andy..." He moved closer, bringing to her the clean male scent that was his own special cologne.

"Did you get the Beavers squared away?" she asked, not for information but to slow the flutter of her heart.

"After a fashion. We're giving them an extra day for half price." He cradled her chin with his hands and lifted her face.

"That's a damn sight better than having them chew down the trees in the atrium."

He groaned at the bad pun. "Shut up and listen to me. You could have taken credit for Jason's idea, but you didn't. And it's not easy to face a bunch of strangers and tell them you've made a mistake. That kind of integrity is a rare commodity in the business world. You're going to be good for Regent."

"I hope so. I have a very fat consultant's fee to earn."

His eyes narrowed speculatively. "We could make it a more permanent arrangement, you know. Getting the wedding center started will be one of my top priorities in the next few months, but after it's up and running, I'll have to go on to other things. If you were the full-time director from the very beginning, we could avoid the hassle of training a new person." The excitement in his voice grew as he continued, "You would have a small staff to start with, probably three or four people, but of course, as the volume of business increased, your personnel would expand. What do you say? Will you take the job?"

Heady visions of an antique French Provincial desk with Andrea Kirkland, Wedding Director inscribed on a discreet brass nameplate and four decorator telephones all ringing at the same time whirled through her head but were rapidly replaced by a more realistic picture: an embattled Andrea Kirkland surrounded by Winona Bellamy clones and reaching for an endless line of glasses filled with Alka-Seltzer.

She perched on the edge of the table, fiddling absently with a pen Lynn had left behind. "I don't know a thing about hotel operations, Matt, and I've never supervised anyone in my life," she hedged.

"So what's Jason, chopped liver?"

"He's not staff; he's my friend. And I also have to think of my obligations at Weddings Unlimited."

Matthew's jaw clenched, and what Andy had mentally dubbed his mogul mask dropped into place. "A little business in a small town may be good enough for some people but not for you. You certainly have more ambition than that," he said stubbornly.

"Thank you for the instant analysis, but beside the fact that I hate brussels sprouts and boiled spinach, you don't know a damned thing about me," she flared. "You're letting the Donaldson Control Syndrome run away with you again."

Mr. Mogul instantly gave way to Andy's favorite shoe salesman.

"You're right," Matthew said contritely. "But I know more about you than you think. You're compassionate, sensitive and loving. I'd bet large dollars that when you were a little girl, your favorite pet was a Persian kitten you called Fluffy."

"Siamese, and his name was Screwball," she corrected with a grin. Then a shadow edged into her gray eyes, and she drew a deep breath. "Maybe in time I could handle the job, but we both know I'm not qualified for it now."

He moved to her side, grasping her shoulders gently. "Would you at least let me expand your consultant contract to cover more than the Whitney-Bowman reception? I need your help to plan the center."

"Let me think about it. I don't want to take the job for the wrong reason."

"Which is?"

Andrea met his gaze honestly. "Because I like being with you," she answered with no hesitation or coyness.

His lips brushed hers; then he pulled back. "Do you have any idea how happy that makes me—how much I've come to care for you?"

"Before you show me, let's promise each other that we won't ever let the work make us argue again."

"It's a deal," he answered, pulling her to her feet and into his arms.

But even with the best of intentions, the promise was not easily kept. Work on the Whitney-Bowman reception progressed at a reasonably smooth pace, first because Andrea's major duty was simply to coordinate units within the hotel that already functioned efficiently, and second, because Matthew's involvement was minimal. The wedding center, however, became an almost constant source of friction between them. During the first week of their working together, apologies were immediately given and eagerly accepted for any breach in their pact, but by February first, detente was increasingly harder to maintain.

"We are going to end up hating each other—I just know it," Andrea muttered to herself, jotting another note on the lengthening list of priority items taped to the wall behind Weddings Unlimited's front counter.

Her gloomy assessment stemmed from the fact that for over a week she and Matthew had not even held hands, and at yesterday's staff meeting they had been open adversaries.

He had dismissed her suggestion of providing free first-anniversary weekends for couples who got married at the hotel with a curt "That's simply not practical, Andrea. In the long run it would be extremely expensive."

"Okay, then—small remembrances for anniversaries instead. And congratulatory cards when they have babies—little things that would show we are aware of their life together after the wedding,'' she had argued stubbornly.

"If we followed that line of logic, we'd eventually have to offer the services of divorce lawyers on the premises," he retorted, moving on to the next item on the agenda.

Her remembered breach of business etiquette after his sarcastic sally now made her cringe and reach for the phone. "Why should I be the one to apologize?" she asked herself, cradling the receiver before the last number was dialed.

"I had every right to call him a pigheaded pessimist," she fumed, stalking across the bridal-shop showroom to snatch up a dress that had slipped from its hanger on the rack. Absorbed by her frustration, she hardly noticed the tinkle of the bell over the front door.

"If you aren't careful, you're going to tear that pretty frock," Henrietta Hewitt informed her.

Andrea's smile reflected her genuine pleasure. "It seems like ages since I've seen you. I've been hoping you would come by."

"I did a few times, but you were either busy or away." The old woman glanced longingly back toward the show window. "I see you sold the veil."

"No such thing." Andrea went behind the counter to retrieve the box a generous impulse had led her to stow there three weeks ago. Handing it to her elderly friend, she said, "I wanted you to have it."

Henrietta's mouth formed an O of surprise. She opened the box and, carefully lifting the tissue, fingered the fragile ornament lovingly. "Thank you very much, but some young bride should have this, not an old lady with nothing left but silly hopes."

"You said yourself that it's never too late," Andy reminded her, teasing. "You can't tell when some Galahad might come along and sweep you off your feet."

Miss Hewitt's laugh was rich and melodic, wind chimes weathered to mellow by the passage of years. "Sancho Panza is more like it. My knight is balding, overweight, and his armor is rusting about the knees."

Andrea was intrigued. It had not occurred to her that the gift would be anything more to Henrietta than a symbol of past dreams, but it sounded as though she could have a more practical purpose in mind for the veil.

"Fifty years ago, though, it was a different story. Oh, my, yes, it was. Nehemiah Gill cut a dashing figure in those days. Dark, curly hair, shoulders that put a blacksmith to shame and a big, booming voice that made the choir loft shake on Sunday mornings. Your Matthew puts me in mind of him then...." She trailed off, and lost in thought, wandered over to the mannequin couple posed together on a dais in the center of the shop. Running her fingers lightly over the sleeve of the groom's morning coat, Henrietta continued, "Our wedding was to be the June after I graduated from high school, but I got it in my head to go to college. He was ready to start a family, so he married someone else."

"You must have been devastated," Andrea murmured.

"I made do—although I never stopped loving him, and it was so hard to come back here and teach the children that could have been mine." The old woman sighed. "Nehemiah seemed contented enough with his life until his wife died eleven years ago. Shortly after, I discovered he still cared about me, too."

Andrea supplied the story with a happy ending. "And so you two got back together."

Miss Hewitt snorted. "I wouldn't exactly compare Sunday afternoon visits and an occasional trip to the shopping center to the grand passion we used to have," she answered. Then, more wistfully, she added, "We still have our moments, though. I'd marry him tomorrow, but the stubborn old fool won't pop the question."

Andrea chuckled, hugging the frail shoulders. "Haven't you heard of women's lib? If you want Nehemiah, why don't you ask him?"

"Oh, no! Proposing to a man might be fine for you youngsters, but it wouldn't be proper for me." Her tone was emphatic, and she replaced the lid on the box. "I should be ashamed bothering you with that nonsense when you obviously have problems of your own. What's troubling you, dear?"

Henrietta's gentle concern was so similar to what Rosa Mascari might have offered that Andy blinked back a sudden spate of tears. Her "Nothing" was followed in rapid succession by "I don't know" and "Everything."

"That covers most of the territory. Where would you like to start?" Miss Hewitt said.

"With the work at the Regent and the new business Weddings Unlimited has lately, it seems that there is too much to do, Henrietta. Jason doesn't complain, and he's doing a heck of a job, but I feel guilty for laying so much of the responsibility on him."

The older woman dismissed the explanation with an impatient wave of her hand. "That young man's not happy unless he has fifteen things going at one time. When he was a boy, he had a lemonade stand, a paper route and a dog-walking service, and he still found time for Little League baseball. But if it concerns you, why not hire a part-time worker so that both of you can occasionally take a breather?"

The solution was so simple Andrea almost laughed. "You're a genius! I'll put a help-wanted ad in tomorrow's paper."

"No need for that. When do I start?"

Andy's jaw dropped. "You?"

"Why not? I have excellent references," she said dryly, adding with a hint of wistfulness, "and if I spend my mornings at the Ark and my afternoons here, I'll have less time to moon over Nehemiah Gill."

She watched numbly as Miss Hewitt hung her coat on the rack behind the counter and marched to the front door to turn the cardboard sign so that the "Closed—Back in Fifteen Minutes" side faced the street. "And while I have my first official coffee break, you can tell me what is really on your mind."

"Yes, ma'am," Andrea said meekly, following her new employee back to the workroom.

Once the initial hesitancy was conquered, the story of the conflicts with Matthew came tumbling out. "We simply can't work together," Andy finished glumly.

"Pooh." Henrietta pursed her lips, and her eyes narrowed. "Work isn't the only problem, and you know it. Are you in love with Matthew?"

"Of course not.... I don't know.... Maybe...."

"If your business decisions are as uncertain as your personal ones, I won't be employed very long," Miss Hewitt snorted.

"I care for him a lot, and I'm pretty sure the feeling is mutual." She picked nervously at a hangnail on her thumb.

"What have you done about it?"

Andrea's lashes shaded her eyes from the other woman's probing gaze. "We haven't really had the opportunity to be alone together, and to tell you the truth, I'm glad. I'm not sure I want us to make love."

Henrietta's expression reflected her surprise. "Why on earth not?"

"Because our relationship probably hasn't got much of a future, and I don't believe in casual sex." Pain edged its way across Andrea's face. "Eventually, I want to have a family—it's very important to me—and I don't think Matt even likes children. Every time the subject comes up, he goes into deep freeze."

"Your babies are a bit premature, missy. In my day, we concentrated on the man before we turned him into a father. You certainly aren't going to have much of a future if you wait for it to build itself." She gathered up the coffee mugs, taking them to the sink to rinse them. "You have some hard thinking to do, so I'll go tidy up the showroom and take care of any customers that might wander in," she said briskly.

Andrea grinned. "I bet your students never dared to throw spitballs. You must have been a holy terror in the classroom."

"Tried my best." Henrietta chuckled as she went to start her new job.

After two false starts, Andrea managed to dial the number at Matt's Prescott office.

"I'm sorry I called you names in front of the staff yesterday. It was stupid and childish, and believe me, it won't happen again," she said as soon as he answered.

"Don't apologize; you were right. Your ideas about the center are damned good," he insisted.

She laughed. "Wait a minute. Before we get into an argument over who was most at fault, I have something to tell you. I'm resigning from the wedding-center project."

There was dead silence at the other end.

"I can't seem to concentrate on four things at the same time, and the center is the only one that's expendable."

"If that's really what you want, I won't try to change your mind." He sounded relieved. "But are you sure the other three things are that important?"

"It would be irresponsible for me to quit the Whitney-Bowman reception at this late date, and without Weddings Unlimited, I'd have to go on welfare. And . . ." She twisted the telephone around her finger so tightly her circulation was endangered. "And you're very important to me, Matt. I can't risk losing your friendship over something as dumb as the Regent's wedding center."

"I didn't want to take that chance, either. That's why I called Lynn MacNamara this morning and put her in charge of the project."

"Oh, Matt. . ." She stopped until the lump in her throat went away. "*E.T.* is on at the Rialto, and the matinee starts in fifteen minutes. Do you want to play hooky this afternoon?"

"I'll bring the Kleenex if you buy the popcorn."

Smiling, she hung up and went to find her mentor. "I finished my homework, teach, and I'm going out for recess with the cutest boy in the class."

"In that case, you deserve an A plus," the old woman said, patting her shoulder.

Chapter Six

The rest of February and half of March passed with the speed of a cartoon roadrunner. In spite of the additional help provided by Miss Hewitt, Andrea's workweeks at Weddings Unlimited stretched to six days, and Sundays were necessarily filled with the minutiae of keeping life in reasonable working order.

Cash flow, or the lack of it, was no longer her major problem; time for romance was now the scarce resource. But the inventive and truly determined can stretch even the most parsimonius of budgets to include a little luxury. Andrea learned to hoard seconds with Matthew as avidly as Midas counted his fortune. Even though they were no longer working on a joint project, she still had twice-weekly meetings with the reception staff, and he was more than happy for her company on the drives between Richmond and Laurel Valley. Those trips became pure gold, reserved to squander on laughter and a growing closeness. And there were smaller, though no less precious, coins: late-night phone calls, secret jokes and shared glances that started by accident and continued by design.

"No more scrimping and saving after this," she promised herself as she watched the ebb and flow of the Whitney-Bowman affair from a little-used balcony overlooking the grand hotel ballroom. "Miranda and Philbert, you're on your own—I've got bigger fish to fry."

At the moment, the catch of the day, resplendent in a perfectly tailored tux, was making a circuit of the floor below. Matt's pace was unhurried, and he was seemingly unaware of the bevy of nubile debutantes practically swooning in his wake. He scanned the room casually but carefully, and Andrea knew he was watching for signs of impending trouble.

Or was he?

His gaze traveled upward as surely as the needle on a compass seeks the North Pole, and their eyes locked. The crooked grin and covert wink he telegraphed made Andrea feel as though she had just hit the jackpot.

"Did I hear you say you were going to fry fish?" Lynn MacNamara asked, appearing at Andrea's side. Her tone was incredulous, and her eyes danced with devilment as she offered one of the glasses of champagne she was carrying.

"I've changed my mind. Frog legs are today's special," Andrea supplied, favoring the other woman with a smile. In the two months they had worked together they had developed a surprisingly strong friendship.

"What's with the amphibian fixation? You and Kermit have been a steady item for two or three weeks," Lynn observed, pointing to the charm on the chain around Andrea's neck.

Andy touched the tiny gold frog, a Valentine's gift from Matt, with gentle fingers. "This little guy makes me believe there's a happily ever after," she answered, remembering the touch of Matthew's hands as he clasped the whimsical trinket around her neck just before Jennifer's birthday party.

One of the few occasions they had agreed to let their busy schedules slip had been Valentine's Day. In Mrs. Pickering's absence—she had been away tending an ailing aunt—the combined Valentine-birthday celebration was held at Mr. Jimbo's, Laurel Valley's one-and-only ice-cream parlor. At first Jennifer had been exuberant, greeting each present she opened with giggles of delight. But as the party went on, she grew strangely subdued.

"What's wrong, Jenny?" Andrea finally asked.

"I'm a one" was the cryptic reply. The teenager's eyes had shaded to violet as she surveyed the group around the Formica table. She patted the dolls propped up beside her and said with a deep sigh, "Barbie and Ken are a two, Sara and Jason are a two, and you and Bubba are a two. When will it be my turn?"

There had been no good answer to the poignant question. Andrea felt a twist of sympathy as she watched the pain on Jennifer's face reflect in Matthew's eyes.

Fortunately, the moment had been brief; Jenny's attention was claimed by the couple at the next table. "Those people over there are going to be a three," she confided in a stage whisper, pointing to the obviously expectant woman.

Matt had been startled. "Why do you say that?"

"Don't you know anything? She's preg-a-nant!" Jenny viewed her brother with haughty exasperation. "You had better talk to Mrs. Pickering, Bubba. She'll tell you all about babies."

Although Andrea had joined in the laughter of the others, in a secret corner of her heart she was troubled. Matt was wrong about his sister; she was not a little girl at all. Her mental faculties might never function like those of an adult, but she was a developing woman, and she was bound to have some of the needs and hopes that went with it.

She shook her head now to clear it of the disturbing exchange. "I should have bought the pearl earrings," she mused aloud.

"Did I miss some of this conversation?" Lynn's face wore a startled expression.

"Sorry—I was babbling to myself," Andy admitted.

"The mind is a terrible thing to waste." The wry observation was accompanied by an exaggeratedly solicitous pat on the shoulder.

Andy chuckled. "Don't start with me, lady. I'm dangerous when my brain is on overload."

"You do look tired," the redhead observed, sobering. "Go upstairs and grab a nap, will you? Everything is under control now."

A vision of the luxurious room on the tenth floor that had been reserved for her use until after the reception was tantalizing, but Andy shook her head. "You know how fast things can go sour. Suppose Master Todd Chadwick Whitney the Fourth gets loose again?" she said, recalling with a shudder how much havoc the five-year-old ring bearer had managed to wreak in the few short hours he had been in the hotel. Nearly every member of the staff now knew him, either by sight or reputation.

"Don't even think it! Being around that kid has made me a staunch advocate of birth control."

Andrea laughed. "Give him a break. He's just curious and active."

"That's what Hitler's mother probably said." Lynn leaned over the railing, peering down into the crowd. "I don't see him, but I think we're safe for the moment. Last time I noticed, Todd number two had him in tow. You know, I think the little brat's scared of his grandfather."

"Wouldn't you be? Even the governor jumps when Senator Whitney speaks," Matthew chimed in from behind. He moved between them, tucking an arm companionably around each waist. "Midget Menace notwithstanding, you two have done a hell of a job. A few more like this one and Regent's reputation is sterling."

"Twenty-four karat," Lynn corrected, raising her champagne glass in a toast. "Okay, friends, my booze break is over. I've got to go soothe a ruffled photographer. Fifteen minutes ago he was making very loud noises about suing."

Andrea frowned. "What happened?"

"Todd dropped his camera bag in the goldfish pond," Matt's assistant supplied with a chuckle as she hurried away.

"If you ask me, that boy should be locked up until he's thirty," Matthew said darkly.

Andrea winced. In the time they'd had together, she had avoided only one topic, but it was an issue they had to confront sooner or later. Sooner suddenly seemed preferable. "Matt, I know you dislike children, but—"

"Whatever gave you that idea?" he interrupted, his eyes puzzled. "I used to be the best baby-sitter in my neighborhood. Normally, I love to hang around with kids."

"You do?"

"Sure. I even coached peewee football my senior year at UCLA. But even you have to admit that Todd is a real pain in the behind."

"He's not intentionally bad," Andy defended halfheartedly. "And besides, having little children in weddings isn't fair.

When you're only five, how can you be expected to perform on cue, behave and stay clean all at the same time?''

"That sounds like a lecture from Bridal Consultant 101," Matt teased.

"Confessions of a former flower girl. I made my debut in the business when I was three. Almost wrecked Aunt Lillian's marriage, though." She leaned against the railing, grinning at the recollection. "I got halfway down the aisle when panic set in and I ran screaming for my mother. In the process, I knocked over one of the candle stands, got a lump the size of a lemon on my head and nearly set the church on fire. Compared to that, dunking a camera bag is bush league, wouldn't you say?''

Andrea had expected some sort of reaction, but she was not prepared for the one she got.

"I wish I had known you then," he murmured, his face suffused with tenderness. "We could have made mud pies together. And later I would have taught you to ride a bike, teased you about your braces, carried your books to school and—"

A discreet cough interrupted just as she was sure he was about to take her to the prom.

"Excuse me, Mr. Donaldson, but I think this is something that needs your attention," the approaching bellman said diffidently. His white-gloved hand was clutching the left arm of a thoroughly soggy, dirty and frightened little boy.

"Please don't tell Gandy. I won't be bad no more." Todd Chadwick Whitney IV removed his right thumb from his mouth to wail.

"One of the janitors found him behind a dumpster in the basement. None of us can figure out how he got there."

"I'm not sure we want to know, Art," Matthew commented dryly.

"I suppose I should have taken him to his mother, but he started crying so hard about somebody named Gandy, I didn't have the heart. Want me to clean him up?" Art asked.

"We'll manage. You do good work, my man," Matthew complimented.

"Thank you, sir." Pocketing the bill his employer slipped him, Art gave a snappy salute and strode away.

Retrieving his handkerchief, Matthew knelt down beside the youngster and wiped at the tears streaking the grubby face. No sooner was one dried than three more took its place.

"I fell in the pond. Then I went to hide so Gandy wouldn't fuss, 'cause he told me to stop messing wif' the goldfish, and..." Lack of breath and a mournful hiccup kept Todd from finishing the garbled explanation.

In his miniature tuxedo, the child resembled a grimy penguin. "First off, let's take him to my room and give him a bath. Then we can decide whether or not to burn the outfit," Andrea suggested.

"Sounds right to me." Heedless of his own clothes, Matthew scooped the boy up in his arms. "All right, partner, we're going to bail you out this time, but you have got to promise to behave yourself all the rest of the day. Is that understood?"

Todd eagerly agreed.

And if you believe that, I got a terrific deal on the Brooklyn Bridge for you, Andy thought.

"That means no more trying to catch the goldfish in the lobby." Matt's tone was stern, but his mouth twitched as though he was holding back amusement.

Assent was slow to come. The boy wrinkled his button nose in indecision. "Kin I just pet 'em?" he negotiated.

"Nope. And you can't pick any more flowers from around the pond, either," Matt cautioned firmly as he led the way to the service elevator.

The continuing list of prohibitions elicited a mental snort from Andrea. *Don't you know you're fighting a losing battle? He'll be fifty-three before you exhaust all the possibilities.* She laughed to herself. The knowledge that Matthew really did like children produced a heady mixture of relief and elation.

In the corridor, the approaching sound of voices—Senator Whitney's stentorian tones rising above the rest—stopped them dead in their tracks.

"Quick, in here!"

Matt grabbed Andrea's hand and pulled her into a dimly lit storage room used for cleaning supplies, steadying her before she could trip over a push broom.

"Don't ever join the CIA. You'd make a terrible secret agent," he murmured right before he banged into a scrub bucket.

She clasped her hand over her mouth to choke back a peal of giggles. "But the free world is safe as long as you're on the case, huh, Double-Oh-Seven?" she shot back. The two of them rocked with silent laughter.

When the coast was clear, they whisked Todd up to Andrea's room, peeled him and popped him into the tub.

Matt gingerly gathered up the boy's clothes. "The valet service will have these done before you're through scrubbing him."

"What do you mean, before I'm through? We're in this together, buster," she said indignantly, rescuing a bar of soap Todd was about to jam into the spigot. "If you're not back in one minute, I quit!"

The deadline should have been shorter. By the time Matthew reappeared sans coat and ready for action, the scrubbee had managed to splash a considerable amount of water on both the floor and the scrubber.

"Good thing this is wash-and-wear." She stood up, wrinkling her nose at the now damp front of her outfit. "If I had known this would be a rerun of the *Poseidon Adventure* I would have dressed for the occasion."

Matt grinned, tossing her one of the fluffy terry-cloth robes the Regent provided for its visitors. "You make a beautiful mermaid."

"No, she don't. She's got people legs, not a fishtail," Todd said scornfully, swinging the washcloth in a sloppy circle above his head.

"And you won't have any tail at all if you don't calm down, mister." Matthew caught the cloth and, wringing it out, tackled the prominent Whitney ears.

In spite of himself, the squirming youngster was soon squeaky clean again. Without the layer of grime, he was a beautiful child, auburn curls shining and hazel eyes taking up half his cherubic face.

"You promise not to tell Gandy?" he asked fearfully as Matt lifted him out of the suds and enveloped him in a towel.

"Cross my heart and hope to eat a worm."

"Okay, part-mer." Todd stretched to wrap his small arms around Matthew's neck.

For a timeless moment, Andrea watched entranced as the man returned the little boy's embrace, nestling his face against the mop of wet ringlets. Matt's eyes were closed, and his features were tight with an expression she could not identify. In that instant she realized that she was irrevocably, totally, in love with him; the knowledge spilled into her consciousness like the blessing of rain after a long drought.

The remainder of Master Whitney's rehabilitation passed in a rosy haze.

"This was above and beyond the call of duty. No more work for you today, my good woman. You're officially off the time clock," Matt told her as he prepared to return the refurbished child to his grandfather. "Get some rest. I'll drop by with a full report as soon as the reception is over."

"Kin we take one more look at the fish?" Todd asked as Matthew carried him out.

Andrea watched the door close behind them, unable to neatly pigeonhole all of the emotions she was feeling. Love—this bona fide, "from this day forward" variety—was a new and strange sensation that would take some getting used to. What she had felt for Patrick was a shadow, a mere caricature by comparison. At the moment she could not even recall his features. A host of other faces, all variations on a dual theme, now peopled her imagination: a sturdy toddler with Matthew's jaw and her chestnut hair, a laughing, dimpled baby with eyes the color of a winter's twilight—an even half dozen, of course.

She drifted along in slow motion, trying a multitude of equally happy scenarios on for size while she swabbed and refilled the tub. And when our children grow up and we retire, we'll sail around the world in a houseboat, she thought, planning their future mentally as she stripped and slipped into the caress of a bubble bath.

Andy eased the snapshot of Matt holding Todd from the album in her memory and relished each detail, wondering why artists seldom chose fathers and their children as subjects for their paintings. When she reached the faces in her internal portrait, she sat up abruptly. The expression across Matthew's strong, irregular features had been one of anguish; she was sure of it.

But why?

The shiver that shook her shoulders was caused by a nameless premonition rather than the scented, frothy water, but by now the bath had lost its appeal. Hurriedly finishing the task, she stepped out of the tub and wrapped the soft folds of a thick towel around her slender figure.

"You're a nut case. The kid probably bit him or something," she told her reflection as she sat down in front of the mirrored dresser and began brushing her hair with short, brisk strokes. "And while we're at it, shouldn't you find out how the man feels about you before you start decorating the nursery? Has he mentioned a single, solitary word about love yet?"

The image in the mirror slowly shook her head.

"Okay, so quit going off the deep end and get dressed before he comes back!" She slammed down the brush and, after slipping on a set of lacy undergarments, dug through her suitcase for Levi's and a cotton sweater.

Matt probably wouldn't be back for another hour or so, she decided, laying the clothes at the foot of the bed. She could either get dressed and twiddle her thumbs while she waited or take a quick nap.

The lure of the king-sized expanse was too tempting to resist. Snuggling into the pile of pillows, she fell into a sleep that was punctuated by fitful dreams.

In one particularly vivid fantasy she stood at the doorway of a three-story army boot, wiping her hands on the apron that covered her feed-sack dress while she watched Matt's sister, Jennifer, lead a giggling band of children in a merry game of ring-around-a-rosy on the front lawn.

"We're a five, we're a six, we're a seven, we're a eight . . ." Jennifer chanted gleefully.

"You're much too old to play games, Jenny. There are dishes to wash and beds to make and—"

"Bubba says I don't have to," the teenager interrupted, sticking out her tongue.

"He's wrong, he's wrong, he's wrong..." Andrea's words echoed over an inexplicably empty yard as the children disappeared.

Where did they all go?

And why didn't Matt come home? It had been nearly ten dream years since he left to buy new shoelaces for the roof.

"I have to find them all," she muttered, starting down the geranium-bordered walk.

But every step was like lifting her feet out of molasses, and every minute she grew more afraid and alone.

"Room service." The gravelly bass and an insistent rapping on the door yanked her up through the surrealistic layers of the nightmare.

"In a minute," she mumbled fuzzily, feeling as though she were a deep-sea diver who had surfaced too fast. She squinted at the window, bright with the panorama of sunset when she last checked but now pitch-black. The knock was repeated, and Andrea's hand was on the knob before she realized what she was doing. "I didn't order anything," she yelled through the door.

"I know; it was my own idea. Open up before I get a hernia," Matthew responded from the other side.

"Oh, my God!" Andy muttered, simultaneously attempting to smooth her hair and wipe traces of sleep from her eyes. In the nick of time she remembered that she was still in her underwear. Snatching the terry robe from the armchair where she had discarded it earlier, she put it on, jerking the belt into a hasty knot.

"I was about to use my passkey," he grumbled when she finally let him in. Pretending to stagger under the load he was carrying, he set a large tray on the table in front of the window and with an elaborate bow lifted its domed cover. "Roast Virginia quail with peach garnish, sweet-potato pudding, buttered asparagus and wedding cake for dessert. At this hour there's nothing in the kitchen but leftovers."

Andrea feigned a sigh. "Meager, but I suppose we can make do." She loosened a sliver from the tender quail breast and popped it in her mouth. "Umm, that's scrumptious. What time is it?"

"A little past one. The reception lasted till almost midnight."

He had changed into jeans and a pale blue sweatshirt, and it was obvious that he was not long out of the shower; the hair at the nape of his neck still looked damp.

"So, what were you, the quarterback?" Andrea said, referring to the legend Property of the UCLA Bruins emblazoned across his chest. It was an idiotic question, but it kept her mind off the way the muscles of his upper body strained against the cotton fabric.

"No, I was fourth-string. I didn't get in a minute of playing time, but the year we went to the Rose Bowl, I did manage a 'Hi, Mom,' on television. She wasn't watching, though."

She bent to sample the pudding, neatly licking off a dollop that was sliding over the edge of her spoon. "If my only son were fool enough to fling his body under a pile of linebackers, I wouldn't watch, either."

What they were saying was the least of what was happening between them. The intensity he generated was electric, almost palpable in the lamp-lit atmosphere of the room. She lowered her lashes, but she could still feel the hungry touch of his eyes.

Giving up all pretext of casualness, he removed the utensil from her hand and pulled her to him. "I hope you always look this way when you first wake up. You have pillow creases on your cheeks, blanket fuzz in your hair, and you're the most beautiful sight I've ever seen," he said softly. It seemed forever, yet not long enough as his lips traced a path along the curve of her cheek to her waiting mouth. "So lovely, so lovely," he whispered, languidly brushing her lips.

The territory into which they were wandering was uncharted and potentially perilous. Though the sweet urgency of Andrea's emotions dictated that she continue the journey with him, a small corner of her mind still counseled caution. She pulled back to catch her breath.

"Dinner's getting cold," she murmured.

"Do you care?" He nuzzled aside her terry-cloth lapel to explore the mysteries of her throat.

"Not really." She silenced the internal warning and gave in to the moment, no more able to stop the way her fingers stole under his shirt to discover the strong, sweet length of his spine than she could have kept her heart from beating. And even if she had tried to will her body not to melt against the firmness of his thighs, it would not have obeyed.

Had she been less occupied with these other things, though, she would have noticed him tugging at her belt and would not have been quite as surprised when the knot slipped loose and he pushed the robe from her shoulders. It fell in a heap around her feet.

In Andrea's very brief audition of different ways she could play the scene, the role of the Victorian virgin lost hands down; her feelings for this man eliminated the need for false modesty or pretense. As his hands moved slowly past the soft swelling of her breasts to the curve of her waist, she could hardly bear the sweetness of her need for him.

"I want you so much," she whispered.

The sound Matthew made was passion and awe and pleasure and gratitude and joy all rolled into one. He swept her from her feet and laid her gently on the bed.

Her arms encircled the breadth of his shoulders, pulling him down to her. And as he shifted against her, there was not the slightest question in her mind about the effect she was having on him. "I wouldn't mind if you slipped into something more comfortable," she murmured into his college insignia.

Matthew massaged the small of her back, his fingers leaving tiny wavelets of pleasure in their wake.

"I really didn't intend to turn dinner into a seduction scene, sweet," he murmured, nibbling the lobe of her ear.

She rose up just enough to leave a feathery trail of kisses along the bridge of his nose. "Neither did I, but since we're here..."

"I'm not exactly prepared. Is everything okay with you?"

She did not understand at first; then it dawned on her that he was alluding to birth control. "Oh, don't worry; this is a safe day."

"Are you sure?"

"I'd better be. We're not quite ready to become a three—yet."

Matt was still as stone. After what seemed like a very long time, he raised her to a sitting position, leaving one arm around her shoulders. "That won't ever happen. I can't have children, Andy," he said quietly.

Now she was confused. If that were true, why would he be concerned about prevention?

The question must have shown on her face, because he answered, "No, I'm not sterile, but I will be as soon as I get up nerve enough to have the operation," he explained.

Andrea felt cold and for the first time nearly naked. She tugged at the corner of the bedspread and wrapped its quilted protection around her. "Why would you do that?" Her voice came out thin and small.

"Because Jenny's condition is hereditary, and my children would have a twenty-five percent probability of being born with it."

The room undulated in sickening waves. Andrea felt as though a gigantic fist had collided with her stomach. "But that means there is also a seventy-five percent chance of them being normal," she reminded him shakily.

"It's a lottery I refuse to play." He held her face, tilting it so she had to look at him. His eyes were stark with misery and his indrawn breath harsh as he continued. "Jenny isn't nearly as disabled as she could have been. My great-uncle was typical of the worst-case scenario. He was fifteen when he died, but he never grew beyond the mental age of six months. He couldn't walk or talk or speak one intelligible word."

He released Andrea and, getting up, picked up the robe and arranged it gently about her shoulders. "I want you more than I want to keep on living, but we can't risk having a child like that. I couldn't live with it, and God knows I wouldn't put you through that hell," he said, grazing her forehead with his lips.

"I understand." She rose, slipping her arms around him and holding on tight. There was only compassion in the gesture. "And don't worry about tonight. There'll be other times."

"You bet there will," he said tenderly, his voice muffled as he pressed his face into her hair. "And I'll make an appointment with my doctor next week. It was stupid of me to put it off this long."

"No!" The objection tore at her throat. "Please—not yet."

He pulled back to gaze at her levelly. "Andy, I saw how you were with Todd. You'd be a terrific mother, and you've already told me that having children is important to you."

Honesty had always worked for Andrea, so she stuck with it. "You're important to me, too." She looked up at him, her smoky eyes wide with the wonder of it. Tracing the college emblem on his shirt with one finger, she said lightly, "When you were a Bruin and the other team kicked off to you, you had four chances to go ten yards, right?"

He looked puzzled. "Right, but what has that got to do with us?"

"We just got the football, Matt. Wouldn't it be dumb to punt on first down? We don't have to make any heavy decisions about the future right now. For the time being, let's just enjoy each other."

He smiled, tightening his arms about her waist. "What ever you say, coach."

"You'd better get out of here before you get sacked," she said, pushing him gently away.

The bright smile she pasted on held up just long enough for him to leave.

"I love you so much, Matt," she wanted to say as the door closed behind him, but the words caught in her throat. And then she cried. Not for herself or even for him—but for all the beautiful children in her fantasy.

Chapter Seven

"I've got to get out of here." Andrea stood up abruptly, knocking over the stool on which she had temporarily piled the shipment she had been unpacking. The satin and *peau de soie* bridesmaid gowns slithered to the floor in a sighing pastel heap.

Startled, Jason rescued them. "What's bugging you, Andy? You've been jumpy ever since the Bowman reception."

"Why does something have to be wrong? I'm just naturally clumsy," she snapped as she grabbed her purse and headed for the front of the store. "If anyone comes looking for me, tell 'em I moved to Missouri."

"Even Matt?"

"Especially him," she called back over her shoulder. She closed the door none too gently and strode along the sidewalk as though the Devil himself were nipping at her heels.

She was not mad at Matthew, just tired of the wary sidestep they had been dancing lately—each trying to pretend that what had happened last week at the Regent had not affected their relationship in the least and both knowing very well it had. The morning after, she had waited in the room an hour past the time when he was to have called her. When she finally tracked him down in the lobby, he and a cadre of security guards were trying to soothe a guest who claimed money had been stolen from his room.

"Sorry, Andy. I can't go back to Laurel Valley until this is straightened out. Take my car and I'll pick it up tonight at your place. I may be late, but don't wait up—I have a duplicate set of keys," he had said, studiously avoiding her eyes.

The Mercedes stayed parked on Petunia Lane well past ten o'clock. "If I pretend I've been asleep when he comes, maybe he'll take the hint and not stay," she had told herself, not yet ready to face the possibility of taking up where they had left off the night before. But the yawning stretches she had rehearsed went unused; the next time she looked out the window, the car was gone.

"I didn't want to disturb you," Matt had answered her somewhat peeved query when he finally called.

"What on earth is wrong with him?" she muttered to herself, absently moving aside to let an oncoming pedestrian pass. *A better question is, What's wrong with you?* she paused to ask her reflection in the department-store window. When she was with Matthew, she was sure she did love him, but when they were apart, doubts homed in like flies around an open sugar bowl.

"It shouldn't be this complicated. Either I do or I don't," she mused aloud.

"How's that?" a fellow window-shopper queried curiously.

Andrea's eyes shifted their focus from her image to the nursery furniture displayed on the other side of the glass. "Could you tell me where the nearest drugstore is?" she asked to forestall a conversation.

"Down two blocks and turn left. You can't miss it."

"Thanks," Andy said, thinking as she hurried down Broadway that she did need dental floss. If she concentrated on that specific purpose for this little trek, maybe she'd stop making a fool out of herself in public.

Fordham's Pharmacy, two blocks off Broadway and nestled between the barber shop and the Southern Comfort Tea Room (homemade apple cobbler a specialty), was a holdover from the era of rumble seats and band concerts in the park. Large glass apothecary jars filled with ruby-, emerald- and sapphire-colored liquids decorated the window out front, and inside, the shelves were absent of the clutter of inflatable toys and rubber shower shoes found in modern chain stores. Except for the soda fountain and the spindly wrought-iron tables and chairs in the center of the black-and-white checkered marble floor, every-thing was dedicated to curing human ailments of one sort or the other; this was an old-fashioned, no-nonsense drugstore.

The air smells like vitamin capsules and ice cream, Andrea mused, scanning a shelf of cough syrups. She picked up a bot-tle and studied the fine print on the label.

"My mama swears by mustard poultices. Says they clear your chest and sinuses at the same time." A middle-aged woman with Mary Rose stitched in aqua on the breast pocket of her yellow nylon uniform looked up from her inventory of analgesics and waved her ballpoint pen at the item in Andrea's hand. "And the makings are a sight less expensive than that stuff. Course I wouldn't want Mr. Fordham to hear me tell a customer that. How long have you had a cold?"

"I don't have one. I was looking for..." She trailed off, her purpose nearly forgotten, but she managed to recapture it. "Uh—dental floss."

"Dentifrices are in back, between antacids and family plan-ning products," Mary Rose supplied helpfully.

"Oh." Andrea almost laughed at the irony of her destina-tion. The subject of contraception had been on her mind a lot lately; she had been struggling to overcome her resistance to the idea. A short-run solution was no problem, since she was no more ready to have a baby now than was Matthew. But the prospect of an entire life without children of her own was de-cidedly bleak, and she still was not certain she could make a lasting commitment to a man with whom she could not have a family.

As long as I'm here, I might as well browse, she decided, meandering toward the rear of the store.

Fordham's early-twenties ambience was misleading. The store was certainly up on the latest advances in birth control; the discreet niche beside dentifrices contained a plentiful sup-ply of different products.

Putting as much distance as the limited space would allow between herself and the small, flat packets adorned with pic-tures of couples walking hand in hand into the sunset, Andrea glanced surreptitiously over her shoulder to make sure no other customers were near. *This is embarrassing,* she thought as she surveyed the bewildering array on the "hers" side.

"Maybe I should make an appointment with a doctor," she mumbled, her hand moving indecisively from a businesslike box with a clinical-sounding name to one festooned with pastel flowers.

"If you wanted to get to Missouri, you should have turned left at the hot-water bottles. You're headed for Arizona," a teasing voice informed her from behind.

Andrea spun around, almost bumping into Matthew. Eyes glinting with amusement, he caught her arm to steady her. "Jason gave me your message. He also said that you had never run out like that before. Is something wrong?"

"I-I think I h-have a fever. Must be coming down with the flu." The alibi was to explain the embarrassing rush of blood to her cheeks.

"You do look flushed. Aspirin is up by the cash register," he supplied helpfully.

If he saw what I was doing, I'm going to kill myself, she thought, edging away from the shelf she had just explored. "I need floss, too," she said coolly, unhooking a package from the dental hygiene rack. "What are you doing here?"

His mischievous glance flicked quickly over the shelf behind her before it held her eyes. "I ran out of toothpaste this morning."

This time the blush started at the bottom of her feet; by the time it reached her neck, it was approaching the temperature of molten lava.

He touched her shoulder lightly. "I didn't mean to tease. You're very special to make this kind of effort...."

The sound of a spasm of choking from one aisle over stopped him. Mary Rose leaned over the rubbing alcohol, avidly taking in the details of the minidrama. The expression on her face signified that by nightfall every soul in Laurel Valley would know Andrea Kirkland and Matthew Donaldson had a tête-à-tête in Fordham's Pharmacy.

"Buying dental floss is no big deal," Andy interjected quickly. "I'd better get back to the shop now. Lucille Mac-Dougal is coming in at three."

Without further discussion, she replaced the package and fled toward the front of the store. Matthew matched her stride for stride.

"It isn't noon yet. Come on, we need to talk," he said, opening the door before she could reach it. As they stepped out into the sunshine of the morning, he grasped her arm, steering her across Broadway to the small park that faced City Hall.

Selecting an unoccupied bench near the toddlers' playground, Matt drew her down beside him.

"It's your dime—what do we need to talk about?" she asked defensively after a moment of strained silence.

"I came looking for you because I was going to tell you that I don't think we should see each other anymore," he began carefully.

Her mouth went cotton-dry.

His features were twisted by an anxious mixture of uncertainty and hope as he continued. "But when I saw you there in the store, I knew I couldn't say it. I love you, Andy. God help me, I didn't intend to tell you, but I had to."

"W-what?"

He grinned crookedly. "Watch my lips carefully this time—I love you. I have almost from the moment you walked into Winona's library and kicked off your shoes."

The day took on a different shine. Andrea was suddenly aware of the heavy scent of hyacinth drifting from a nearby flower bed, and the spring sun filtering down through newly leafed maple branches overhead touched her skin in warm benediction. "Why weren't you going to tell me?" she asked quietly.

His eyes were fixed on a woman pushing a child in a stroller toward the swing set, and he didn't answer immediately. When the words finally came, they were muted with regret. "Because I thought it would be unfair to you. I can't give you what you need, and I want you to be free to find it with someone else."

She took his hand, clasping the broad fingers tightly. "Don't try to make my decisions for me, Matt. Even if I never saw you again, I wouldn't be free. I love you, too." Her innate honesty prompted her to add, "But I'm not certain what that means. I can't promise that we . . . that I . . ."

He bent to her, his lips stilling the attempted caveat. "I won't rush you, sweet. We'll just take the future day by day and see where it leads us."

"I'll be through with Lucille MacDougal by three-thirty, and if you don't have anything better to do, this would be a perfect afternoon for a picnic," she whispered.

"I promised I would drive Mrs. Pickering to North Carolina to visit her aunt. I'll be back tomorrow evening, though, and we can have dinner," he explained regretfully, his eyes promising much more than a meal. "I do have time to walk you back to the shop, though."

"No, you go ahead. I have a little more shopping to do," Andrea told him, her radiant smile serene for the moment.

Tomorrow would take care of itself somehow, and if it didn't, at least she had today.

"SHALL I PUT the new sample books out on the table or store them behind the counter?" Miss Hewitt asked, the usual note of authority in her voice replaced by hesitancy. She had come in early to start an inventory, but by eleven not a single veil had been counted.

"Wherever you think best," Andrea replied. She glanced up from the pile of bills she was sorting, not able to miss lines around her elderly friend's eyes that seemed to have been added overnight. Henrietta's thin shoulders drooped, and for the first time since they had met, she looked every minute her age.

Andrea momentarily shed the warm glow still surrounding her from the previous day's trip to the drugstore. "How was dinner with Nehemiah last night?"

The old woman's lips pressed into a thin line. "Just fine."

"If that's your version of fine, I'd sure hate to see terrible," she joked.

"Excuse me. I have to take these things to the office." With a noise halfway between a strangled hiccup and a sob, Henrietta snatched the stack of invoices from in front of Andy and marched into the workroom.

Andrea sat still for a moment, uncertain how to handle the situation; then the sound of running water galvanized her into action. She hurried into the workroom, rescuing the bills before Henrietta could douse them in the sudsy sink along with the coffee cups.

"Sit." As her elderly employee stiffly obeyed, Andy added, "Okay, tell me what happened."

Henrietta narrowed her eyes as though daring a single tear to escape the boundaries of her lashes. "I served him poached salmon, fresh asparagus and tossed salad. We had fruit salad for dessert."

"Sounds delicious. And?" Andy prompted.

"It was probably the only decent meal he'd had all week. The old fool takes in far too much cholesterol. He had a heart attack some years back, and he should be a lot more careful about his diet."

Mr. Gill's eating habits were not the issue, but Andrea was willing to let the story trickle out as best it could. "He complained about the food?"

Miss Hewitt shook her head miserably. "No, that part was fine. It was the proposal that went awry."

Andrea's forehead furrowed with puzzlement. "I thought you wanted him to ask you to marry him."

"Not his, mine!"

"Your what?"

Henrietta glared at her. "Please pay attention. I'm the one who proposed, just as you suggested. I told him that we could take care of each other for whatever time we might have left."

Andy vowed silently to leave the lovelorn to Ann Landers from now on. It was evident her advice had not helped the situation.

"He said that if he needed a nurse, he would hire one, and when he wanted a wife, he would do the asking." The flood she had held at bay finally overwhelmed her, and tears coursed down her cheeks.

"I'm so sorry." Andrea hugged the shaking shoulders helplessly. "Don't worry; we'll think of something."

Henrietta straightened up, quickly drying her eyes. "Please forgive me. I didn't intend to do that."

"I should never have opened my big mouth," Andy said contritely.

"Don't blame yourself. Enough nonsense; we have a business to run. Was that the front doorbell I just heard?"

"Sit still; I'll get it," Andrea said, hurrying into the showroom.

"Hi, Andy. I've come to play dolls with you," Jennifer Donaldson informed her, bouncing in with a sunny smile and an assortment of Barbie paraphernalia. She plopped down on the dais in the center of the room and, moving the mannequin bride's train aside, opened a small pink plastic suitcase and began taking out an extensive miniature wardrobe.

Andrea was flustered, to say the least. "When did you come back from your trip?" she asked, glancing quickly at the door for the welcome sight of Matthew.

Jennifer's smile change to a scowl. "I didn't go nowhere. Bubba and Mrs. Pickering did, though. I'm supposed to stay with Addie today till they get back."

"Who?"

"Adele Winslow, the Donaldson's next-door neighbor," Miss Hewitt supplied as she joined them.

"I know you," Jenny said excitedly. "You were at that Ark place Bubba took me to one time. I was sad 'cause my mama went to heaven—that's why I didn't want to stay there."

"Well, we certainly hope you'll decide to come back. Did Addie bring you here?" Henrietta asked.

"Huh-uh. I walked."

"All the way from home?" Andrea said incredulously. Though the distance was not really great, the route was somewhat complicated, and she was surprised that Jennifer had managed to navigate it alone.

"I remembered the way from the time we went to Mr. Jimbo's," the girl answered, as though she had read Andrea's thoughts.

"Did you tell Addie that you were coming here, Jennifer?" Miss Hewitt persisted.

"Nope. She said I should watch *General Hospital* while she went to the grocery store, but I was tired of TV. You can comb my doll's hair if you promise to be careful, Andy. She's tenderheaded somethin' awful."

Jenny posed Ken and Barbie with their arms around each other, while singing snatches from a popular ballad as she danced them around the hem of the mannequin's skirt.

The teenager could not have chosen a worse time for her impromptu visit; the afternoon was entirely booked, and Andrea did not see how she could possibly conduct business with Jennifer underfoot. She stooped down beside the girl to break the news as gently as possible.

"I'd love to play with you Jenny, but Nancy Ellison is coming in about an hour to choose her bridesmaids' gowns; then Mrs. MacDougal wants to go over the final plans for her twenty-fifth anniversary celebration. I'll call to see if Mrs. Winslow can pick you up."

"I want to stay with you," Jennifer said, her lower lip starting to tremble. "I thought you were going to be my best friend, Andy."

"And so she is," Miss Hewitt interjected. "But even best friends can't always be there when we want them to. I have an idea, though. This afternoon at the Ark we're going to make a double-double chocolate layer cake. Would you like to come along and help?"

"Can we put pecans on top?" The name of the nuts came out "pe-cay-uns."

"Surely, and you can bring back slices for Andy and your brother."

An eager Jennifer scrambled up and held her hand to the old woman. "We'll let Barbie and Ken stay here so Andy won't get lonesome."

"We'll be back around three. Phone Adele before she calls out the state troopers," Miss Hewitt cautioned as they left for the independent-living program.

Andrea had looked up the Winslow's number and was dialing when Nancy Ellison wandered in, her round face uncharacteristically subdued. "I know I'm early, but I'd like to get this over as soon as possible," she said.

"Be with you as soon as I finish this call." After the tenth ring, Andrea decided that Mrs. Winslow was probably still at the grocery store and cradled the receiver. Turning her attention back to her waiting customer, she studied Nancy curiously. "Is something wrong?"

The ash-blond debutante shrugged off her Burberry trench coat and slumped onto a stool beside the counter. "The lavender I wanted for the bridesmaids will clash with Courtney's red hair, and Patricia Wilson is dying to wear a picture hat, but short as she is, she'd look like a mushroom." Her hands plucked nervously at the strap of her purse as she added, "And we just got an addition to Grandmother Wright's guest list. This wedding is turning into an absolute circus, Andy! How are we going to cram two hundred people into that tiny church?"

Andrea wanted to remind her that the tiny church had a capacity of at least three hundred fifty, but she could not edge it into the continuing flood of complaints.

"And another thing; I absolutely refuse to walk down the aisle with Mrs. Flemming caterwauling in the choir loft. Can you get another soloist?"

"I'm sure we can," Andy said, the seeds of an inspiration taking root. "Have you ever heard Jennifer Donaldson sing?"

The prospect brought some of the animation back to Nancy's face. "She's terrific! Do you think she'd do my wedding?"

"It won't hurt to ask," Andrea hedged, wondering if Matthew would agree. "But worrying about the details is my job, remember? All you have to do is relax and get married."

"How can I relax with Doug insistin' that we move to New York? I'm not going, you hear? I must have been brain dead to get mixed up with a damned Yankee!"

Andrea recognized all the symptoms of a galloping case of prenuptial jitters. The Nancy she had first met would have lived in East Hell if Douglas Wright were there. "Nance, stop fighting the Civil War for a minute and tell me the real reason you're upset."

The other woman's hazel eyes filled with tears. She hesitated a long minute before she answered. "I'm just plain scared. 'Till death do us part' could be a long time. Suppose we stop loving each other?"

"The choices are fairly simple: you can stay together and try to work things out, stay together and be miserable, get a divorce or kill each other," Andrea said dryly.

"Lot of help you are," Nancy pouted. "I'm serious, Andy. All I want is to make Doug happy. What if I can't?"

"Everybody's future is a gamble, Nance, but if you don't play the game, you'll lose for sure. The important thing is that you love each other."

Will you listen to who's talking? an inner voice mocked.

"I wish I were as together as you are. I bet you never have doubts about your relationship with Matthew Donaldson." The socialite raised her eyebrows, some of her old perkiness peeking through the gloom. "It must be gettin' serious—I heard you went shopping over to the drugstore yesterday."

Andy blushed bright scarlet. "That salesclerk—Mary Rose What's-Her-Name—has a big mouth."

Nancy glanced at her obliquely. "This is none of my business, but I'm going to butt in, anyway. If I were you, I wouldn't rely on the stuff at Fordham's. Paula Giladeaux is my doctor, and if you want me to, I'll make an appointment for you. She won't spread the news around town, either." She squeezed Andy's hand, continuing, "And neither will I."

"You're a good friend, Nance. I'll give Dr. Giladeaux a call next week." Andrea stood up briskly. "Ready to tackle the bridesmaids' gowns now?"

"If you don't mind, I'm not exactly in a white-satin mood. Mind if we put if off?"

"No problem. You let me know when you're ready," Andy said, shooing her out with a grin.

Feeling tons lighter, she picked up the phone and dialed the Winslows' number. A familiar voice answered before the first ring was through.

"When did you get back, Matt?"

"Fifteen minutes ago." The fear in his voice poured through the receiver. "Andy, Jennifer's disappeared. She left here sometime between eleven and noon, and nobody has seen her since. Addie already called the police, and they're out searching the woods in back of the house."

"It's okay; she's with me," Andrea reassured him quickly. "At least she was. Miss Hewitt took her..."

"I'll be right over," he interrupted.

"...to the Ark," Andy informed the dial tone. *Why can't the man listen? I'd better call back,* she told herself, exasperation making her forget the Winslows' number. By the time she found the scrap of paper on which it was written, the phone started to ring.

It was Mrs. MacDougal canceling her appointment. "Thank goodness for small favors," Andy muttered, preparing to redial. But it was already too late; Matthew was hurrying through the door.

Wordlessly, he took her in his arms and hung on for dear life. She could feel the trembling of his muscles, and his breath came in ragged gulps. She patted his back gently, as though he were a frightened child, but her inner emotions were far from maternal.

When he had recovered his composure, he loosened his grip. "You have no idea how scared I was. Sorry for grabbing you like that, but I was in a dire need of a hug."

She grinned up at him. "Glad to oblige."

He dropped his arms, the beginnings of anger glinting in the depths of his eyes. "Where's Jennifer, in the back? I've got a lecture for that young lady that she'll never forget!"

"I tried to tell you on the phone that she is at the Ark." Andy checked her watch. "Miss Hewitt should be bringing her back any minute now."

His expression was guarded. "The Ark?"

Andrea filled in the details, finishing with "Please don't be too hard on her, Matt."

Obviously upset, he ran his hand through his hair and paced back and forth in front of the counter. "I know you did the best you could under the circumstances, but I wish you had put her in a cab and sent her back to Addie's," he said. "It's going to take a week to calm her down."

"Why?"

"She hated the Ark when I took her there. She wouldn't stop crying."

"But she has changed since then, Matt. She was perfectly satisfied to go with Miss Hewitt."

He acted as though he had not heard a word she said. "I'm sorry she got in your way. I'll have to watch her closer from now on to make sure it doesn't happen again."

"I don't think that's the answer. She needs more freedom, not less."

"I know you mean well, but you don't understand her problem at all. What she really needs is discipline. If I don't get tough with her now, she'll never learn that she can't wander off by herself."

The ends of Andrea's patience began to tatter. "What are you going to do, take away her Barbie dolls for the next month? My God, Matt—let her grow up, will you? I think she's much more mature and capable than you give her credit for being."

He drew back as though she had slapped him. "I've lived with Jennifer's problems all my life, remember? I know her better than you ever could."

"Maybe so, but you're so busy concentrating on the damned problems that you overlook her potential!"

What promised to be the first round in a championship bout was ended by the bell above Weddings Unlimited's front door. Arms laden with brown bags, Miss Hewitt and the subject of the dispute returned.

"Uh-oh, am I in trouble?" Jenny asked, peering at her brother wide-eyed.

"You bet your sweet life you are! How many times have I told you—"

"Would you please take this for me, Matthew? I'm not as strong as I used to be." Handing him the sack of groceries she was carrying, Henrietta cut short the tirade with a sweet smile. "We would have been back sooner, but we had some shopping to do. You have no idea how long the lines in the Phillips Foodland are these days."

"I'm sure they are. Now, Jennifer, would you explain to me—"

"I brought you a piece of cake, Bubba," Jenny said, digging into her bag to retrieve a slightly crushed foil-wrapped package. "Andy's is in there, too, so don't eat it all."

Taking a cue from the other two women, Andrea decided that the best way to defuse Matthew's anger was to go on the offensive; fast talk and action were the options of choice here. "I think I'll sample my piece right now," she said, removing the cake from his hand with a swiping motion that would have done Garfield the Cat proud.

"This is delicious," she pronounced after a quick nibble. "Here, have a bite, Matt."

Before the beleaguered man could get his wits about him, he had a mouthful of chocolate crumbs. "Gwood, brut Jenni-pherr, doo..."

"You shouldn't talk while you're eating, Bubba." Jenny's manner was primly reproving. "Everybody at the Ark liked me. Wanna know why, Andy?"

"I can't wait for you to tell me."

"'Cause I can crack eggs with one hand without wasting a bit," Jennifer informed them proudly. "I learned it watching the cook show on Channel thirty-two."

"And that's not all. Matthew, did you know your sister can recite the recipe for crabmeat Mornay? Show him, honey," Miss Hewitt prompted.

Jennifer happily complied, right down to the last instruction, "Sprinkle with Parmesan cheese and bake until lightly browned."

Matthew looked dumbfounded. Swallowing, he set the groceries on the counter behind him and faced them with a broad grin and both hands raised in surrender. "Okay, okay—I give in! What chance do I have against three scheming women?"

"None at all, and I'm glad you're smart enough to recognize that," Henrietta said, chuckling. The amusement left her face as she continued. "Jenny and I had a chat about the worry she caused by leaving home without permission, and I expect you have strong words to that, Matthew."

"A few, if I can ever get them in edgewise," he agreed dryly.

"I'm sorry, Bubba, and I won't do it again. Can I please go back to the Ark tomorrow?"

"It's not that easy, Jenny. There are a lot of forms we have to fill out, and we probably have to wait until there's room for you," her brother told her.

"I think I can help snip through the red tape," the elderly lady offered. "Meanwhile, Jennifer is always welcome to visit anytime she likes."

"That's very kind of you, but—"

The redoubtable Miss Hewitt cut his sentence in half with a gimlet stare. "I was sure you would approve."

Andrea covered her mouth to suppress a giggle.

"One thing more, Matthew. We bought these groceries because we knew that Mrs. Pickering would be tired tonight. Jenny wants to fix dinner all by herself—aren't you pleased?"

"Yes, ma'am," he answered in a small voice.

"Will you come, Andy? I already asked Miss Hewitt," Jennifer chimed in.

"Not this time, pumpkin. But we'll all have a dinner party at my house soon, okay?"

Henrietta glanced from Matt to Andrea and back again, smiling in obvious satisfaction. "We'll wait for you in the car, Matthew."

"Scratch one intimate dinner date, but I promise to make it up to you," he murmured as the two left.

"I'll hold you to that. I'm glad Miss Hewitt will have company tonight. She doesn't need to be alone."

"What's wrong?"

"I'll fill you in later. Just be extra sweet to her, will you?"

"If I don't, she'll probably rap my knuckles with her ruler." Matt chuckled and, tilting Andy's chin, brushed her lips lightly. "Do you have a suitcase?"

"Of course I do."

"Good. You have exactly sixteen hours and eleven minutes to pack it. Leave out the fancy stuff, though—jeans and sneaks ought to do it. We have to get an early start, because it would be a shame to waste a second more than we have to. I'll pick you up at seven."

"What are you talking about?"

He held on to her as though he might never let go. "If you don't have anything better to do tomorrow, we'll drive to Williamsburg as soon as the sun comes up."

"I was planning to wash my hair, but I suppose I could put if off," she said with a sigh. Giving up the pretext of casualness, she returned his embrace. "Tell me again."

"I love you, and I want you more than anything I have ever wanted in this life." His voice was warm cognac and firelight.

"I love you, too, Matt."

"Does that mean you'll go with me?"

"Be at my apartment by six," she answered softly. "We wouldn't want to miss the sunrise."

Chapter Eight

At five-thirty Andrea latched the lid of her overnight bag and, for the sixth time in the past fifteen minutes, went to the window overlooking Petunia Lane to make sure Matthew had not arrived earlier than expected.

"I really should clean up this mess before I leave," she said, eyeing clothes and cosmetics scattered over the bedroom from four different stages of packing. Round one had ended with a suitcase, dress bag and cosmetics tote, all crammed to the seams. But heeding Matthew's earlier advice, she had ruthlessly weeded out the "fancy stuff" and reduced the load to the bare essentials—including, of course, her laciest lingerie and perfume guaranteed by its manufacturer to "make him remember this night for all eternity."

Too obvious—the rest of his life will be long enough, she decided, rummaging around on the dresser for the light floral fragrance she usually wore. Applying a final spritz to her neck, she tucked the atomizer into an inside pocket of the overnight bag next to the pastel Fordham's box that had promised her twenty-four carefree hours.

She knelt on the window seat and, opening the casement, stared out into the soft mauve of the waking April sky. The eastern horizon was tinted with the vermilion assurance of a perfect day. "At least the weather will be good," she said with a sigh, settling down to wait.

The flight of butterflies in her stomach—actually, more like a flock of starlings—quieted somewhat at the touch of a gentle breeze. It had rained early during the night, and the air was fresh rinsed and scented with new greenery.

"For Pete's sake, pull yourself together. This is not the first time you've gone away for the weekend with a man," she scolded herself.

The admonition had a negligible effect, since it was precisely the memory of her only other three-day tryst that had her so on edge. The winter before last, Patrick had taken her to a posh resort in Vermont for, as he put it, "the Green Mountains, fantastic skiing and, of course, the great Harahan."

The advertisement had been a snow job; since they traveled both ways at night, she had seen very little of the Vermont countryside, and the pair of skis on which she had spent a miniature fortune hardly touched the white powder.

"Harahan wasn't all that great, either," she said grimly, thinking of his arrogant disregard of her needs.

One of her more painful recollections was of standing at the front desk, crimson with embarrassment, while he registered.

"King-size bed, right?" he had asked the desk clerk archly.

"Heart-shaped, just as you requested when you made the reservation, sir," the man replied with a smirk in Andrea's direction. It did not take an Einstein to deduce the main purpose of the trip from Patrick's perspective.

"I promised myself I wouldn't go through it again. Why am I doing this?" she mumbled, now more uneasy than ever.

One immediate answer was the depth of her feeling for Matthew, but even that did not allay her anxiety. Before Vermont, hadn't she believed she was in love with Patrick?

Her confusion was far from resolved when Matt pulled up to the curb out front. Instead of blowing the horn, he got out of the car and waved up at her window, pointing first at his watch and then to the sunrise.

Signaling that she had seen him, she headed for the door, grabbing her suitcase and a light jacket on the way. Her steps slowed as she started down the stairs. It occurred to her that this was Friday, and though there was not much on Weddings Unlimited's calendar, the MacDougal "retread" was scheduled for the middle of next week, and some problem that needed immediate attention might arise. She stopped on the landing, deciding she could not possibly go to Williamsburg. More than a little relief mixed with her regret as she mentally sped through a series of excuses to give Matthew.

"If Miss Hewitt and Jason can't do it, it won't get done. Stop stalling, Kirkland; this weekend will be totally different," she ordered herself, skipping every other step on the way down.

Matt was lounging against the fender of his car, one sneaker-clad heel absently bumping the tire. In the dim light, Andy could not tell whether the expression on his face was one of impatience or not.

"Sorry to keep you waiting. I forgot something and... whoops!" Intent on the apology as she got into the automobile, she almost squashed the bouquet of narcissus lying on the passenger seat. Cheeks pink with pleasure, she rescued the blossoms and buried her face in their sunshiny sweetness. "If I took these upstairs and put them in water, they would last the rest of the week."

"Uh-uh. They're strictly for now. Don't you know what day this is?"

She glanced at him curiously. "April third, I think."

"Wrong. It's officially the twelfth of Never." Matt started the engine, sliding back the transparent roof panel to let in the morning sky. After he pulled away from the curb, his hand moved from the wheel to encircle her wrist. "And you won't be needing your watch, because there is no such thing as an hour. Today, flowers don't wilt, nobody catches cold, and—"

"And Mondays don't exist," she finished, taking off the timepiece and tucking it in her purse.

A pleased expression modulated the angularity of his jaw-line. "That's my girl. And since we have no schedule, whenever something along the road catches your fancy, you holler and I'll stop."

Both the content of the offer and the accent that crept into his voice were so Southern, she could not repress a smile. "I'm squirrely about rusty old wash pots and handmade quilts, so every time a country flea market comes along, you'd better be ready to hit the brakes."

"Fine with me. Springtime in Virginia is just naturally meant for browsin'."

"Your roots are showing," she teased, relishing a mental comparison between his attitude and Patrick's you've-seen-one-tree-you've-seen-them-all cynicism.

"They usually do when I'm this happy. How about a little traveling music?" he asked, waiting for her nod before slipping a cassette into the tape deck.

Andrea relaxed, allowing Debussy and the breeze that gently tousled her brown curls to work their soothing magic. The past night had been both physically and mentally hectic, and loss of sleep was beginning to take a toll. Stifling a yawn, she pointed to a small, elaborately wrapped package on the dashboard. "What's that?"

"A present for you. Open it."

Inside was a box of Jujubes. Andy poured a few out into her palm and peered at them skeptically. "Thank you—I think."

"Those things have a strange effect on women. I discovered the secret when I was ten." He reached over to pop a red bead into her mouth. "After eating just one, Sue Ellen Colodney let me kiss her passionately during a matinee of *Beach Blanket Bingo.*"

He brought the car to a stop at a highway interchange and bent forward to test his theory. "See? Works every time."

The taste of him was ten thousand times better than the fruity candy. Discarding the Jujubes, she went for the sweeter flavor.

"You're not the only one with a past. Arnold Funderbunk bought me a tub of buttered popcorn every Saturday," she murmured as he pulled back into the sparse traffic.

"Did you kiss him?" Matt's brow beetled in mock jealousy.

She shook her head. "I was afraid my braces would get caught on his lips. Zack Langley was the first boy I ever kissed."

"Let me guess—Zack was the best-looking guy in your high school. He had a straight A average and was the captain of the football team."

"You just described Arnie. Zack had glasses an inch thick and ears like Alfred E. Newman. He was one of the Grimsley High Gamecocks, though."

"Quarterback?"

"Team mascot. He would flap his wings and run clucking around the field every time they made a touchdown."

Matt threw back his head and laughed. "Somehow I can't picture you with a nearsighted chicken."

"Neither could my mother and father," Andrea said drowsily. "I think the main reason I dated Zack was to bug them."

He reached over to lightly pinch her cheek. "Typical smart-mouthed teenager, huh?"

She snorted. "'Andy's Rebellion' started way before puberty. My parents and I never got along. Still don't, as a matter of fact."

"Why?"

"For starters, they had to get married. Back then, illegitimate babies were a big no-no in middle-class Cincinnati. And in addition to being an embarrassing accident, I wasn't the world's most adorable child. I had colic, a cranky disposition, and I was allergic to nearly every food known to mankind. When you get right down to it, I was a mess."

"Even if that's true, which I doubt, you overcame it all nicely. You're a beautiful woman, both inside and out." His tone was light, but his eyes were filled with understanding. "You must have had a rough time."

"It wasn't all that bad. In their own way they do love me, and I had more toys and clothes than I knew what to do with." Andy picked up her bouquet and fingered the petals absently. "I didn't even know what I was missing until the Mascaris moved next door. Each one of those eight kids knew he or she was Rosa's favorite. Tony—that's Papa Mascari—worked two shifts, but when he came home, he had time to listen to everybody's problems, even mine."

"That is the kind of family you want, isn't it?"

Too late Andrea saw where her reminiscences had led. *Good work, big mouth,* she chided herself.

"Yes, but Mama and Papa Mascari loved each other; that was the main thing. The kids were the frosting, not the whole cake," she said firmly, wishing she were as convinced as she sounded. Would Tony and Rosa have been as happy if they had been childless?

Andrea pushed the question from her mind and reached for Matthew's hand. "Hey, we're forgetting the ground rules! If the twelfth of Never doesn't have a tomorrow, it must not have a yesterday, either. I promise not to mention the words 'Cincinnati' or 'Mascari' again."

The car was headed due east, and she lowered her lashes against the brightening glare of the new sun. The comforting feel of his fingers entwined in hers, and the smooth gliding motion of the car had a soporific effect; her eyelids did not move again until the warmth of his mouth coaxed them open.

"Breakfast time," he murmured.

They were stopped in front of a roadside café, and her head rested against his shoulder. She sat up, stretching to relieve the tightness in her cramped muscles. The digital clock on the control panel said 09:32. "Is this Williamsburg?" she asked, glancing at the narrow tree-lined lane behind them.

"No, I took a detour. We are in tidewater country, near a town called Gloucester."

She brushed at the curls tumbling over her forehead, hoping they would fall into a reasonable semblance of order. "Never heard of it. What's here?"

"Daffodils," he replied cryptically, getting out of the car. "C'mon, I'm starving."

Della's Dew Drop Inn had the best breakfast this side of the Mason-Dixon line, or so the neon sign perched on top of the red-trimmed, white-frame building boasted.

"This is a truck stop, isn't it?" she said, eyeing a neighboring eighteen-wheeler dubiously as she preceded him to the door. Her imagination peopled the inside of the café with tobacco-chewing rednecks who answered to CB handles like Easy Rider, and she secretly longed for the plate-glass familiarity of a fast-food chain.

But the interior was nearly deserted, and the spanking-clean tile floor and cheery chintz that curtained the windows relaxed her considerably. The bouquet of aromas wafting from the open kitchen in back made her salivary glands tingle.

As they slid into a booth, a teenager with skin the shade and texture of caramelized sugar brought napkin-wrapped silver and steaming mugs of coffee.

"What can I get for you this mornin'?" she asked, retrieving an order pad from the pocket of her starched apron.

At Matthew's prompting, Andrea scanned the hand-lettered menu on a large board over the counter.

"Half a grapefruit and wheat toast with no butter for me," she said, eschewing the fancifully labeled offerings; Cousin Lettie's redeye gravy might be a delicacy to the initiated, but she was not about to take the risk.

"That's all?" The waitress looked faintly horrified.

"I'm not much of a breakfast eater," Andrea felt compelled to explain.

Matthew's order encompassed most of the list.

"Do they really fry the apples?" Andy asked *sotto voce* as the young woman hung their orders on a carousel behind the counter.

"I suppose so. Della Shoffner doesn't go in for false advertising. The waitress must be one of her daughters; there's a definite resemblance," he said matter-of-factly.

The observation startled her. "You're a friend of the family?"

He smiled crookedly, the expression deepening the off-center dimple in his chin. "I feel like one, although Mrs. Shoffner probably doesn't remember me. I came here a little over a year ago. It was raining catfish, I had a flat tire, and I was about as blue as I could get. Della and her good food sure helped."

Andrea added sugar to the fragrant beverage in front of her. "What was wrong with you?"

"Mother had just died, and I knew Jenny would be coming to live with me." He spread his fingers on the table, staring down at the square-cut nails somberly. "I was also in the process of breaking my engagement to Kristin Drake. It wasn't an easy time."

Andrea's antenna homed in on the name. The illusive Kristin had popped up before, usually introduced by an incautious remark from Jennifer, but in the past Matt had always avoided the subject.

He didn't now. "Kristin wasn't anxious to be saddled with a retarded sister-in-law, and she couldn't deal with my refusal to put Jenny in a home. It didn't take long for us both to realize we didn't love each other enough to solve our differences."

The conversation was cut short by the reappearance of the heavily ladened waitress. Setting a large tray on the table, she proceeded to lay out a meal in front of Matthew that would have sated three famished lumberjacks.

"Are you sure I can't bring you something else?" she asked Andrea worriedly.

"This will be just fine."

"The fried apples will be along in a minute. Mama is just finishing a fresh batch," she said, bustling off again.

"Surely you're not going to eat all that," Andrea said, viewing his breakfast with alarm.

"Got to keep up my strength. Pass the jelly, please."

She slid a rack holding marmalade, strawberry preserves and grape jam across the table, then nibbled at a wedge of her toast. "What's the white stuff?"

"You've been in the South over nine months, and you never had grits? That's uncivilized!" He dipped up a spoonful and held it in front of her lips. "Open wide, lady. Your education is about to begin."

She wrinkled her nose but obeyed and was surprised to find she liked the buttery flavor and hearty texture of the food. "Not bad. Reminds me of Cream-of-Wheat without milk and sugar." She cast a wistful glance toward his appetizing plate, adding, "That bacon is cooked crispy, just the way I like it."

Matt's chuckle was honey sliding over gravel. He lifted half his portion and gave it to her.

"The first time you came here, were you going to Williamsburg?" she asked between crunches of the tangy meat.

"No, I was on my way to a cabin an old buddy of mine owns. Well, he calls it a cabin, but it's really a vacation home with all the conveniences—he even put in cable TV last summer. The house sits on the banks of Mobjack Bay in a grove of pine and dogwood, and the view is spectacular in the spring."

Why was he telling her all this? "You sound like a real estate agent," she commented dryly.

"I wanted you to know it isn't a rustic dump. Nehemiah let me rent it again for this weekend." He cut squiggly trails through the grits with his fork. "If you don't like it, though, we can stay at Yorktown Commons in Williamsburg. I made reservations just in case."

I'll sleep in a pup tent as long as we don't have to register, she thought, hastily assuring him, "The cabin sounds lovely. Now stop destroying the grits, because I'd like another bite." After dipping a healthy portion of the remainder, she waved her spoon toward a fluffy mound of scrambled eggs. "You need help with those, too?"

The arrival of a tall black woman carrying a fragrant bowl of cooked apples temporarily halted the food raid. She could have been anywhere from thirty to sixty; age did not show on the long oval of her face. Her eyes were deep set and shadowed, as though she had seen too much of the harder side of living. But the smile that played at the corners of her full mouth said she had successfully coped.

"I spotted you when you came in, but I was too busy to stop and say hello. Is everything all right, Matthew?"

The words held much more than a restaurateur's casual inquiry about the service.

"Couldn't be better, ma'am, and I'm pleased that you remembered me." Matt was obviously taken aback.

The woman's brows arched in mischief. "Who could forget a mug like yours? If you're staying over at Gilly's place again, be sure to drop by for dinner tonight. There's homemade ice cream and Miss Lavada's pound cake for dessert."

"We probably won't be back from Williamsburg until late, but if you're still open, we'll stop for a doggie bag," Matt promised.

The woman glanced pointedly from him to Andy and back again. "Your manners are slipping. Aren't you going to introduce me to your friend?"

He hung his head like a small boy. "I'm sorry. Mrs. Shoffner, this is Andrea Kirkland."

The inspection was quick but thorough. Andy had to steel her muscles to keep from squirming, but she met the hooded gaze squarely. An audience with Queen Elizabeth couldn't be much worse, she thought, resisting an idiotic urge to get up and curtsy.

"Glad to meet you, and I'd be pleased if you called me Della." She smiled warmly, enclosing Andy's proffered hand in both of hers. "I can see that you're enjoying breakfast, but why are you sitting way over there? You can reach his plate much easier from his side of the table." The café owner's posture made it clear that she intended for Andrea to move.

Andy was not about to argue. As she slid into the cozy space beside him, Matthew slipped his arm about her waist to settle her comfortably. When the switch was over, he did not bother to remove it.

Della regarded them approvingly as she whisked away the dry toast and grapefruit. "Want me to send out more biscuits and a little Smithfield ham? If you all go to the Williamsburg Pottery Factory, you'll need some extra energy."

"This should hold us, Della. Particularly since Andy's not much of a breakfast eater," Matt teased.

Andrea made a face at him, halting an attack on the mixture of cinnamon, sugar and crisp, tart fruit to query, "Is this pottery factory something we should see?"

"Only if you like shopping and bargains. One hundred thirty acres of goodies—you name it, they sell it. Your feet usually give out before your money does," Della said over her shoulder as she strode back toward the kitchen.

"She's sort of intimidating, but I like her. Think I passed muster?" Andy said when the other woman was out of earshot.

"She probably wouldn't have made you move if you hadn't."

The sensuality of Matt's fingers caressing the space between her belt and rib cage diminished her appetite—for breakfast. Colonial Williamsburg had also lost some of its luster; her mind traveled on to the less historic but certainly more attractive lure of the cabin. A migrating warmth in her midsection made Andrea banish the intriguing thought and inch away from the firmness of Matt's denim-clad thigh. If she sat this close much longer, her legs would not be able to hold her when she got up.

The interesting condition must have been contagious, because Matthew straightened up abruptly and reached for his glass of ice water. She could see a fine sheen of perspiration on his forehead.

"Want to hit the highway again? We have a lot to get in today," he said after a long swallow.

"Ready anytime you are," she replied, meaning every word.

Mrs. Shoffner rang up their bill on the cash register, handing Matthew a wax-paper-wrapped parcel along with his change. "A couple of chicken sandwiches for later on. No need to eat greasy hamburgers if you don't have to," she explained, waving away his offer of payment.

The sun had nearly reached the tips of the stand of pines behind the café as they sauntered out. Filled with the contentment only a clear mind and a full stomach can bring, Andrea slung her light jacket over her shoulder. It seemed almost a shame to leave the hospitality of Gloucester.

"I bet the temperature gets up into the seventies today," she said, reluctantly shutting the car door.

"At least. Maybe we should go by Gilly's place and open a few windows before we head out. The house has been closed all winter, and the air is bound to be a little musty," Matthew commented as he backed out into the road. "We probably should check the coffee supply, too. If I don't have a shot of caffeine before the rooster crows, I turn into the Wolf Man." He twisted his features into a menacing, white-toothed grimace.

"Then by all means, stop. I didn't pack my silver bullets," she agreed with a chuckle.

As they rounded a bend, the woods along the narrow lane thinned into open fields lushly carpeted with canary yellow. A seemingly endless orchestra of daffodils lifted their trumpets in silent overture to the glory of the morning.

Andrea forgot to breathe.

"Another present for my lady," Matt murmured, his fingers electric on the nape of her neck. "In the thirties, daffodils were Gloucester's cash crop, the same as cotton and tobacco are in other parts of the South. Now most folks just grow them for the sheer pleasure of a day like this. If we had waited a little later in the month for this trip, we could have caught the annual show."

I couldn't have waited one more hour for this trip, she thought, loving him so much the emotion spilled from her heart into her eyes. "The flowers are wonderful, but they're not nearly as special as you," she said.

"I love you, Andy" was his soft reply.

Cabin was a totally inappropriate designation for the Colonial-style cottage in front of which they stopped ten minutes later. It was at the end of a long, winding driveway, its rear guarded by a glade of budding dogwood and the dormers of its facade facing the gray-green waters of Mobjack Bay.

"If we brought in the bags now, there would be more room in the trunk for all the stuff I plan to buy at the pottery factory," Andrea suggested as Matthew lifted the multipaned windows in the living room and unlatched the outside shutters.

A rush of salt-scented air rewarded his efforts. "Good idea. I'll get them while you check the supplies in the kitchen. It's through the door by the bookcase."

Andy nodded, gazing around the spacious but cluttered room. The cottage was obviously a man's hideaway. A scuffed leather-upholstered recliner had a place of honor in front of the fieldstone fireplace, and the magazines on the massive oak coffee table were of interest only to the avid outdoorsman.

As she passed the floor-to-ceiling shelves, packed with an assortment of paperbacks and masculine gadgets, the uses for which she could only guess, a small ornately scrolled silver frame caught her attention. She picked it up to study a sepia photo of a couple posed with a convertible roadster.

The face of the girl perched on the fender was eerily familiar. Her high cheekbones and sharply chiseled nose somehow looked out of place under the lustrous dark bangs, but there was no mistaking those eyes.

"Henrietta," Andy exclaimed.

"She was beautiful fifty years ago," Matt said, coming up behind her to lock his arms about her waist. "And she still is. If I were old Nehemiah, I'd snap her up before she got away again."

"This is Mr. Gill's house?" The question was unnecessary; Andy suddenly remembered Della calling it Gilly's place.

Matt nodded assent. "Do you know Nehemiah?"

"No, but Miss Hewitt mentioned him. How did you two come to be friends?"

"Last year we both were regulars in the Saturday night poker game down at the volunteer firehouse. I don't see him much anymore, since I found a better exercise for my hands than shuffling and dealing."

His demonstration made her blush. "Cut that out; I'm ticklish," she warned, but she did not back away. "Why won't Nehemiah marry Henrietta—doesn't he love her?"

"Is the pope Catholic? Come on, there's something I want you to see." Taking her hand, he escorted her through the kitchen and out the back door.

The yard behind the cottage was a jumble of new life. Violets and the beginnings of a bumper crop of impatiens vied for space under the bud-ladened branches of azaleas, and rows of hyacinths paraded along the weathered length of a stockade fence.

And, of course, there were daffodils.

Matthew led her to a gold-speckled, grassy rise that sloped to the banks of the bay. At the top, he sat cross-legged on the ground and pulled her down beside him. "Nehemiah bought this place ten years ago as a surprise engagement present for Henrietta. She always wanted a gazebo, so he built that one," he said, pointing to a weather-beaten latticed structure under the drooping arms of a willow.

Andy's brow wrinkled in puzzlement. "Were they supposed to get married ten years ago?"

"Not exactly. He had a heart attack, and the doctor told him he would have to be careful for the rest of his life. He didn't want to be a burden to Henrietta, and he never proposed."

"Well, she just did, and he flat turned her down. She probably wouldn't have done it if I hadn't opened my big mouth," Andrea said miserably.

He plucked a flower and, brushing her hair aside, tucked it behind her ear. "Nehemiah is a proud man. He visits Henrietta because he can't deny himself the pleasure of being with her, but he doesn't want her to marry him out of pity."

"Pity, my foot—that woman loves him! I can't bear to think of them living the rest of their lives alone."

He lay back in the grass, and drawing her to him, kissed the dampness from her lashes. "My instincts tell me that I'll eventually get suckered into some wild matchmaking scheme, so I might as well give in now. If I promise to help you get them together, will you shut up and kiss me?"

For an answer she pecked the tip of his nose.

"You can't expect a first-rate Cupid to work for less than union wages," he protested.

"I'm willing to negotiate."

The contract Andrea offered was eminently fair to both parties.

Her lips moved over the contours of his face, tentative at first, lingering at the apex of his brow, then sliding down into the hooded valleys of his eyes. Encouraged by a complete lack of opposition, she became a more intrepid agent, boldly insisting that the warm fullness of his mouth yield to her demands. Her fingers stumbled over the buttons of his shirt, but the luxuriance of the silken curls beneath the cotton fabric lent them fresh purpose, and they drifted slowly downward over the lean planes of his body.

With a low moan, he now became the chief arbitrator, shifting so that she was pinned beneath him. Tenderly he shackled her wrists with his fingers, replicating, then adding his own intricate stipulations to her version of the transaction.

"I love you so much," he whispered, his hand becoming inexplicably hesitant. An unspoken question darkened his mahogany gaze to ebony.

"Don't stop. We really are safe this time."

The command was tempered with a quiet smile of reassurance, and as negotiations moved closer to final settlement, she ventured a breathless "Shouldn't we go inside?"

Matt's eyes glinted with amusement as he slipped the blouse from her shoulders. "Not unless you think the squirrels will object. Nehemiah's nearest neighbors live five miles away, and—" The sight of rose-tipped ivory pouting beneath the lacy bra cut short the sentence, and his touch roughened with wanting.

Andrea shivered, her senses taking on an acuity she had never experienced. The inverted bowl of azure above them pressed closer, became transparent—she could almost see the light-spangled void beyond. Moments later, as he entered her, the boundary between them and the world outside blurred until she could no longer find it. The whisper of the wind was their breathing, and the dark fragrance of the rich Virginia soil mingled indistinguishably with the heady scent of their combined perspiration. She was unable to separate the faint cries of gulls wheeling overhead from the tiny sounds coming from her own throat.

They tried to harness the energy of the sun that had risen within them, to slow its inexorable advance so that they might relish the serenity of morning. But neither could find the power to tame the star. At its zenith, they yielded gladly to midday, glorying in the blaze of white heat that fused them into a single entity.

In the afterglow they clung together, whispering words that meant nothing and everything, gently tending the embers with small, secret touches.

After a long while, Matt raised himself up on one elbow. Brushing the sweat-dampened tangle of chestnut from her forehead, he grinned down at her. "Management drives a hard bargain."

Andy nodded, her eyes smoky with deviltry as they traveled the muscular length of his body. "Apparently labor isn't satisfied with the outcome, though. Shall we take it to arbitration?"

He laughed, hugging her. She could feel the quickening pace of his heart as he responded with a feigned sigh, "I guess we have no other choice."

Chapter Nine

"And we must've gone through every single one of the thirty buildings at the Pottery Factory. I've never seen so much stuff in all my life—crystal, china, candles, jewelry, furniture—all jumbled up in the most wonderful chaos imaginable. Do you know they have a whole workshop that sells nothing but Christmas decorations? Matt bought me the cutest set of wooden elves. And I went absolutely bonkers over the hand-made soap." Andrea paused in her glowing recital of the weekend's highlights to dig into the shopping bag she had carried to work Monday morning. Drawing out two rectangular boxes, she presented Henrietta with a choice. "I didn't know which scent you'd prefer, so I got primrose and orange blossom. You can have both if you like."

The elderly woman went unhesitatingly for the pink box. "You were sweet to think of me, Andy. Primrose will do just fine. I don't have much use for orange blossoms these days," she said with a regretful smile. "It sounds as though you had a marvelous time. Where did you stay?"

"Gil—" In the nick of time, Andrea broke off the name, hastily substituting, "...er, a small place near the bay. We got to Williamsburg early Saturday morning, and when we walked down Duke of Gloucester Street, it was as though we'd been transported back through time." She sighed dreamily, then said, "Matthew would've made a spectacular colonial gentleman, don't you think? He has the perfect legs for knee breeches and tight hose. And I would love to have worn long skirts and farthingale."

"Spoken like a person who's never encountered whalebone corset stays" was her employee's observation.

Andy grinned. "I guess you're right, but life was so much simpler in those days—no traffic, no pollution . . ."

"No indoor plumbing, no food processors. I'm just as content with things as they are. Women worked a lot harder and died very early back then," Henrietta said dryly. Her eyes grew distant, and she absently replaced the lid on the box of handmade soap. "If you stayed near the bay, you must've been in tidewater country. I've never visited there, but Nehemiah is partial to that part of the state—he owns a house near Gloucester."

Andrea could not lie to her friend. "I know. We stayed in his cottage. It's a wonderful place, Henrietta, and he keeps a picture of you in the living room."

"I don't want to hear about it." Miss Hewitt got up abruptly, walking over to a dress rack to straighten garments that were already perfectly aligned.

Andy followed, catching the woman's shoulders and turning her around. "You have to listen. No matter what Gilly said when you proposed, he loves you. I'm going to get you two back together if it's the last thing I do."

"Don't even try it." Henrietta's eyes glinted with anger. "No more schemes, Andrea. That man is a closed chapter in my life."

Andy stepped back, raising her hands in defeat, but there was still a secret trump left to play. "Have it your way. If you want to let that wonderful gazebo he built for you go to waste, there's not much I can do to stop you."

"He built me a gazebo?"

Andy inspected her nails carefully. "Uh-huh. He told Matt it was nowhere near good enough for you, though. Gilly thinks you deserve the Taj Mahal."

"He actually said that?"

"Would my Matthew lie?" She smiled, adding, "Out back of the cabin there are violets, azaleas and a whole hill covered with daffodils. I know that you like working with flowers, so I got you a sweatshirt to wear when you're gardening. It would be perfect for Gloucester."

A second trip to the brown bag produced a white cotton sweater printed with a green-thumbed hand and the slogan Virginia is for Gardeners.

Miss Hewitt fingered the lettering wistfully. "Hrumph. If I know Nehemiah, he stuck in every plant on the face of the earth. The yard is probably a mess."

"It's a little crowded, but you could straighten it up in a hurry." Andy's forehead creased into a worried frown. "What do you call those little bugs that suck the sap out of roses?"

Henrietta's face paled noticeably. "Aphids?"

"Yep. I'm no expert, but I think Gilly's bushes have a bumper crop."

"That will never do! We'll have to..." The woman trailed off, frowning at Andrea. "I may be old, but I still have enough sense to know when I'm being manipulated. Not another word about Nehemiah Gill, do you hear? I wouldn't marry him if he got down on his knees and begged."

"What if he just asked nicely?"

The green eyes softened. "That's another story altogether. But I want you to promise that you won't interfere in any way. I don't want him unless he comes to me of his own accord."

"Okay, I promise. But I've never even met Mr. Gill. How could I possibly interfere?" she asked innocently.

"I'm sure you could find a way if I'd let you." Miss Hewitt folded her gardening shirt and stowed it carefully behind the counter. "I'm off to the Ark now. If you're still in the mood to mend broken hearts, you can work on Jason's when he comes in. He moped around all day Saturday—I think he and Sara had a spat."

"I'll give it my best shot," she said.

But the press of a busy afternoon made Andrea forget her pledge. When Jason finally made an appearance, she was on her way to the station wagon with a load of boxes.

"Can I help you with those?" he offered after her brief greeting.

"No, but Lucille MacDougal's wedding gown is hanging on the rack in the workroom. Would you bring it out for me?"

"Sure." Shoulders slumping, he went to comply.

When he returned with the garment bag, Andy noted with some concern the unaccustomed dourness turning down the corners of his mouth.

"Where are you off to?" he asked.

"Tara Estates. I'm going to deliver the outfits for the MacDougals' twenty-fifth anniversary celebration." Andrea closed the tailgate, adding dubiously, "I sure hope the tuxes fit. Lucille couldn't get her husband and son to come in and try them on."

"It won't matter much. The whole thing is going to be a bust, anyway," Jason predicted sourly.

"Thanks for the vote of confidence, good buddy." Andrea's tone was tart, but her smile removed any sting from the words. "Before I leave, please tell me what's wrong with you."

"Nothing. Why are you going way out to the MacDougals when they could just as easily come into town and pick up that stuff? They're taking advantage of you."

"I know, but I don't mind," she answered. Any other time the chore would have irritated her, but she was still riding a crest of elation left over from the weekend. She tucked her briefcase behind the driver's seat and slid under the steering wheel. "I have to pick up Matt at his office, anyway, and he won't be ready until eight."

"It figures you two would have plans tonight." The tone of the observation spoke reams of disappointment.

"I'm only dropping him off to pick up his car at the garage. He's spending the evening with Jenny," she said with a trace of regret, thumbing the key in the ignition. The engine of the wagon coughed and grudgingly turned over. While she waited for it to warm up, she stuck her head out of the window and peered at her assistant sympathetically. "I heard you and Sara had a fight. Is there anything I can do?"

"Nope," he answered tersely, shoving his hands deep in his pockets.

"There's no sense in both of us spending the evening alone. Why don't you meet me at Chang Lee's around eight-thirty? I've got a craving for Chinese."

"Sounds good." A trace of the old irrepressible Jason crept back into his mournful eyes. "Isn't it kind of early for cravings?"

She gave him the raspberry and pulled off in a sputtering cloud of exhaust.

Twenty minutes later she had successfully navigated the confusing maze of Tara Estates, Laurel Valley's new (and only) subdivision, and slowed to a stop on Butler Court.

"I'll bet the MacDougals' doorbell plays the theme from *Gone with the Wind*." She laughed to herself as she retrieved the garment bag containing the wedding gown and walked up to the white-columned facade of their plantation-style split-level.

She was wrong. It jingled a bar of "Dixie."

The skinny teenager who answered the door stared at her sullenly as Andrea explained the purpose of her visit.

"Yo, Mom! The wedding crap is here," he yelled over his shoulder.

"Unload Miss Kirkland's car for her, Junior, and bring the suits up so you and your father can try them on. We want to make sure everything fits before she leaves." His mother's honeysuckle voice wafted from the top of the marble staircase.

The boy shot Andrea a dirty look but complied.

A second long-distance message was addressed to Andy. "Make yourself at home in the parlor. I'll be down in a minute."

The wait was longer than advertised, but at least it was interesting. Andrea spent much of the time studying the life-sized oil portrait of Wild Willie MacDougal—King of Kars, as he was billed in his television commercials for Laurel Motors.

Love is truly strange, she thought, wondering why Lucille, a nervous, birdlike woman, had been attracted to the flamboyant car dealer in the first place. And how they had stayed together for twenty-five years was a complete mystery.

"I'm sorry to hold you up, but Wilfred broke a hook on his cummerbund," Mrs. MacDougal apologized as she hurried in.

She's been crying, Andrea speculated to herself, feeling a tug of sympathy as she noted the red-rimmed eyes behind Lucille's gold-framed glasses. "That's quite all right. Does the tuxedo fit properly?"

The woman seemed not to hear the question. She wandered over to the sofa, perching on the edge of a cushion as though afraid to dent the gold velvet upholstery. "My husband has to go on a business trip. We're not going to have the ceremony," she commented dully.

Before Andrea could react to the unexpected announcement, heavy footfalls on the stairs leading down to the foyer heralded the entrance of the King of Kars. Ample jowls quivering with importance, His Majesty strode into the living room.

Andrea swallowed the bubble of merriment rising in her throat; in the powder-blue tuxedo, Wilfred MacDougal resembled a six-foot Easter egg.

"Snappy outfit. Since it's already rented, I'll wear it on my next TV commercial," he said, adjusting the cuffs with a flourish. "Lucille did explain that the shindig has to be called off, didn't she? It conflicts with my annual convention in Detroit."

Three hundred engraved invitations, enough flowers to fill the National Cemetery, and an irate caterer flashed through Andrea's mind in rapid succession. It seemed incredible to her that the MacDougals hadn't bothered to check their calendar before they planned the event. "Canceling at this late date presents a rather large problem, Mr. MacDougal. You'll lose the deposits you've already made, and some of the service providers will probably insist on full payment."

He shrugged. "My accountant will find some way to write it off as a business loss. Sorry to put you to all the trouble for nothing, little lady, but you'll be well paid for your time." He walked to a desk in the corner and, pulling out a checkbook, glanced at her expectantly. "How much are we talking about for you to let me off the hook?"

It's not me you have to worry about, Willie, Andrea mused, watching Lucille's complexion change from pallid to a furious mauve.

"The convention's just an excuse. You never wanted to celebrate our anniversary in the first place," his wife accused.

"That's not true, angel. We'll have a blast in Motown," Willie said soothingly.

"I'm not going to Detroit." Lucille stood to face him, her legs trembling. Gall that must have been a long time building poured over her face and into her voice. "For twenty-five years you've put Laurel Motors before your family. I went to the kids' school plays and took them to the orthodontist while you sat around that dealership laughing it up with the salesmen. All I ever asked from you was this one thing, and you thumb your nose at me."

Both of them appeared to have forgotten the third party in the room.

"I told you from the beginning that the ceremony was stupid. And as for Laurel Motors, don't forget that my cars paid for the fancy private schools and all those damned braces in the first place. And the mink I bought you last year."

"There's not enough fur in the world to make up for your neglect. I'm leaving you, Wilfred MacDougal!"

"Here we go again." The disgusted observation came from Junior, slouching against the doorway while he flipped through a dog-eared copy of *Rolling Stone*. "Mom, ya gotta admit that Pop's got a point. Why should y'all repeat a lot of junk you didn't even mean the first time?"

The boy's gaze shifted to Andrea, and for a brief second the sullen eyes glistened with pain and pleading. Herself a battle-scarred veteran of parental discord, she remembered all too well the hope that somebody—anybody—would intervene. Responding to the mute appeal, she pasted on a bright smile and ventured into the fray.

IN THE SERENITY of Matt's small office at Prescott College, Andy tried to emphasize the more humorous aspects of the story, but the brush with disharmony had left a sour cast to her thoughts.

"Solomon wouldn't have touched the MacDougal case with a ten-foot pole, but I take it you managed to resolve it. What did the trick?" Matt asked. Rising from his swivel chair, he walked to the window to stand beside her, his eyes filled with admiration.

"A simple appeal to Wild Willie's basic greed." Andrea's grin was justifiably smug at the brilliance of her coup. "I pointed out what a wonderful public relations event the anniversary celebration will be—particularly if the reception is held in the Laurel Motors showroom. After the ceremony Wild Willie will take the guests from the church to the party in a fleet of convertibles. The marching band from Prescott Senior High will lead the parade."

"Majorettes included?" Matt's question was accompanied by a deep chuckle.

She nodded, joining in his laughter. "Lucille wasn't too crazy about the idea until she realized that it was a way for her to participate in the family business. I suspect she's going to be a lot more than a silent partner from now on."

His arms slipped around her waist and at his touch the distaste she had felt for the episode started to dissipate.

"My lady is the best cupid in the business," he murmured, nuzzling her neck. "Ever think of adding marriage counseling to your repertoire?"

She shook her head vehemently. "That was my last shot at it, and I probably wouldn't have butted in in the first place if it hadn't been for Junior. The situation's not good for any of them, but he and the girls are the real victims. Growing up in the middle of a parental war zone isn't easy."

"That sounds like the voice of experience. Did your parents fight?" he asked gently.

"Yes, but nothing physical—they did yell a lot, though. It was confusing, but I got to be an expert at patching up disagreements." Again disturbed by the memory, she turned to stare absently at the lights twinkling over the darkened campus.

"What did they argue about?"

"You name it: the weather, the price of hog-belly futures, professional football..." She stopped, and feigning a scowl, demanded, "By the way, how do you feel about the Cowboys?"

"Hate their guts. I'm a Redskins fan," he responded quickly.

She looked pleased. "So am I."

"Jason told me." Leading her to the leather chair beside the desk, he sat down to make a lap for her. "Actually, I've rooted for Dallas since I was a kid, but I'll gladly give up my ten-gallon hat for the sake of peace. Why haven't your folks gotten a divorce?''

''Habit, social pressure—who knows? Maybe in some strange way they even care for each other.'' She looked at Matt curiously. ''Didn't your parents ever fight?''

He chuckled, but there was no humor in the sound. ''Only once, and it wasn't really much of an argument. Mother finished what she had to say in ten minutes, and Dad just stood there listening. A few months later, he took off. I haven't seen much of him since.''

Andrea was startled; she had assumed from earlier conversations that his father was dead. ''Where is he now?''

''In Georgia.''

The sound of the clock in the chapel tower tolling the half hour punctuated the uncomfortable silence that followed his terse revelation. Andrea was tempted to probe further, but the granite set of his jaw told her the subject was best left alone. ''Speaking of fights, Jason and Sara apparently had a lulu, and I have to go talk him out of hara-kiri. C'mon, I had better get you to the garage.''

She reached for Matt's hand, in the process knocking over a folder that was at the edge of the desk. The photographs of various styles of houses and floor plans that were inside scattered over the floor.

''That was really clumsy of me,'' she said contritely, scrambling to pick them up. ''Everything's all out of order. I hope this isn't some poor student's senior project I've messed up.''

''Don't worry about it. It's just some information I had a real estate agent put together for me.''

Andy got down on her hands and knees to retrieve a picture that had landed under the desk. Apparently unable to resist the tempting target, he patted her fanny.

''You're a lewd and lascivious old man,'' she informed him. ''Don't tell me you're planning to offer housing services as part of the wedding center's package to newlyweds.''

''No, the information is for me. I've pretty much pinpointed the section of Richmond where I'd like to settle, and now I'm trying to decide on the style of the house. I've always been partial to English Tudor." He knelt beside her on the floor and, sorting through the photographs, selected one to hand to her. "What do you think of this one?"

"It's very nice," she said, hardly bothering to look. "Matt, why are you suddenly interested in a home in Richmond?"

"I work there, remember? The Regent exchange program here at Prescott is over on the first of May, and even though Dean Gamble has offered to let us stay until the beginning of next fall's term, I'd like to get Jenny settled somewhere permanent as soon as possible."

The room took on an air of unreality; Andrea felt as though she were watching the scene from a long way off. "But she's doing so well at the Ark."

"That's the main reason I have to move as quickly as possible. She's only been there for a couple of weeks, and if she gets too attached to it, it'll be doubly hard for her to leave. Thanks to you, I know now how important it is for her to be in an independent-living program, and Richmond has one of the best in the area." He caressed Andrea's cheek gently. "Things won't change that drastically, anyway. Mrs. Pickering's already agreed to go with us. There may be a few problems at first, but I think it'll work out, don't you?"

On the face of it, his plan was completely logical; the trouble was, "us" didn't include Andy. But she felt she had no right to interfere at this juncture. "Of course it will, and I'll help all I can. After all, we'll still be seeing each other, won't we?"

"You bet we will."

She had known from the beginning that Matt's job at Prescott was only temporary, and she had successfully pigeonholed the disturbing fact in the section of her mind labeled "Things To Worry About Tomorrow." That compartment was about to spill over, and though a month would not add much extra space, it was better than nothing. "I wish you could wait until early June, though. Nancy Ellison wants Jenny to sing at her wedding, and I was hoping to persuade you to let her take the job," she said as she finished tidying the contents of the folder and rose to her feet.

"I'll think about it, but are you sure you want to risk hiring her, Andy? You know how unpredictable my sister can be," Matt said dubiously.

She saw a reprieve and grabbed for it. "I think she would do just fine, and I'll take complete responsibility for getting her to and from rehearsals. You wouldn't have to do a thing. Please let her do it," she begged earnestly.

"When you put it like that, how can I refuse? I was always a sucker for big gray eyes." Matt grinned as he opened the door and escorted her into the echoing hallway and toward the stairs. "Speaking of the real estate, I went by to return Nehemiah Gill's key this afternoon, and he said he was putting the cabin up for sale."

"Why in the world would he do that?" Andrea's startled response drew curious stares from a pair of coeds passing them on the stairs.

"He's moving to Seattle to live with his daughter in two weeks."

"Does Henrietta know?"

Matt shrugged. "I doubt it. I don't think he's seen much of her lately."

"Well, she'll never find out, because we're going to stop him!"

"I don't see how."

As they walked to the car, the cool evening air took some of the sting from Andy's cheeks but did little for the weight in the pit of her stomach. Climbing in, she revved the motor absently.

"You should have your transmission checked. Sounds like it's slipping," Matt commented.

"It's near terminal, but never mind that." She was so absorbed in Henrietta and Nehemiah that she slammed the gear into reverse instead of coaxing it. The transmission wailed in anguish. "This problem calls for drastic action," she said grimly.

"Wild Willie would probably give you a decent deal."

She cut her eyes at him. "You know very well what I mean."

Matt shrugged. "Even if we could stop him from leaving—and there's not a snowball's chance in hell of that—it wouldn't do any good. When he refused her proposal, Henrietta told him she never wanted to see him again."

"I've already taken care of her. You worry about him."

"I think it could be a mistake for us to interfere."

"But you promised!" Coasting gingerly to a stop at a red light, she turned to him, persisting, "I would try to talk some sense into him myself, but I don't even know him."

Matt sighed. "Okay, you win. But if I can't convince Gilly soon, you're on your own. Starting Friday, I'll be in Washington, D.C., for a five-day Regent district seminar."

The unexpected revelation temporarily pushed the Henrietta-Gilly dilemma into limbo.

"Can't you send somebody else?" she asked as the traffic light turned green.

Matthew shook his head. "It would look strange if the district manager didn't show up for his own meeting."

"Since you're in charge, can't you cut it short? Five days make nearly a whole week!"

He pinched her cheek lightly. "I'll do my best to make it four days if you stop tying up traffic."

Eyeing the lengthening line behind her guiltily, Andy inched through the intersection and parked in front of Shannon's garage.

"Will you call me when you're not busy?" she asked plaintively.

"At least three times every night. Between you and my sister, I'll owe my soul to Southern Bell." Matt chuckled, but the amusement in his face was tinged with worry. "Jenny hates it when I travel. Being at the Ark will keep her busy during the day, but she's at loose ends when I'm not home evenings."

"She might not be if I were there," Andrea said impulsively. "It would halve your phone bill, too. You could talk to both of us at the same time."

"That would be terrific, but your schedule is heavy enough without adding baby-sitting to the list."

"If Jenny would like for me to stay, I'd be spending time with a friend, not baby-sitting," she said emphatically. "And first off, you have to ask her. I'm not about to impose myself on her."

"I know what her answer will be. She's come to love you almost as much as I do."

Andy grinned wryly. "I'm no Barbie, but I think we'll have a good time."

His eyes were bottomless as he looked at her, and when he spoke again, his voice was vibrant with emotion. "You just lifted ten tons off my shoulders. It'll be a relief to know I won't have to worry about Jennifer while I'm away."

"Don't be too sure. We'll probably experiment with every new makeup on the market. Are you ready for Jenny in eye shadow and mascara?"

"I guess so, but absolutely no purple hair." He opened the door to leave but did not.

"What's wrong?"

"I'm trying to figure out how to say, 'thank you, I love you, I need you, I want you,' all at the same time."

"Start at the top of the list and work your way down."

It did not take long for his kiss to progress beyond gratitude; exploring all the nuances of love took quite a bit longer, though. And when he headed toward need, Andrea realized that the chances of her getting to Chang Lee's at all, much less on time, were growing slim.

"I believe you," she gasped, laughing as she gently shoved him toward the garage.

BY THE TIME Andrea reached the restaurant, Jason was already munching on an egg roll.

As she sat down and reached for a menu, he said, "Don't bother; I already ordered one of everything. We're having sweet-and-sour shrimp, ginger beef with mushrooms, Hunan chicken, pork Szechuan, lo mein noodles with—"

"Pepto-Bismol," she finished. "I said I had a craving for Chinese food, not a blood lust."

"You know how much I eat when I'm this miserable." As though to prove the point, he reached for the basket of crackers in the middle of the table.

"No, I don't. I've never seen you this miserable before." She removed the packet from his hand before he could tear through the cellophane. "Okay, what's this all about?"

His answer was delayed by the arrival of a huge tray of dome-covered dishes. The waiter's smile turned to consternation as he viewed the two of them. "They told me the rest of your party had arrived. I'll take these back to the kitchen until you're ready."

"I am the rest of the party." Andrea struggled to hold back a laugh as the waiter left, shaking his head in disbelief.

Jason's hand snaked toward the nearest dome, but Andy fended it off with a rap of her chopsticks. "First, talk. You can eat while I'm deciding what you should do about your problem."

"This is worse than old Hewitt's senior English class." He feigned pain, but humor glinted in his amber eyes. "Okay, teach, I'm putting my future in your capable hands."

Mention of Henrietta set off a warning bell in Andy's head. Though she had succeeded with the MacDougals, her advice had already ruined one relationship, and she didn't want to press her luck. "Well, er, I probably won't help much, but I'm a good listener," she told him.

"Sara is in line for a promotion at the bank, but I can't convince her to take it. She wants to be free to travel with me after I graduate," he said, picking at a grain of rice that had fallen on the red tablecloth.

What the hell is happening? Is everybody in town fixated on moving? Andrea wondered, viewing her friend with no little alarm. Jason has become a more or less permanent fixture in her life, and the arrangement was comforting. "I had no idea you were planning to leave."

"I don't want to, but where would I get a hotel job in Laurel Valley?" he countered glumly.

"You could commute to Richmond. Matt does." As soon as the words were out of her mouth, she remembered the temporary status of that arrangement. "At least he did. He'll be back at Regent full-time after June," she amended glumly, then brightening, added, "But Richmond isn't the moon—we'll still see just as much of each other."

Jason snorted. "Don't count on it. If you want to get ahead in hotel management you put in twenty-eight-hour days."

The assertion confirmed Andrea's worst fears, and her mouth went dry. "It'll be different with you and Sara, though. You'll be married, and even though commuting might strain your budget, you'll be together every night."

"I don't want to settle for that. The worst part is, I don't even want to be in the profession anymore. There's too much pressure and not enough time to spend hanging around with people you care about."

"Are you ready to throw away all the work you've put into grad school?"

It seemed to Andrea that her voice was coming from someone else as she reached absently for one of the entrées. She tried to concentrate on what Jason was saying, but widening ripples of dismay blocked out his answer. She knew in the marrow of her bones that what her assistant had said was true, so she did not waste time debating it. The more important question was how would she react when Regent started to gobble up more and more of Matthew's time?

Not well, she admitted to herself.

Marrying him could solve the problem. The internal speculation stopped her spoon midair.

She ruthlessly squashed the small voice. *Don't be silly—I've only known him for four months.*

Jason's voice cut through the fog. "Hey, save some lobster Cantonese for me."

Andy looked down in distaste at the mound of food she had piled on her plate, and she pushed it toward him. "You can have it all, Jase. I've lost my appetite."

"Me, too. Let's ask for doggie bags."

When the waiter came back with their packaged food and the check, Jason dug out his wallet, gesturing for her to put away her credit card. "The meal is your fee for listening to my troubles. What do you think I should do?"

She was ashamed to admit she had not heard all of the story and even more guilty for letting her own problems interfere with helping him. In an attempt to delay her answer, she cracked open one of the crispy sweets the waiter had left with the bill.

The words on the oblong of paper she unfolded leaped out at her: "You're going to embark on a profitable business venture with a friend."

The solution to both their problems was so simple she almost laughed. "Jason, old buddy, what do you know about franchising?"

"Enough. We covered the basics last semester, but if you're suggesting I open up a fast-food joint, forget it."

"Not hamburgers—matrimony! Look, the business is already in the black, and eventually there'll be plenty of money to expand the operation to Richmond. Of course, the plan depends on my finding someone who is willing to split the work and the profits straight down the middle." She extended her hand to him. "What do you say? Is it a deal?"

"You're offering me a partnership?"

"You betcha!"

"I'd like to take you up on it, but I don't have the cash to pay half of Weddings Unlimited's fair market value," he answered after a moment's hesitation. "Your offer means a lot to me, though."

She opened her purse and, pulling out a dog-eared one-dollar bill, handed it to him. "You owe me two quarters and a penny."

"What for?"

"I'm selling you half of the business—I'll have the legal papers drawn up tomorrow. You're the one who saved the Whitney-Bowman reception, and that brought in all the new business. If it hadn't been for you, the fair market value of Weddings Unlimited would be exactly forty-nine cents by now."

He leaned across the table to shake her hand, then signaled the waiter. "Would you bring us two plates, please? We're ready to finish dinner now."

The man bowed slightly, looking confused as he removed the bags from the table. "I'll have your food reheated for you. Would you like more tea?"

"At least two pots, and could you throw in another order of egg rolls? My partner and I have a lot to talk about," Jason said happily.

Chapter Ten

The procession of balloon-and-crepe-paper-festooned convertibles that had rolled triumphantly down Broadway toward Laurel Motors at high noon on Wednesday was like none the town had seen before. In truth, there had been few spectators; most of the population were either in the cars or following behind as though the Pied Piper, rather than an ordinary drum major, headed the parade. The MacDougals' twenty-fifth anniversary celebration was definitely a Laurel Valley happening.

No corner of the King of Kars' Kastle had escaped the prodigal hand of the florist. Even the grease racks in the service bays, scrubbed nearly to bare metal for the occasion, were garlanded. The establishment was so overdecorated that it transcended bad taste to take on a grandeur all its own.

"Wild Willie sure knows how to throw a party," Matthew murmured in Andrea's ear as, at the halfway mark of the reception, he led her back through the phalanx of new cars that ringed the showroom floor.

"A buck says he has a cameraman filming it for his next commercial," she puffed, slightly winded from the strenuous dance they had just finished. Leaning against a sleek new station wagon, she peered at the price list pasted to the rear-quarter glass. "Hmm, this sucker is loaded. Wonder what kind of discount W.W. would give me."

"The Volkswagen factory offers terrific deals if you don't mind picking up the car in Germany," Matthew commented, studying the tips of his nails.

She looked askance at him. "Why should I mind? Don't I always shop for coffee in Rio? I'd just love to lay out all that money for a plane ticket to Europe," she said sarcastically.

Except for the faint twitching at the corners of his mouth and the glint in his eyes, his face was perfectly serious. "Air fare is cheaper when you travel with a close relative. And I understand the factory is just a stein's throw from a castle on the Rhine that offers a fantastic honeymoon package."

Andrea's jaw dropped, and she couldn't even manage a gibe for the terrible pun. If this were the prelude to a proposal, what would her answer be? Her heart knew, but her brain still was not sure.

The internal warfare must have showed on her face, because Matt quickly dropped his gaze.

Wild Willie could not have picked a better time to pop up.

"Today will go down in automotive history, and I have this little lady to thank for it," the car dealer boomed, patting Andy's shoulder with his left hand while offering the right to Matt. "Glad you could make it, Donaldson. Hope I'm not interrupting anything important."

"We were talking about cars," Andrea said hastily.

"Well, this one is perfect for the young couple just starting out." Wilfred beamed, patting the shiny fender of the wagon. He leaned toward Matt, voice sinking to a conspiratorial murmur. "Plenty of room for groceries and kids—you know what I mean? I can make you a damned good deal on it, Donaldson, and I'll throw in one of our deluxe infant seats to sweeten the pot."

Andy did not know which was more irritating, MacDougal's chauvinistic assumption that the male half of the couple was the better target or the familiar, wary stiffness that crept into Matthew's face at the mention of children.

"A sizable discount would be of more use to me right now, Mr. MacDougal. I'm interested in a multipurpose vehicle for Weddings Unlimited," she interjected, handling both of them with one neat swipe.

The King of Kars had the grace to blush. "Twenty percent below cost on anything you want, little lady, and I owe you a lot more than that. If you hadn't talked some sense into us, this anniversary could have been the end of our marriage instead of the start of a better one. I decided that Lucille could be a big help to me—bring in all the bridge-club trade. From now on she'll be here at the dealership part-time."

"That's a terrific idea. I'm happy that things worked out for you," Andrea said more graciously. "I'll come in next week to look at your vans."

Craftiness edged in to replace some of the gratitude on Willie's face. "You do that, and remember, anywhere from fifteen to twenty percent off is yours for the asking."

"I should've pinned him to the wall while I had the chance. By next week, I'll be lucky to get twenty percent above cost," Andrea said in a low voice as Wilfred ambled off into the crowd, slapping every back in sight.

"Maybe you should do a little comparison shopping. You don't want to get stuck with a lemon," Matthew said softly.

Wild Willie's deal isn't the only one I might lose out on, she thought, reading a meaning in his words and expression that had nothing to do with automobiles. She ran her fingers over the chrome of the station-wagon door. "Let's get out of here, Matt. I think we need to talk."

"Your clients might take a dim view of their consultant walking out in the middle of the reception."

"I do have a partner, you know," she reminded him, taking his arm and steering him toward the nearest exit.

"Before MacDougal butted in, you were going to ask me to marry you, weren't you?" she said as they got into his car.

"Yes, but I'm glad he stopped me. I said I wouldn't push you about the future, and I intend to keep my word," he answered, his eyes fixed firmly ahead as he wheeled out of the parking lot.

"I love you, and I'd hate living in Laurel Valley with you in Richmond."

He reached for her hand, and drawing her closer, kissed its palm. "I want you to marry me, but that's not a good enough reason. You would be giving up your dream of having children—that's a very large price for a future with me. Are you sure you can pay that much?''

"You may be blowing the problem out of proportion, Matt. Genetic counseling could—''

He cut her off sharply. "Don't you think I've been to doctors? No one can predict when the defect will occur, and there's no way to avoid it.'' Then, more gently, he added, "We could adopt as many as you wanted, though.''

"I suppose so.'' The thought had occurred to Andy, but it was not very appealing; Zack Langley had been adopted, and it was less than a happy placement. "But no matter how you get babies, they don't come with a money-back guarantee. What if we adopted and later discovered something was wrong with the child?''

"We would love it and do everything we could to help it.''

"Wouldn't we do the same thing for one of our own?'' she persisted.

"There's a very large difference between taking care of a handicapped child who is already here and giving the world another one, Andrea.'' His eyes were bleak but determined as he slowed to a stop in front of her apartment. "You have no idea what stresses that can put on a marriage. Dad left because Mother blamed him for Jenny's condition. I'd rather lose you now than have you come to hate me.''

"I could never . . .''

"I don't want a promise you might not be able to keep. All I ask is that you think very carefully about what you would be giving up,'' he said, brushing her lips with a brief kiss.

"You, too. You might change your mind.''

The assertion was in no way intended as a threat, but Matthew apparently viewed it as one; his face tightened. "To believe that would be fooling yourself, Andrea—I have no intention of fathering children. Even if you can't accept that decision, I hope you will eventually come to understand it.''

"I'll try my very best to do both,'' she said softly.

A BEAMING MISS HEWITT bustled into the shop early the next Monday morning; not a trace of the gloom she had pulled about her like a shroud since Nehemiah Gill's refusal remained. "Isn't it a grand day?" she chortled, waving her left hand in an exaggerated gesture toward the gray mist pressing against the front window.

"If you happen to be Donald Duck," Andrea answered sourly. "Personally, I hate rain."

"I think it's very romantic. Reminds me of little diamonds falling from heaven."

The somewhat flowery phrasing sounded strange coming from the usually brisk schoolteacher. Andrea glanced quizzically at her bright eyes and glowing smile but made no comment. Her own lack of enthusiasm for the day was partially due to fatigue. Keeping Jennifer's mind off her brother's absence was turning out to be more than a notion. And not only had the weekend been hectic, but during the two nights Andy had spent quartered in Matthew's room, sleep was hard to come by. Between restless dreams she had stared into the darkness, searching every shadow for answers that still eluded her.

"I thought surely I would beat you in today. I wanted to surprise you by having the inventory finished," Henrietta said with some disappointment.

"Jenny and I have been here since seven-thirty. She insisted on coming with me this morning."

"Where is she now?"

Andy nodded toward the back room. "She's pressing the gown Susan Shannon rented for her senior prom."

"Unsupervised?" Miss Hewitt's brows peaked in alarm.

"She asked to help, and she can't hurt the dress or herself. I set the iron on the lowest heat possible," Andy hastened to assure her. "I felt sure she could do it alone, and I wanted to show that I trusted her."

"I applaud your intentions, but don't go overboard, Andrea. Too much confidence can be just as harmful as too little. You shouldn't push Jennifer along too far, too fast. Would you like for me to go check on her?"

"She'll be all right," Andy said stubbornly.

"Whatever you say, dear."

As Miss Hewitt adjusted the pins in her silver upsweep more securely, a flash of light from her left hand caught Andrea's attention.

Her eyes widened. "Is that an engagement ring?" she queried incredulously.

"It's about time you noticed; I was getting tired of being coy," Henrietta said dryly, spreading her slender fingers to show off the marquise-cut stone in its elegant filligree setting. "Nehemiah came to visit last night, and before I could get my wits about me, I had a diamond, and he had my promise to be his wife."

Andrea grinned broadly. "Galahad swept you off your feet, after all. What changed his mind?"

The old woman shrugged happily. "Who can tell about men? He wants us to be married as soon as possible, and so do I— we've wasted far too much time already."

"Well, let's get to it! We have a wedding to plan." Andrea picked up the nearest book of fabric samples and thumbed excitedly through it.

"No such thing. A simple ceremony in the pastor's study is just as binding as a huge to-do, and it's plenty good enough for two old folks like us. I bought a rose crepe two years ago that will do just fine."

Andy was dismayed. "I thought you wanted to wear the veil."

"That was a dream. Reality is ever so much more wonderful."

The remark hit a target for which it was not intended. *But dreams are important, too,* Andrea mused stubbornly.

"You're the closest I'll ever come to a daughter, Andy. If it isn't an imposition, I'd like you to stand up for me."

Her answer nearly tripped over the sudden lump in her throat. "I'd be honored, Henrietta. Have you set a date?"

"Next Thursday, if it will fit into Matthew's schedule. Nehemiah has already asked him to be best man."

Andy gaped at her. "Wait till I get my hands on that fink— I talked with him late last night, and he didn't say a word!" She stopped, remembering parts of the sweet conversation. "He did seem awfully interested in how you were, though."

"I think your Galahad may have given mine a slight nudge," Henrietta mused aloud with a smile.

"Lord, I love that man," Andrea said in a tone meant for herself but obviously picked up by her sharp-eared friend.

"He is very special, isn't he? Wouldn't it be grand if we had a double ceremony?"

Andrea dropped her gaze. "Next Thursday is your day, Henrietta. But if mine ever comes, I'd like to have you beside me."

"That should be when, not if," the elderly lady instructed. Instead of continuing the lecture, she sniffed suspiciously. "What's that?"

Andrea glanced at the workroom, the apparent source of the hot brown smell wafting through the air.

"Oh, my God!" they muttered in unison, scurrying toward the back.

Jenny was standing so close to the door they nearly stumbled over her.

When Andy lifted the unattended iron—now set on Linen—the bodice of the gown, draped over the board, sported a scorched replica of the sole plate, complete down to the last steam vent.

"I told you not to touch the dial, Jenny." Andrea could not hide her irritation.

"The wrinkles wouldn't come out. I'm sorry I messed up the dress," the teenager quavered. "I just left it for a minute, and it started to burn."

"Why did you leave it?" Miss Hewitt probed gently.

Jennifer's long lashes shaded her azure eyes. "I wanted to hear what you all were talking about." Apparently curiosity was stronger than guilt, because she asked excitedly, "Are you really gonna get married, Aunt Henrietta? I didn't know old people were supposed to be brides."

The last threads of Andy's patience snapped. "What a thing to say, young lady! It's bad enough that you ruined the dress, but you certainly shouldn't have been eavesdropping."

"I'm sorry," Jennifer repeated. "What's e-vas-dropping?"

"Listening to other people when they're not talking to you," Miss Hewitt explained carefully.

Jenny's heart-shaped face was still puzzled. "I do that all the time. I didn't know it was bad."

"It isn't bad, but it's not very polite," Andrea said reprovingly.

"But how else would I find out things? People hardly ever talk to me."

"I sure do, and so do your brother and Aunt Henrietta," Andy said.

"Y'all aren't people; you're my friends," Jenny answered miserably, twisting her fingers together. "Except when I'm at the Ark, everybody acts like I can't hear good, 'cause they talk real slow and loud. If I didn't e-vas-drop, I wouldn't ever know any secrets."

Touched by the pathos of the admission, Andrea put her arms around Jennifer. "Well, from now on, you won't have to. I'll tell you my secrets, and you can tell me yours. That's what best friends do, you know."

"Tell me one now—are you going to marry Bubba?" Jenny demanded with a giggle.

Andrea was temporarily thrown for a loss. "I love him very much," she hedged, blushing.

"Everybody knows that," Jenny replied scornfully. "I want you to tell me what you're gonna do about it."

Andy gulped. "I'm not really sure yet."

"Well, you'd better hurry and make up your mind. You're almost as old as Aunt Henrietta," Jenny informed her solemnly.

"I couldn't have put that better myself," Miss Hewitt said dryly. "Run and get your purse, Jenny. You and I are going to the Ark early today. We want to get there in plenty of time for our bus trip."

"She's going to teach us how to put the money in the hole and get off at the right place, Andy," the teenager confided, pelting off to the front.

"If it's all right with you, I'd like for Jenny to have some supper with Nehemiah and me this evening. You have some more homework to do, and I want to introduce her to her new uncle."

"Henrietta, you're an absolute angel! I could sure use a breather," Andrea whispered fervently as they went back to the showroom.

"Mail's here!" Jennifer bounced up with a bunch of envelopes the postman had pushed through the slot in the door. "Is there a letter from Bubba?"

"I don't think he'll have time to write, but we'll talk to him tonight."

"Are you gonna tell him about the dress?"

"Nope—that's our secret," Andrea answered with a smile.

After the two of them left, she locked the door and turned the Closed sign over. "Now, I'm going to put my feet up and have an uninterrupted cup of coffee," she announced to the mannequin couple on the dais, stretching luxuriantly. The silence of the shop was a relief after two days of chatter and activity; her pajama parties with Jennifer had been fun, but the girl's boundless energy had taken a definite toll.

"And you want six children—what would you do if they all started talking at once?" she muttered to herself, flopping down in the swivel chair by her desk and wondering how Mama Rosa survived the onslaught of eight young Mascaris.

She sorted through the mail, relegating circulars to the wastebasket with the ease of a Las Vegas dealer, but Matthew's bold, back-slanted script on the envelope bearing the elaborate Regent crest stopped her cold. "Don't be so damned anxious," she scolded herself, laying it aside until she finished the task. The last letter was obviously a wedding invitation.

She read the return address incredulously: Mr. and Mrs. Anthony Mascari.

Both pieces of mail were tempting, but the Regent envelope got first priority.

"No matter what you're doing right now, stop and call me" was the cryptic message.

The phone in Matthew's room was answered after the first ring.

"Took you long enough. Mr. Webster brought the mail ten minutes ago," he said lazily.

"Five," she corrected. "How did you know?"

"Laurel Valley schedules never change. I love you, sweet." She was engulfed in the wave of tenderness that poured through the receiver.

"Me, too," Andrea mumbled, now unaccountably shy.

"Aren't you going to congratulate me?" It was not hard to tell that Matt was extremely pleased with himself; canary feathers fairly floated through the receiver.

"For what?"

He answered with a gloating question of his own. "Isn't Henrietta's ring a beauty? I love it when my plans come together."

"Your plans? Are you saying that you're responsible for Nehemiah's proposal?"

"More or less." She envisioned him studying his nails modestly as he added, "Last Friday night before I left, I went over to his house for a friendly game of seven-card stud. After I let him pick my pockets, I challenged him to one last hand. But to make the game more interesting, I changed the stakes. His half of the anti was an IOU for one proposal of marriage."

Andrea gasped. "Henrietta was part of a poker bet?"

"I had three ladies and an ace showing, and another ace in the hole. I figured I couldn't lose. . . ."

"You can skip the play-by-play. The important thing is that you won," she interrupted. Then she added dubiously, "Don't ever tell Henrietta, though. She wouldn't be exactly thrilled to know Nehemiah is marrying her because he lost a card game."

Matthew chuckled sheepishly. "He didn't lose. The old fox cleaned my clock with four deuces."

"Then how—"

"After the game, we shared a glass of his home brew and talked about it. He didn't need much convincing—mostly I listened to him go on about how much he loved her."

"You really are terrific."

"I know," he said smugly.

She glanced at the receiver as though it could transmit the suspicion in her eyes. "What was your part of the bet?"

"Well, er, that's what I wanted to talk to you about. See, I promised Gilly a bachelor party, and I need a naked lady to pop out of the cake."

"Don't look at me!" she said with alarm, unconsciously fastening the top button of her blouse.

"You don't know how much I want to."

His tone was roughened by need, and the imagined flame in his dark eyes produced her involuntary shiver of pleasure.

"I have a fairly good idea," she responded when her racing pulse was once again under control. Scurrying for safer ground, she changed the subject. "Henrietta asked me to be her maid of honor."

"I'm glad."

"Why?"

"Because we'll be in a wedding together" was Matt's wistful answer.

JENNIFER'S GAZE FLICKERED from the clock behind the airline counter to the milling Saturday afternoon crowd in the Richmond airport. "You said Bubba would be back when the big hand got to the three, Andy, but it's on the six now, and he's still not here," she complained.

The Regent conference in New York had stretched past a week, and though she had seemed reasonably happy most of the time, Matthew's sister was apparently reaching the limits of her patience.

"The flight is late. We might as well make ourselves comfortable," Andrea replied, steering the disappointed girl to empty seats in the lounge.

"I wish he would hurry, don't you?" Jenny said with a sigh.

Andy's nod of assent was heartfelt; she could hardly wait to see him. Thanks to Mama Rosa, her decision was finally made.

"I can't believe it—in three months, I'll have Tony all to myself again" had been Rosa's surprising response to Andrea's congratulatory call on the upcoming marriage of the youngest Mascari.

"But won't you miss having all of them with you?" she had asked.

"No matter where they are, they never leave me. But now I can be a bride again, and I'm going to enjoy it."

A tug on Andy's sleeve brought her back to the airport.

"What are you thinking about? You look awful happy," Jennifer observed crossly.

"It's a secret, but if you promise not to tell, I'll share it with you." She leaned over to whisper a few words in Jenny's ear.

"You are?" The teenager's loud exclamation turned quite a few heads in their direction. She clapped her hands over her mouth, whispering through her fingers. "When?"

"Tonight, as soon as he takes me back to my apartment. And don't you say a single word or you'll spoil the surprise."

Jenny pinched her lips tightly between her thumb and forefinger and nodded. When the ritual was over, she pointed to a pregnant woman with a young child squirming in her arms who was walking toward them. "That lady's gonna have a baby. Can we have one, too?"

"We sure will—maybe even two or three," Andrea confided in a low tone, rising to offer the woman her seat and thinking ruefully that she would never experience that special glow that seemed to accompany motherhood.

Adoption does have some advantages, though—at least my ankles won't swell, she reminded herself, crushing a tendril of wistfulness ruthlessly.

"My name is Jennifer; what's yours?" Matt's sister asked the mother companionably, peering wide-eyed at the toddler.

"Barbara." The woman fumbled tiredly through the diaper bag at her feet for a bottle, which she then offered the fretful little boy. He rejected the milk with a roundhouse swing that knocked the plastic bottle from his mother's fingers.

Jenny caught it before it hit the floor. "Can I hold the baby? I could feed him for you," she said eagerly.

Andrea tensed, not sure what the reaction would be, but the explanation she hastily searched for was unnecessary; from her actions, Barbara found nothing unusual about the offer from the smiling teenager.

"I don't think he's wet, but you'd better put this blanket on your lap just in case," the woman said, gratefully surrendering her now squalling youngster.

"'Hush-a-bye, don't you cry, go to sleep, little baby. When you wake, you shall have all the pretty little horses.'"

Jenny's song had an immediate quieting effect. Before she finished naming the promised stable, the toddler's suckling was a contented counterpoint to the sweetness of the old Southern lullaby.

"He just yells louder when I sing to him. You have a terrific voice, Jennifer," the child's mother complimented.

"Thank you. I'm going to sing the solo at Miss Ellison's wedding, and she's gonna pay me real money. I'm gonna get a new green dress that goes all the way to the floor and high-heeled shoes like Barbie's, too. Isn't that right, Andy?"

Barbara's oblique gaze flickered over the teenager, then lit questioningly on Andrea, who, nodding quickly, dropped her lashes to avoid the probing.

"Let's talk about it later, Jenny," Andy said evenly, unwilling to identify the warmth in her neck as embarrassment, though she knew it was. The past week had made her painfully aware of the reality that had confronted Matthew for so long. Jennifer's naïveté with strangers and penchant for making them friends could cause anxious moments.

Jenny's face grew subdued as she continued. "Mrs. Flemming got all huffy yesterday when I told everybody in the beauty shop about my solo. She said I was dumb and that a person who couldn't even read music had no business singing in public." The glance she turned toward Andrea was filled with misgivings. "You don't think I'm gonna mess up the wedding, do you, Andy?"

"Of course not. You'll be as perfect as you were at the Christmas concert," she replied heatedly, forgetting for the moment that this conversation must sound very bizarre to an uninitiated third party. Her jaw hardened at the recollection of the middle-aged soloist's vicious behavior in the salon. "Mrs. Flemming is a jealous, spiteful woman with a very big mouth."

The answer was apparently reassuring, because Jennifer giggled. "Is that why you told her her curlers were twisted too tight?"

"Good for you, Andy," Barbara chortled approvingly.

Andrea's cheeks flamed fire-engine red.

"Passengers on flight 349 from New York City are now deplaning at gate twenty-six A."

The nasal announcement from the public-address system mercifully ended the discussion, and a ripple of activity spread through the waiting crowd.

"That's Bubba's airplane!" Jenny's excited tone startled the drowsing baby in her arms.

After a loud burp, he began to cry again, and his mother reached for him with a hasty "Thanks for giving me a rest, honey."

"Do I look all right, Andy?" Jennifer's hands flew to her golden hair, now cut to a shoulder-length style more appropriate to her age. Not waiting for an answer, she started toward the gate with an impatient "Come on, we'll miss him."

"I'll catch up with you. Be sure to wait behind the rope," Andrea called after the hurrying figure, wanting to give her a moment alone with Matthew.

Jenny turned back to yell, "Don't worry, I won't tell."

"Her brother is so lucky—she's a very sweet kid," the pregnant woman said as, rising to her feet, she gathered her things and prepared to leave. "Nice talking with you. Give old Flemming hell," Barbara advised as she waddled away.

Andrea's introspection on the basic decency of her fellow humans was shelved by the sight of Matthew's vigorous wave.

When she joined the beaming duo, his greeting was a circumspect kiss on the cheek, but considering the lazy heat that curled through his gaze, the gesture was a remarkable exercise in restraint.

"Is that the best you can do?" she murmured.

"My best would get us both arrested. Do you want to take the chance?"

"I look terrible in stripes," she answered.

Jennifer's elbow dug into Andy's ribs. "Couldn't you ask him now?" she whispered.

"Ask me what?"

"Nothing. It can wait," Andrea said quickly with a warning glance in his sister's direction.

The drive back to the Donaldsons' home seemed endless, and by the time the festive dinner Mrs. Pickering had prepared was over, Andy was willing to risk Devil's Island for an hour alone with Matt in her apartment.

Jenny seemed equally anxious. "That's enough dessert, Bubba. Andy has to go home," she ordered, whisking away his half-eaten portion of Baked Alaska.

"What are you two up to?" he asked, grinning. His hand reached under the table for Andrea's.

"Nothing. I need to water my plants." She returned the pressure of his fingers happily.

"Upstairs in my suitcase there are some new records for you, pumpkin. You can listen to them now, and when I come back, we'll have a long talk, okay?"

His sister paused in her jubilant dash for the steps to comment, "We should put an extra bed in my room when you come to live with us, Andy. Bubba hogs the covers something awful."

"I swear I didn't put her up to that," Matt said, frowning as he opened the front door. "I wish she'd learn not to say the first thing that pops into her head."

As they walked down the driveway, Andrea drew her features into a scowl. "You can have the blankets, but touch my pillow and you're a dead man."

"I won't bother your pillow if you promise to wear socks to bed. Your feet are cold." He mugged, pulling her to him.

"Tsskkk." The nonverbal comment issued from the vicinity of the rosebushes in the next yard.

"Afternoon, Addie." Matt dropped his arms, a grin creasing his face as Mrs. Winslow straightened up from the thorny screen.

"I was putting out beetle traps," his neighbor explained sheepishly.

Andrea could feel Mrs. Winslow's gaze boring into her back as she got into the car. "How long do you think it will take for our pillow talk to make the rounds?" she asked, snickering.

"Twenty-seven seconds. Addie's got the fastest dialing finger in the east. Let's make her day," he said, leaning over to tease Andrea's lips with the tip of his tongue.

She groaned at the shiver that zipped up her spine. "That's as cruel as waving a hot-fudge sundae at a weight watcher. You have no idea how much I missed you."

"Show me." He drew her to him in an embrace that would deservedly earn a place in Laurel Valley history.

Andrea could not hold her question any longer. "Matt, will you marry me?"

His eyes searched her face intently. "Are you sure that's what you want?"

"Absolutely certain." She snuggled her head against his chest so that the next line came out muffled. "Since my immediate plans include seduction, the least I can do is make an honest man of you."

Chapter Eleven

The shadows of late afternoon had lengthened into twilight, and from outside Andrea's open bedroom window came the noises of regular people doing mundane things: Mr. Zaccaro's electric trimmer buzzed irritably at a vagrant branch that had the temerity to spoil the sculpted symmetry of his hedge; Timothy Hodge's mother shouted dire consequences if the boy dared to make supper late; and, radio blasting at top volume, Peter Diggs's Trans Am screeched to a stop in front of Samantha Crump's house. Hardly background music for a romantic love scene, yet in Andrea's view, this symphony of the ordinary was preferable to a thousand Hollywood violins; it affirmed the reality and continuity of living.

She watched the slow rise and fall of Matthew's breathing as he lay beside her. He slept on his stomach like a little boy, head cradled in the crook of one arm and blunt fingers curled into fists. Moving slowly so she would not waken him, she loosened the tangle of covers from his legs and pulled the sheet up around his shoulders.

Their shared intimacy had been profoundly moving; after the immediate urgency of need was satisfied, they had fashioned renewed desire into a singing sword that cut through all layers of pretense and ego. Withholding nothing, they started as two and continued as one. Andrea knew with a certainty accorded only to morality that from this day forward part of Matthew would always remain with her.

He stirred, his mouth curving in the half smile of a vagrant dream. She could not resist its sweet invitation.

"Thought I was asleep, didn't you?" he said fuzzily, reaching for her without opening his eyes.

"Naah. You only snore when you're awake."

Her lips wandered down his neck, reveling in the softness at the base of his throat. She realized that no matter what ceremony they had later, she could never be any more committed to him than at this moment, and she felt compelled to express that knowledge. "Matt . . ."

"Hmm?"

"You can make that appointment with your doctor if you still want to," she said gently.

His lids edged open, the depths beneath alert and questioning. "You don't object anymore?"

She shook her head. "I want us to be free when we love each other. I'll go if you'd rather not." She was amazed at how easily the words came now and how much she really meant them.

"It's my problem, not yours, sweet, but the offer means more to me than you can ever know." He pulled her to him, rocking her gently. "What changed your mind?"

"Not what—who. I had a long talk with Rosa Mascari, and she told me something that nearly knocked me out." She ran her hand over his chest, loving the springy texture of the black hair twining around her fingers. "When she and Tony were first married, they didn't think they could have children. But after they adopted the twins, they were more relaxed, and the next six just came right along."

"That happens a lot. Why were you surprised?"

Andy propped herself up on her elbow and, smiling, looked down at him. "Mike and Donald were always treated just like the other kids in the family. If anything, Mama Rosa might have been a little partial to them, but I thought that was because they were the oldest. I had no idea they were adopted."

Matt brushed aside the tangle of curls and rose up to kiss her forehead. "You were afraid you couldn't love a child who wasn't your own?"

"More the other way around. Zack Langley's parents always made a big deal of how they had chosen him over all the other babies at the agency, and he couldn't stand them. He told me he would rather have been raised in an orphange." She sighed, stroking the thick, strong line of his brow with the tip of her finger. "Boy, do I feel dumb."

"Why should you?"

"I wanted to have a lot of children because I thought that is what made the Mascaris so happy. I, of all people, should have realized that blood alone doesn't make a family." She grimaced wryly, adding, "Henrietta Hewitt told me weeks ago that I had my priorities backward, but I'm just now able to see what she meant."

"Tell me."

"You come first. I never loved you because I wanted your children—I wanted your children because I loved you." She lay back down beside him, snuggling into the warm haven his arms provided. More words would have gotten in the way of the lovely contentment they shared. Not moving, they held each other quiety for a long while.

Andrea was the first to break the silence. "Guess what? I'm hungry."

"Lord save me from an insatiable woman. This will probably be my doom, but at least I'll die happy," Matt sighed, grinning lazily as he shifted her toward him.

She wriggled out of his grasp and sat up laughing. "Bacon-and-eggs-type hungry, fool! As much as I love you, I don't think I could prove it again right now."

He rose up on his elbows. "You just had dinner."

"That was—" stretching across him, she switched on the lamp and checked the clock on the nightstand "—three hours and seven minutes ago," she said, amused by the instant reaction her motions elicited.

"Is it past eight?" His brows peaked incredulously.

"Time flies when you're having fun."

Matt grinned at the hackneyed adage and, retrieving the clothes he had discarded earlier, donned his slacks. "I had no idea it was that late. If I know my sister, she's tired of the music by now, and ticked off because I'm not home yet."

Andrea removed her robe from the closet and slipped it on. "Right now she's too busy to miss you."

"Doing what?"

"Exercising. I got her a Jane Fonda tape for the video recorder, and when she finishes that, she'll take a bubble bath and set her hair. I give you my word—until ten, you would just be in the way." She walked over to the dresser to run a comb through her tangled curls.

"I don't believe it." He picked up the receiver and dialed. "Hi, Mrs. Pickering. Would you call Jenny to the phone?"

There was a pause, and his jaw dropped open. "I see. No, don't disturb her; everything is fine. In fact, everything is terrific. Andrea and I are getting married. Don't tell Jennifer, though. I want to break the news...."

He listened, a dazed grin spreading over his features. "She already knows...? Thank you; I think it's wonderful, too.... Yes, I certainly do know how lucky I am. I'll tell you all about it soon; I should be home around..."

"Ten," Andrea mouthed silently.

"Ten. Okay, see you then."

As he hung up, he had the look of a man who had just had a close encounter with a Martian. "I don't believe it," he repeated numbly. "Jenny won't budge when I try to get her to do calisthenics."

"Aerobic dancing is much more fun than two-a-day football drills, especially if you make it part of a regular routine. I try to work out at least three times a week."

"It shows," he said huskily, running his hands along the satin length of her thighs.

"Oh, no, you don't. Food first, then we'll decide what to do the rest of the evening."

He patted her rear. "I already have some interesting ideas."

She laughed, and catching his hand, led him toward the kitchen. "Can you cook?"

"When I'm pressed."

"Consider yourself pressed. The stove and I aren't on speaking terms," she admitted, perching on the stool beside the counter. "Last week I tried to make the blueberry muffins we had before we left Gloucester, and they were a total disaster."

"What did you do with the recipe Della gave you?"

"I followed it closely, but I guess I never caught up with it."

Matthew chuckled. "Toast is fairly foolproof. You can make it while I take care of the rest."

She slipped two slices of bread into the broiler with a flourish while he opened the refrigerator, taking out a bowl filled with a greenish-brown fuzzy mixture.

"What the hell is this?"

"Oatmeal and avocado face mask," Andrea said vaguely, entranced by her lover's spare, efficient motions and the way the overhead light defined the musculature of his naked torso. She brought herself back to the conversation with difficulty and peered into the dish he was holding. "It's supposed to be more effective after it ages, but I think I overdid it."

"How long has it been in there?"

"About a month," she answered, wrinkling her nose. The ripeness of the mixture blocked out the warning plume of smoke from the broiler.

Matthew lifted his eyes to the ceiling in mute appeal.

"I'm going to offer Mrs. Pickering a lifetime contract, because after we're married, you're not going to set foot in the kitchen," he said, brushing her cheek with his lips on his way to rescue the charcoaled bread from the broiler.

"Suits me just fine. I—"

A Gestapo-stern rap on the front door cut her off.

"Nobody knocks like that but Agnes-Avant-Your-Landlady," Andy said. Her "Who is it?" was distinctly annoyed.

"Agnes Avant, your landlady" was the muffled reply.

"Just a minute." Andrea jumped up from the table with an anxious scan of Matt's disheveled appearance. "I'll go change and get your shirt. That woman is dying for an excuse to break my lease."

"What do you care? You won't need it much longer."

"It's the principle of the thing. Damned if I'll let her get the best of me," she muttered, sprinting back through the living room. She scooped up the trail of clothes that she had left earlier and scrambled into them, not forgetting to toss Matt his shirt with a whispered "Don't forget to tuck in the tail."

When she opened the door, she was breathing hard but was reasonably composed. "What can I do for you, Mrs. Avant?" she queried coolly.

The landlady positioned her head so that the kitchen was in her line of sight. "I came to look at the gas line on the stove. Some of the tenants complained of a leak."

"Well, I haven't had a bit of trouble."

"Ah'm real pleased to hear that, but I have to inspect, anyway."

They stared at each other; then Andy stepped aside. "Certainly. Mr. Donaldson and I were having a bite to eat. Would you care to join us?" she asked sweetly.

Mrs. Avant's face furrowed with speculation as she nodded in Matthew's general vicinity. "No, thank you."

Instead of heading for the range, the woman stood by the sink, arms folded across her ample bosom and beady gaze slithering over Matt's tousled hair. "This is a small town, Miss Kirkland, and—"

"Is it really? I had no idea."

"We have values and sensibilities that someone from the North might not understand," Avant continued as though she had not been interrupted. "Of course, it's not my place to tell you how to conduct yourself, but . . ."

"You have surely got that right."

". . . there *is* a clause in your lease pertainin' to gentlemen visatahs."

Matthew stood up, and ignoring Andrea's signal to keep out of it, moved over to her side. "That certainly doesn't include fiancées, does it, Mrs. Avant?" he said, turning on his best New Orleans charm.

"This is mighty sudden. I haven't heard a word about y'all bein' engaged," Agnes said suspiciously.

"You're among the very first to find out. Miss Kirkland and I have been keeping the news our little secret."

"Not for long—soon the whole town will know," Andrea interjected grimly.

Agnes fairly licked her chops over the juicy tidbit. "Don't worry, your little secret is perfectly safe with me."

Andy's smoky eyes glinted with silver slivers of irritation. "I bet. Now, if there's nothing you have to discuss besides your lovely city and my morals, we can say good-night. I certainly don't want to keep you from any important phone calls."

Agnes-Avant-Your-Landlady's face darkened almost to purple. "Well, I nevah! If I were you, I'd be more careful who I insulted," she fumed.

"That's very good advice. You and your relatives should follow it." Andrea strode to the front door and held it open. As the other woman stalked out into the hall, she added, "By the way, I'll be moving soon. I trust you won't have trouble filling this charming apartment."

The landlady's "No, indeed" was truncated by the slamming door.

"Lord, I hate gossips!" Arms akimbo and mouth pressed into a thin line, Andrea glared at Matthew. "Do you realize that before ten o'clock everybody in town will know we're getting married?" she said, stalking toward the kitchen.

Matt followed her, grinning devilishly. "Saves us the expense of putting an announcement in the paper. What was that all about, anyway? You were really going for the throat," he commented as he cracked the eggs and whisked them into sunshiny froth.

"She ought to mind her own business."

"Ag-gu-nus never complained about me being here before."

"You aren't the problem. I am. Avant is Mrs. Flemming's sister-in-law, and every Thursday they both have their hair done." Andrea replied, extracting the silverware from the drawer.

"That's nice to know," he said mildly. "Is there a point to this story?"

She hesitated, not wanting to tell him of the ugly incident in the beauty salon but knowing he was sure to hear of it later. As she set the table, she quickly sketched the bare bones of the scene, eliminating details of the dialogue she thought he would find painful. "It wasn't the best way for Mrs. Flemming to find out she had been replaced as soloist for Nancy's wedding, but it wasn't Jenny's fault. She was so proud of her new job that she wanted to share it with everyone," she finished.

"I was afraid something like this might happen." Matt's face was grim. "I don't think Gilly and Henrietta would mind if Jenny sang at their wedding. That way, she won't be disappointed about Nancy's, and you can smooth things over with Mrs. Flemming and Agnes."

"Hold it—I'm not about to knuckle under to those witches! Besides, Nancy specifically asked that Flemming not do the solo."

"You shouldn't alienate them, though. Your business depends on the goodwill of the community."

"I don't care. Jennifer is my soloist until Weddings Unlimited closes or she gets tired of the job—whichever comes first."

"You said everything was perfect while I was away. Is there anything else you'd like to tell me?" Matt said warily, dividing the omelet and sliding a steaming plate in front of her.

"There were a few rough spots at first. Jenny wasn't too happy about loading the dishwasher and cleaning her room, but—"

"The housework is Mrs. Pickering's job," he interrupted.

Andrea shrugged. "I thought the responsibility of doing chores would be good for her."

His fork stopped halfway to his mouth. "Look, sweet, I appreciate what you're trying to do. Jenny needed a new hairdo, and the makeup looks wonderful on her, but—"

"You forgot the pierced ears," she reminded him gently. "Matt, I didn't do anything that can't be undone, and I checked out every move I made with Rene Hill, the director of the Ark. She thought my instincts were pretty good."

He swallowed hard. "So do I. I may be a bonehead, but even I can see that Jennifer is happier than she has been since Mom died. It's just that when I went away, she was content with Barbie, and now she's a Fonda fanatic. Change isn't easy for me." Matt's smile chased the shadows from his mahogany eyes, and he reached for her hand. "Will you come home with me? I want to be with you tonight."

"That wouldn't be a good idea with Jenny and Mrs. Pickering there."

"I'll stay on the living room couch."

"That doesn't sound like much fun."

"I walk in my sleep."

She laughed. "You talked me into it."

Every window in the house was lighted when they returned to Faculty Row, and they were barely out of the car when the reception committee met them.

Jennifer wrapped her arms around her brother. "Were you surprised, Bubba? I knew she was gonna ask you, but I didn't tell."

"Lord-a-mercy, I'm happy for you. You're just a precious couple," Ida Pickering joined in tearfully.

"Congratulations! When's the big day?" Mrs. Winslow added her two cents from the porch next door.

Andrea and Matthew looked at each other. "We haven't decided yet," they chorused.

"It's gotta be June sixth." Jennifer's tone brooked no disagreement.

"Why my birthday, pumpkin?" Matt asked.

"So you won't forget to buy Andy a present every year like the husbands do on tee-vee."

He threw back his head and laughed. "You are one terrific kid."

"I know." His sister dug in her jeans pocket and, producing a small box, handed it to him. "Give it to her now," she ordered.

"Yes, ma'am." Matthew turned to Andy, his love shining in his eyes as he took out a square-cut diamond in a simple platinum setting and slipped it on her finger.

"It was my mama's," the teenager said proudly.

The lovely ring glittered in the light from the front porch, a myriad of tiny rainbows dancing in its crystalline heart. As Andrea looked at it, the colors blurred, fusing into a shimmering haze.

"Why are you crying?" Jennifer anxiously touched Andy's cheek.

"Because I finally have a family of my own" was her soft answer.

THE CREAM-COLORED DRESS with its high Victorian collar and leg-of-mutton sleeves suited Miss Hewitt perfectly; she looked as though she had stepped from the pages of a Regency novel. It had almost taken an act of Congress to get her to wear it, though.

"I'm much too old for all this foolishness," she had insisted even as Andy was zipping up the back of the gown.

No force on earth could have gotten her to change her mind about the size of the ceremony; besides the wedding party, there would be only two other people in Pastor Pickins's study—Jennifer and Jason. And Andrea's plan to organize a reception had also been met with polite but firm refusal.

"Who would come?" Miss Hewitt had asked. "Folks in this town have better things to do on a Thursday afternoon than celebrate a marriage that should have taken place years ago."

Andrea adjusted the circlet of silk flowers that crowned Henrietta's silver hair and, fluffing the veil so that it floated in a transparent cloud, stood back to admire her handiwork. "Now isn't that better than the rose crepe you were so set on?"

"Hmmph." The elderly woman dabbed nervously at her mouth with a corner of her lace handkerchief. "Do I have on too much lip rouge? I can't go out there looking like a clown!"

Andy took the bride's shoulders firmly, and turning her around, marched her toward the pier glass in the corner of the small dressing room. "See for yourself. You're absolutely beautiful."

Henrietta's eyes widened as she scanned her image. "I am, aren't I?" she said in a stunned tone. "That groom of mine is in for a real shock."

"Nehemiah Gill has always known how lovely you are. By the way, he's really gorgeous. I fell in love with the man the minute I laid eyes on him."

Henrietta's sidelong green glance was mischievous. "Would you like to trade?"

"He wouldn't give me a second look with you around." Andrea took both of Miss Hewitt's hands in hers. "If you and Gilly are back from your honeymoon by the sixth of June, will you be my matron of honor?"

"Of course I will. I've waited nearly fifty years for somebody to ask me that." The old woman sighed happily.

"Weren't you ever in a wedding party?"

Henrietta chuckled. "Not as a matron." The strains of Brahms's Fantasy in C issuing from the phonograph in the next room sent her fingers fluttering to her throat for a last-minute touch to the cameo Nehemiah had given her.

"It's time," Andrea said gently, presenting her with a bouquet fashioned of gardenias and baby's breath.

"Just a minute." Henrietta hurried to the table where she had laid her purse before she dressed. Her hands were shaking slightly as she found a key and gave it to Andy. "Gilly and I want you and Matthew to use the cabin anytime you like while we're in Europe. Never can tell when you might need to get away from it all."

"You're the dearest friend in the world. I don't know what I'll do without you for a whole month."

"You'll manage quite nicely, I'm sure," Henrietta said dryly. She smoothed the skirt of her gown and, straightening to ramrod posture, tucked her arm through Andy's. "Well, let's not dawdle. Gilly and I don't have a minute to waste."

The big man waiting beside Matthew was obviously moved by the sight of his lovely bride. When she walked to his side, his eyes glazed over, and he tugged at the collar of the formal shirt he was wearing. Henrietta's small hand was dwarfed by her groom's broad fingers, and he held it as though it were made of rose petals.

Pastor Pickins cleared his throat and began, "Dearly beloved, we are gathered here..."

The next part of the ceremony was lost to Andrea as Matthew's gaze sought and found hers and a current of warmth flowed between them. *This is for us, too,* his eyes seemed to say.

"Who giveth this woman to be joined with this man?"

The question met with silence, and the good reverend mopped his brow with his handkerchief. "Sorry, I guess I should have skipped that part."

The bride smiled. "Don't you dare leave out a single line, Billy Pickins—except that one about obeying. I giveth myself."

Nehemiah was so nervous that he muffed the handoff from his best man just before the exchange of rings; the gold band he was to give to Henrietta bounced on the carpet and rolled out of sight under the desk.

Jennifer was first to reach it. "And don't drop it again, Uncle Gilly," she said reprovingly, scrambling up from her knees to return it to him.

"I'll do my best," he said shakily.

When the vows were over and Nehemiah lifted his new wife's veil to brush her lips with his, Matthew turned slightly, nodding to his sister.

"We've only just begun to live—white lace and promises, a kiss for luck and we're on our way..." Jenny's clear, true voice needed no accompaniment; it elevated the simple ballad from standard to classic.

A wide grin spread over Gilly's face. He circled Henrietta's shoulders with his right arm, gesturing with his left for the teenager to stand beside him. Hesitant until he found his range, he inserted a booming bass, adding depth and richness to the delicate fabric Jennifer wove.

Pastor Pickins's tenor was way off-key, but his intention was good. And one by one, the others joined in.

Except for Andrea. Try as she might, she could not force a sound past the obstruction in her throat.

"Thank you all for caring so much. I can't imagine a more wonderful way for us to begin our life together," Henrietta said when the song was finished.

"Don't be too sure," Jason said cryptically, bending to place a kiss on his former teacher's cheek.

"What are you up to?" Henrietta pinned him with a suspicious stare as the wedding party prepared to leave the manse.

"You'll see." Andrea's partner strode to the front door, and opening it wide, yelled, "Hit it, gang!"

After a few preliminary squeaks and toots, the high school band assembled outside on the lawn struck up a lusty—if slightly ragged—version of the March from *Lohengrin*.

Jason turned back to the newly married couple with a smug grin. "You wouldn't come to the reception, so we brought it to you."

The Gills were pelted with a veritable blizzard of rice when they stepped out onto the manse's wide veranda.

"Oh, my goodness" was all the bride could manage in response to the spectacle that confronted her.

April had taken care of the floral arrangements—the low-spreading azaleas were in full bloom and lavender blossoms crowned the trees that had given the small town its name—but the rest of the decorations had been provided by the Gills' friends and neighbors.

The street was cordoned off with pastel streamers, and crepe-paper wedding bells hung from every bush and tree in sight. Someone had even tied a bunch of pink balloons to the stop sign on the corner. And the limousine parked in the pastor's driveway (Courtesy of Laurel Motors, a large placard on the side insisted) trailed old shoes and tin cans galore. Laurel Valley knew how to take care of its own.

Andrea gaped at her partner. "Half an hour ago, there wasn't a soul in sight. How did they manage all this?"

"Elves," Jason supplied with a grin.

"I hope you're taking notes. A potluck reception could start a whole new trend in the wedding business." Matt chuckled, slipping his arm around Andy's waist.

Mayor Bellamy mounted the steps to the porch, and after a bow to the newlyweds, signaled to the crowd for silence. "Miss Hewitt, er, Mrs. Gill, in all of your years of teaching, you touched every one of us—sometimes not too gently, as I recall it," he said, rubbing the knuckles of his right hand. When the murmur of amusement from the crowd subsided, he continued. "As a token of our respect and love, we will now form our version of the traditional receiving line."

At the first wave of Hizzoner's hand, the assembled multitude parted into groups; the second brought forth a sea of hand-lettered signs, one for each year Henrietta had taught.

"I've never seen anything like this in my life," Matthew murmured as the mayor escorted the happy couple toward what was left of the class of forty-two.

"Only in Laurel Valley," Andy replied, her fingers tightening around his. She was touched by a sudden rush of affection for the town and its people, and the thought of moving away was not a welcome one. "Do you suppose this could happen in Richmond?"

"Maybe, but I doubt it. These people aren't a community; they're a family. That kind of closeness is hard to find." He looked down at her and smiled. "There's an English Tudor over on Beech Avenue that has a For Sale sign in front. Are you interested?"

"I would be if the drive from here to Regent weren't so long. You'd spend half the day commuting."

"What's forty miles?" He grinned lazily. "The house is on a cul-de-sac, so we wouldn't have to worry about traffic, and there's an oak tree in back that was just made to hold a swing. Bet there's room for a sliding board and sandbox, too."

She dimpled at him. "How many bedrooms?"

"Enough to start with, I imagine. We can add more on as we need them."

"Later on I'll join the PTA and a few of the women's clubs— the Establishment could use a little shaking up. You can run for mayor." Her smile changed to a grimace. "Staying here will present one major problem, though."

"Which is?"

"I'll have to make peace with Flemming and Ag-gu-nus," she answered, wrinkling her nose in distaste.

He slipped his hand under the weight of her hair and massaged her neck. "I wouldn't worry about it. You could charm a grizzly if you put your mind to it. You'll have to do something about your cooking, though."

She pulled back and frowned at him. "Why?"

"If you take one of your casseroles to a potluck supper, the good folks of Laurel Valley will run us both out of town on a rail."

Chapter Twelve

Armed with two recipes she had clipped out of a gourmet magazine and the grim determination that she would prepare at least one edible meal during her lifetime, Andrea cruised the narrow aisles of Phillip's Foodland, tossing item after item into her basket. Although over a week had passed since the Gills' impromptu reception and her decision to confront the issue of cooking, the press of preparations for Nancy Ellison's fast-approaching nuptials had kept her from doing anything serious about upgrading her culinary skills. But an unexpected cancellation had given her this entire, blessed Thursday afternoon free, and she was going to spend it preparing a New Orleans-style meal her fiancé would never forget.

Pausing beside the spice rack, she ran her thumb down the list of ingredients for sweet-potato pecan pie, one of Matthew's favorites. "This has to be a misprint—no sane person would put mace in food," she mumbled, conjuring up a picture of the spray can she carried for protection on the New York subway. "I'll just throw in a couple of extra teaspoons of cinnamon instead, and he will never know the difference."

The entrée was to be Creole red snapper, but looking at the slick, full-color photo now, it did not seem nearly so appetizing as when she had cut it out; the fish on the platter—head and tail included—was awash in a gaudy sea of tomato sauce, and even though a sprig of parsley had been artfully arranged to cover the snapper's eye, it was obviously still there.

Andrea had sudden qualms about serving food that would stare back at her guests. Things like that had never particularly bothered her before, and as she pushed the cart toward the back of the market, she wondered why she was being so picky.

To be located in a town the size of Laurel Valley, Foodland had a remarkably good selection of seafood; there was even a lobster tank on top of the case where the fish were on ice.

How can anyone eat those things? she thought, feeling queasy at the sight of the crustaceans with their banded claws groveling through the murky water. Forgetting that lobster thermidor was one of her favorite dishes, she turned her back to avoid their beady gazes and waving tentacles.

"What can I do for you today, little lady?" The man behind the counter dried his hands on the front of his white apron and beamed at her.

"I'd like a three-pound red snapper, please."

He shook his head regretfully. "Won't have any till tomorrow morning—the best pick is always on Friday, you know. I do have some nice catfish, though."

If you've seen one fish, you've seen them all, she thought. Besides, catfish was a hallowed Southern tradition, wasn't it? "That will be fine."

The clerk reached into the case and seized undoubtedly the ugliest creature known to mankind. Instead of scales, its body was covered with a substance resembling black Naugahyde, and the gaping mouth—which actually boasted lips, for Pete's sake—had a disgusting growth of whiskers on each side. As the man pulled the monster out of the case, it slithered over its companions with a sickening slurp. Pushing it toward Andy, he asked, "How's this feller here?"

She returned it's dead-eyed stare, her stomach lurching and pinwheels of light dancing in front of her. She bit her lip hard and gripped the handle of the cart, but neither action did much good. She still felt herself sinking into a black vortex.

Two stout arms from behind saved her the ignominious fate of hitting the floor.

"Bend over so the blood can get back to your head," a familiar, high voice instructed.

The advice sounded logical, so Andy complied; after a moment, she felt better and straightened up. "Thank you for your help, Mrs. Flemming," she said with a mixture of gratitude and chagrin.

"I've got a stool back here. Do you want to come sit down for a while?" the clerk asked.

The bouquet of raw seafood permeated the immediate area, and Andrea imagined an inch of slithery scales on the floor behind the counter. The mental image of wading through them to get to the seat almost sent her doubling over again. "I'm fine now. Really I am. I can't imagine what's wrong with me—I've never even come close to fainting before."

"You should go home and prop up your feet. A cup of chamomile tea wouldn't hurt, either," Mrs. Flemming advised.

"Good idea. I could be coming down with a stomach virus," she said weakly.

The other woman folded her arms, her brows winging their way toward her hairline; the expression could not have been more skeptical if Andrea had offered her a deal on the Brooklyn Bridge. "If that's the case, you'll probably be over it in a couple of days. Would you like me to help you finish your shopping?"

"You've done more than enough," Andrea began frostily. Then remembering her resolution to make peace with the ousted soprano, she said. "You're very kind to offer, though. Mrs. Flemming, I've been meaning to call and straighten out our misunderstanding."

The other woman dropped her gaze. "I'm so ashamed of the way I behaved in the beauty shop. I'm just glad the little Donaldson girl couldn't understand what was happening. I didn't want to hurt her—I was angry with you."

"She understood every—"

"Please, let me finish. I know that my voice isn't as good as it once was. That's exactly why I refused the soprano solo at the concert last Christmas. But I do have my pride, and to find out that you had replaced me without so much as a by-your-leave was quite a blow."

Andrea swallowed hard, the solution to this whole unfortunate mess beginning to surface in her busy mind. "I admit I was wrong, and there's still a place for you at Weddings Unlimited—"

"Absolutely not! I don't want your charity or your pity." Mrs. Flemming's faded-denim eyes snapped ominously.

"I wasn't offering either one." Andrea's tone was placating. "You graduated from the Boston Conservatory of Music, didn't you?"

"Yes, I did, and I'm very proud of it. I could have had a brilliant career if—"

"I know," she cut in quickly to forestall a repeat of the woman's life history. She set the hook and slipped on the tempting bait. "I've been told that you have better music credentials and more experience than anyone in this part of Virginia," Andy continued, omitting the fact that the soprano herself was the source of that information.

Flemming nibbled cautiously. "Well, I wouldn't say that exactly."

Andrea played out a little more line. "You must have more students than you can handle."

"I'm a performer—I don't teach," the woman said haughtily.

"What a shame. Working with you would be such a wonderful opportunity for some young person with talent," she mused aloud.

"I suppose it would at that," Mrs. Flemming said with a characteristic lack of modesty.

Andrea reeled her in before she could get away. "For example, you would be a wonderful coach for Jenny. She has a good voice, but it needs the training only a professional like you can provide. Would you consider it?"

"Oh, I don't think so." The woman was obviously flustered. "She can't even read music, you know."

Andy touched Mrs. Flemming's shoulder lightly. "You've heard Jennifer sing, and you know what a gift she has. She'll never be able to attend the conservatory, but if she had someone like you in her corner, she could still develop her ability."

Mrs. Flemming nodded slowly. "I suppose it would be a challenge, and it is my abidin' duty to help the handicapped. We'll try a few lessons, but I won't promise much."

Her attitude was galling, but Andrea knew there was no way to instantly effect a change. A couple of sessions with Jenny should straighten out her new coach, though. "I can't tell you how grateful I am," she said warmly.

"Do you want the catfish or not, miss?" The clerk's face wore a long-suffering expression.

One glance at the slick gargoyle still in his hand brought back Andrea's earlier queasiness. "No, thank you. I'm eating out tonight," she answered, pushing her cart hastily away from the counter.

Mrs. Flemming followed. "I'm glad we've settled our differences. We're going to see a lot of each other, you know. I live on Beech Avenue, two blocks from the house you and Matthew are going to buy."

"We haven't even looked at it yet," Andy protested.

"Well, you ought to. At the price they're asking, it's a steal—even though the gutters are rusting out. Jennifer will be able to walk to her singing lessons, too." She leaned closer, asking in a low tone, "You can let her out by herself, can't you?"

Andrea gritted her teeth. "Certainly. She does very well on her own, Mrs. Flemming."

"Call me Myrtle." The woman beamed, adding in a conspiratorial whisper, "And don't worry, I won't tell a soul what happened today, Andy."

"I'm not sure I understand what you mean."

"Your fainting spell will be our secret. I never gossip about my neighbors." With a final pat, she sailed away, smiling.

Andrea stared after her in puzzlement. Why should her slight dizziness be grist for Laurel Valley's gossip mill? Shrugging it off, she returned all the items in her basket to their proper places on the shelves and walked out of the market sans dinner but buoyed by a sense of accomplishment; she had managed to defuse a bad situation and land Jenny a coach both at the same time.

But her satisfied smile quickly faded when she reached the rear of Foodland. Her abused vehicle was nowhere in sight; the parking space where she thought she had left it was now empty. In fact, the only other occupant of the lot was a sleek teal-blue station wagon parked on the far side.

"Somebody stole my car!" she said angrily, her opinion of Laurel Valley taking a giant step backward.

"It wasn't a theft; it was an act of mercy." The door of the wagon opened, and Matthew slid from behind the steering wheel, grinning.

"How can you joke about something this serious?" she demanded, frowning as he sauntered over to her. "And what are you doing here? You're supposed to be in Richmond."

"I played hooky because I wanted to test-drive your new wheels." He took her arm, and ushering her across the lot, patted the fender of the vehicle he had just vacated. "Can I pick out automobiles, or what?"

She stared at him. "That's mine?"

"Yep. It's the same model we were looking at in Wild Willie's showroom, but I thought this was a nicer color. It's got cruise control, a stereo deck, air-conditioning . . ."

Andrea was suddenly and unaccountably angry. "I don't care if it drives itself. You had absolutely no right to trade in my wagon."

Matt's face was puzzled. "I couldn't have done that even if I had wanted to. It's illegal."

"Then where is it?"

"Jason drove it back to your shop."

"Oh." That bit of information only temporarily dammed the mounting flood of her fury. "How could you make a decision like this without consulting me first?" she demanded. "If I'm going to have to pay for an overpriced hunk of metal the rest of my natural life, I certainly should be the one to choose it."

"I didn't tell you about it because I wanted it to be a surprise. The car is your engagement present," he said quietly.

Andy was stunned. "My engagement present? Oh, Matt, you shouldn't have. It's much too expensive," she said, throwing her arms around him and feeling like an absolute fool.

"You're not exactly marrying a pauper, sweet, and since I didn't have to buy a ring, I figured what the heck," he told her, grinning wryly. "But if you don't like the wagon, Wild Willie said I could return it."

"Don't you dare! I love it."

Matthew lifted her chin and kissed her. "How about a spin around the block?"

After the clunker she had had for so long, the new car was a cream puff to drive. "Did MacDougal try to weasel out of the discount?" she asked, enjoying the instant response of the wheel.

"As a matter of fact, he gave me an even better one—" chuckling, Matt gestured toward a cardboard box in the rear "—and he insisted that I take the infant seat, too." He stopped, looking at her quizzically. "I wouldn't have mentioned it if I had known it would upset you, Andy."

"Why should I be upset?"

"You don't usually cry when you're happy."

Andrea took one hand off the wheel to wipe away tears she did not know were there. "There are times when I'm just weepy and cranky. You'd better get used to it."

"Oh." His features held the resigned look of a male confronted by the inevitability of the calendar. "Are you feeling ill now?"

"No, but I will be tonight around nine."

Matt looked confused. "How can you pinpoint the precise time?"

"I'm exaggerating a bit, but I could almost set a clock by my body," she assured him. "I'll be my old self again Monday."

"I'm looking forward to it, but we'll have to hold the welcome-back celebration until Wednesday. I have to run up to New York for a few days."

"That's nice," she said vaguely.

Disappointment clouded his eyes. "I did expect at least an 'Oh, shucks,' when I told you I'd be away. Can't you pretend you're going to miss me a little bit?"

"Course I'll miss you, dummy. Do you want me to stay with Jenny again?"

"I promised I would let her spend the time with her friend Melissa at the Ark. I'm sure she'd like it if you dropped by, though."

"I'll be sure to do that." She smiled at him, adding, "Now is there anywhere in particular you'd like to go, or should we just keep driving around in circles?"

"Turn right at the next corner, go five blocks and then hang a left. We might as well look at the house." He slid across the space between them and slipped his arm around her shoulders.

"Okay, but let's not rush into this. We might find something we like better."

"We might at that. The house has been vacant for a year, so don't expect too much. It will probably take a lot of work to whip it into shape." He stretched his long legs luxuriously in the ample space beneath the dashboard and mused aloud, "I've always wanted to try my hand at renovation. I'm a pretty fair country carpenter, you know."

Andrea peered at him suspiciously. "You didn't buy it already, did you?" The question was sharper than she intended it to be.

"Of course not." He grinned. "Believe me, from now on I won't even shop for a toothpick without checking with you first."

"I'm sorry, Matt. I'll be in a much better mood next week, and I won't grouch at you again for a whole month."

The English Tudor on Beech Avenue showed the sad effects of neglect; brown paint was peeling from the wooden cross-beams along the dingy stucco of the upper story, the lawn was overgrown with weeds, and the shrubbery that screened it from the house next door looked as though it had never known a pair of hedge clippers. But the lines of the house were well-proportioned and graceful. In a flash of recognition, Andrea could see shining possibilities.

"We could plant daffodils beside the garage and rosebushes there in the sunny spot on the other side of the driveway," she said, pointing as they strolled up the front walk.

"Let's not rush into this. We might find something we like better," Matthew mimicked her earlier caution drolly. He took the key from his pocket and unlocked the door. "Wait," he said before Andy could enter. Scooping her up, he carried her across the wide threshold and kissed her until they both were breathless.

"Just practicing," he said huskily.

"You don't need to; you're perfect already."

She took his hand and drew him from the entry hall into the spacious, high-ceilinged living room. The fireplace, with its solid oak mantel, caught her attention immediately. "Can you imagine how cozy this will be on a cold winter night with the wind howling outside?" she said dreamily, plopping down on the ceramic-tile hearth.

"A whimper is the most you can expect from the wind in Virginia, sweet. We probably wouldn't light the fire more than two or three times a year," Matt teased as he sat beside her, clasping his hands around his bent knees.

Andrea ignored the sally. "The first thing we do is get rid of this stuff. I hate wall-to-wall carpeting." Reaching for a loose corner of the ugly sculptured rug, she gave it a tug, uncovering the beauty of the floor beneath. "Isn't that much better?"

"If you happen to like waxing. Hardwood requires a lot of upkeep," he cautioned.

"I hadn't considered that. Kids are notorious for spilling Kool-Aid and tracking mud," she observed ruefully.

The subdued expression that crossed Matt's features took her by surprise. "The thought of adopting children right away bothers you, doesn't it?"

Matthew stood, and shoving his hands in his pockets, walked over to the diamond-paned double window to stare out. "Not exactly, though I have to admit that it scares me a little. There are a lot of new things I have to learn—" He turned to her, and smiling crookedly, added, "Like how to be a good husband, for instance."

Andrea went to stand beside him, twining her arms about his waist. "That's no big deal. All you have to do is keep loving me."

He stroked her hair absently. "What I'm most afraid of is that you'll be disappointed. Adoption isn't an instant process, Andy. It could be five or six years before we found a baby."

She tightened her hold on him. "I know, but I can wait. And in the meantime, I can learn to make cookies; it will take that long for me to bake a decent batch."

"At least. Now, let's go inspect at the rest of the house—except for one room. We'd better leave the kitchen to Mrs. Pickering," Matt said, pinching Andrea's cheek playfully.

Hand in hand they wandered back to the foyer, and through an unspoken agreement, headed up the broad staircase toward the master bedroom.

"We could have a king-size bed, a triple dresser and two nightstands, and there would still be enough space for a small couch in the far corner," Andy said delightedly.

Matt opened the door to the adjoining bath and wriggled his brows mischievously. "Look at this, will you? It's big enough to put in a hot tub!"

Andy laughed. "Matthew Donaldson, you're a truly decadent man."

"You and this room bring out my best instincts," he said with a laugh, capturing her in his arms and drawing her over to the bench built into the alcove formed by a bow window. As she snuggled happily beside him, he continued, "And you know what? My mother had an antique love seat that would go perfectly in here. It's in storage with the rest of her things, but we could make a quick trip to New Orleans before we get married."

"Nancy's ceremony is only two weeks away, and I won't have a minute to spare before then. Afterward, we'll be too busy getting ready for our own," Andy reminded him.

"Okay, forget the furniture, but if you could squeeze out a little time, I would really like to go to Cincinnati. You don't want your folks to have to meet their new son-in-law at the wedding, do you?"

"My mother and father send regrets with a present to follow. They simply can't make it," she said bitterly, pulling away from him. "They're leaving for Greece the last of May and won't be back for a month."

"That's no problem; we'll postpone it till then," Matt said soothingly.

"The hell we will! I'm not putting my life on hold just so they can float around the Mediterranean and get a perfect tan," Andy asserted grimly. "Who needs them, anyway? Jason is more than delighted to give me away, and I won't be the first bride whose mother wasn't sitting in the front pew."

"I think we should wait. I'm sure it would mean a lot to all three of you for them to be here. Weddings are an important family occasion," he said quietly.

Andrea's reply dripped sarcasm. "I agree. Have you called your father yet?" she asked sweetly, knowing full well that he hadn't.

He scowled, and there was a minute of oppressive silence. "That's different. He can't come."

"Oh, will he be vacationing in the islands, too?"

Matt ran his fingers through his hair, loosening the cowlick that fell so engagingly over his forehead. "No, but there's no way he can show up, because Jenny thinks he's dead. She was only five when he left, and at the time it was the easiest explanation my mother could give her."

Andy stared at him in disbelief. "All these years you've never told her the truth?"

"The truth would hurt much more than the lie. He didn't want her; don't you understand that?" Matthew's breathing was harsh, and his features twisted with long-held anger. "Mother spent the first few years of Jenny's life taking her to one doctor after another. We weren't rich, by any means, and Dad said she was just bankrupting the family by chasing a cure that wasn't there."

"He was right, wasn't he?" she interjected softly.

Matt's eyes glinted obsidian in the fading light of the afternoon. "That's beside the point. He wanted to put her into an institution, and when Mom wouldn't hear of it, he took off."

The famous Donaldson Control Syndrome, Andy mused, adding aloud, "He left you, a seventeen-year-old boy, to support your mother and sister? That was terrible."

"Even he's not that rotten. He sent checks every month, and he offered to pay my way through college, but I didn't want anything from him. He set up a trust fund for Jenny, and if I can help it, she'll never have to use a single penny of his guilt money. He wanted to see her when Mother died, but I wouldn't let him."

"You really hate him, don't you?"

Matthew leaned against the window casing and closed his eyes. "I used to. Now I'm just indifferent."

The poignant expression on his face belied the assertion.

"What's your father like?" she prodded gently.

"Me" came out in a dead voice. "His name is William, and people down home used to call me Little Bill instead of Matthew. I was proud of that then—I can even remember practicing his walk until I got it right."

He's afraid the resemblance is more than physical, Andrea thought, stirring restlessly beside Matt. She didn't relish making him relive the pain of his early years, but she needed to know the whole of the story. "His leaving wasn't all his fault, was it? You told me that your mother blamed him for Jennifer's condition, and it seems to me that wasn't exactly fair."

"It wasn't, but when she confronted him, he didn't even try to convince her. The man who was always telling me to be strong and responsible folded in the middle like a soggy newspaper," he snapped. "Let's leave it at that, shall we? Big Bill Donaldson was buried years ago, and there's no point in resurrecting him."

"People do change, you know. If he wants to see his daughter, it's not fair for you to stop him," Andy persisted.

"You're a fine one to lecture, considering that your partner, not your dad, will walk you down the aisle," he answered, eyes narrowing.

"I may not be crazy about Henry Kirkland, but at least I haven't killed him off" was her heated response. "Think how happy Jenny would be to discover that she had a father, after all."

"If you tell her, I'll never forgive you," he said, and she knew he meant every word.

"I would never do that." Defeated, she reached for his hand. "Please, let's not argue, Matt. In time both of us may have to come to terms with the past, but we don't have to tackle it this minute," she said, a wave of her earlier malaise creeping back.

"We'll have a whole lifetime to sort it out, that's for sure," he agreed, pulling her to her feet. "Right now I'm going to take you home so you can get some rest. You look as though you aren't feeling well."

"To be honest, I'm not. But by the time you get back, I'll be turning cartwheels down Broadway," she promised.

BUT MONDAY MORNING Andrea was having serious doubts about her ability to keep her word; nausea and fatigue had kept her in bed most of the weekend, and when the phone rang at eight o'clock, she felt barely able to lift the receiver.

"Mornin', Sunshine. I didn't wake you, did I?" Matt asked after her groggy hello.

"No, I'm talking in my sleep."

"Is something wrong?"

She swallowed hard. "I must have picked up a virus. Actually, I feel like hell warmed over."

"I'm sorry I'm not there to take care of you, sweet. Those things usually don't last long, but if you're not better by tomorrow, I'll sit at your side all night and feed you chicken soup."

Andy nearly gagged. "It's cruel to mention food to a person whose stomach is crawling with invisible bugs," she groaned.

"I'm sorry. It's a damn shame you have to put up with a virus on top of your other little problem," he said comfortingly.

It took her a few seconds to decipher the euphemism, then quite a few more to deal with the flood of pure panic that inundated her—the "other little problem" had not yet occurred.

"Andy, are you still there?"

She licked her lips to relieve their sudden dryness. "Trouble always comes in twos," she mumbled.

"I thought it was threes," Matt corrected.

"You're right, and if I don't get to work soon, my third disaster is going to be my business. Got to run, love—see you tomorrow," she trilled, hanging up before he could pursue the matter any further.

Dry toast and a cup of tea provided some relief for her churning stomach, and three hours later, when Andrea got to Weddings Unlimited, she was feeling a shade less ragged. She had completely forgotten Nancy Ellison's nine-thirty appointment for the final fitting of her bridal gown, however.

The socialite was standing patiently at the front of the boutique.

"I'm so sorry, Nance. Something came up this morning," she apologized, unlocking the door and ushering her customer in.

"No problem, though. While I was waiting, I went across the street to the malt shop for a banana split."

"How could you eat ice cream at this hour?"

"It beats the heck out of runny fried eggs and greasy bacon, don't you think? And it can't have as many calories as a stack of heavy pancakes dripping with syrup...."

"Sorry I asked," Andrea croaked, turning green.

Nancy's glance was oblique. "You look like walkin' death," she said sympathetically, leading Andrea to a chair beside the dais. "Can I get you a drink of water?"

"I'll be fine as long as you don't mention food. I've got a touch of virus."

"Yuck!" Nancy moved a step backward.

"I don't think I'm contagious," Andrea said, taking in a steadying breath. "The worst of it is probably over by now."

"Stomach flu can be bad news. Have you seen the doctor?"

"If it doesn't get better soon, I'll make an appointment."

"I'll do it for you. Paula Giladeaux is a good friend of mine, and she'll squeeze you in right away." The socialite headed for the counter and picked up the phone.

"I thought she was a gynecologist," Andy said, gulping hastily.

"Old-fashioned GP, but she does specialize in plumbing problems." Nancy paused, her hazel eyes filled with new speculation. "Whatever's wrong, Paula can handle it," she said firmly as she dialed.

Before Andrea could marshal any more arguments, an insistent Nancy bundled her off to the doctor's office.

"I appreciate your seeing me on such short notice, and I feel silly for bothering you with such a trivial problem. I do have a virus, don't I, Dr. Giladeaux?" Andy chattered after a brief examination.

"Why don't you call me Paula?" The attractive physician looked up from the folder into which she had been jotting notes and smiled. "Your temperature's normal now. Has it been elevated at all recently?"

"I don't think so."

"Have you had any dizzy spells?"

Andrea grimaced wryly. "Only when I buy catfish. A couple of days ago I almost fainted in the grocery store, but I think that was because I didn't eat any breakfast. Why?"

One of Paula's eyebrows elevated the slightest bit. "Just exploring all the possibilities. Your monthly period is late, and if you're as regular as you've indicated, you could very well be pregnant."

Andrea shook her head in the negative with much more confidence than she felt. "That's impossible. We've been very careful."

The physician again consulted the medical history she had taken. Closing the folder, she fiddled absently with her pen. "You're not on the pill, and you haven't been fitted for a diaphragm. In most cases, over-the-counter products work well, but they're not a hundred percent effective." She grinned, adding wryly, "I have a four-year-old who's proof of that."

A fine sheen of perspiration glazed Andrea's upper lip. "I want to know for sure. Isn't there a test I could take right now?"

"Yes, but you would have to have it done in Richmond. The lab here doesn't have the necessary equipment." Paula opened the drawer of her desk, taking out a small, square carton.

"What's in the box?"

Paula grinnned. "An early pregnancy test that you'll be able to take at home in another week. I keep a few on hand for patients who might not relish the thought of buying them at Fordham's."

Andrea fingered the test kit absently. "What do I do if I'm pregnant?" The question was addressed more to herself than to the physician. How could she possibly break the news to Matthew?

"That's up to you. Do you want the baby?" Paula asked kindly.

To this point, the notion of pregnancy had been a mere abstraction, but the doctor's words gave it meaning and form. Andrea could almost feel the gentle weight of a sleeping child in her arms. "More than anything in this world," she answered fervently.

Chapter Thirteen

The test was positive, and failing an unlikely glitch in the manufacturer's quality-control system, the other two kits Andrea covertly purchased in a nearby town confirmed the validity of its results.

Awareness of the new life inside her was at once a miraculous and terrible secret; her emotions vacillated wildly between elation that the love she shared with Matthew was now tangible and the despair of not knowing what to do about it. Living minute by minute was the only way she could control her confusion; at this point, she would not—could not—consciously consider any "what ifs." But the dread possibility that her child might be handicapped gained entrance to the dark hours after midnight, and most dawns her pillow was wet with tears.

At nine-thirty on the morning of Nancy Ellison's wedding, Andy sat in front of her dressing table, peering into the mirror. She and her image had had quite a few long conversations since the visit to Dr. Giladeaux's office; the more rational one of the pair kept insisting Matthew be told immediately. Though she knew it was a vain hope, the real Andy was holding out for some magic that would instantly dissolve his fears about having a baby and make the revelation a joyous present for him.

"It may be a shock at first, but he loves me, and nothing can change that," she told her reflection dispassionately as she got up to finish packing a garment bag with the pale pink dress she had chosen to wear to the early-afternoon ceremony.

Baloney! Everything is different now. And your Mary Sunshine act is wearing thin—he's already beginning to suspect that something is wrong.

The peal of the telephone relieved her from the immediate responsibility of a rebuttal. Guessing that the caller was Matthew, she quickly assumed a guise of bright normalcy.

"Something has come up. I'll probably be late for the wedding," he said after her cheery hello.

His terse, distraught tone turned the inside of Andy's mouth to cotton, and she sped through a number of ways in which he could have stumbled on her secret. All of them were improbable, so she relaxed.

"You won't miss Jenny's solo, will you?"

"No, but right afterward I'll have to leave for the airport. I'm flying to Atlanta this afternoon. Could I drop her by your place so she can go to the church with you?"

She groaned inwardly at the request. It was already hard for her to concentrate on work, but with the teenager as an additional distraction, it would be well-nigh impossible.

"I'm leaving in fifteen minutes. Jason could pick her up later," she suggested.

"That won't do. Mrs. Pickering has gone to have her hair done, and Jenny is keyed up about the wedding. I wouldn't want her to be here alone. I realize that this is an imposition, particularly since you haven't been feeling well lately, but—"

"It's not an imposition," she cut in quickly. The state of her health was not the most desirable topic for discussion at the moment. "Didn't I promise to be responsible if you let her sing the solo?"

"Thanks, sweet. Do you want her to get dressed now?"

"No, it's too early. Let her wear jeans and she can change in the dressing room at the church." Even to her own ears her voice sounded too bright and brittle. She toned it down to add, "Is something wrong at the Regent?"

There was a slight hesitation, and when he finally spoke, it was almost in a whisper. "Jenny's in the next room, and I don't want her to overhear me. I'll discuss it with you this afternoon before I leave."

"How long will you be gone?"

"No more than a couple of days, if things go well." His voice roughened, and Andrea thought she detected an undercurrent of despair as he continued. "If not, I just don't know."

Matthew's job was important to him, but Andrea had never heard him speak of business matters with such intensity, and it was beginning to concern her. Maybe this was more than a crisis at the hotel. "Is there anything I can do to help you?" she asked, responding to the almost palpable tension coming through the line.

"Knowing you're there is more than enough. I love you, Andy," he said softly as he hung up.

SHE WAS WAITING FOR THEM at the front of her apartment, fully intent on ferreting out more details of Matthew's mysterious errand, but there was no opportunity; he simply deposited Jennifer and her things, speeding away with a brief wave in Andrea's direction. And questioning his sister while they were on the way to Valley Baptist proved a useless exercise. All Jenny knew was that Bubba had to go to Georgia.

"I'm beginning to hate the Regent Hotel," Andy muttered to herself as she pulled the sleek station wagon to a stop in front of the church.

Jason was already inside when she and an excited Jennifer, ladened with garment bags and totes filled with cosmetics, walked through the vestibule. From the harried expression on his face it was easy to deduce that the four-hour wedding countdown was not progressing smoothly.

"You aren't supposed to be here until eleven, Andy. I thought I told you yesterday that I would handle the early details," he said accusingly.

"I know, but I felt guilty dumping it all on you. How is it going?"

"Pretty well, if there hadn't been a mix-up at the florist shop," he said ruefully, gesturing toward a meager display of carnations and gladioluses propped along one side of the entry hall. The arrangement nearest Andy bore a wide purple ribbon with the legend Farewell, Harley—We All Loved You emblazoned in gold.

"Arnold, the delivery man, is reloading his truck now. We should have our flowers in forty-five minutes," her partner told her.

"I hope so. Nancy's mother is superstitious, and if she saw these wreaths, she'd probably cancel on the spot," she said grimly.

"Too bad old Harley doesn't have the same option," Jason observed with a grin as a gray-uniformed man ambled in to retrieve another armload of arrangements.

"This time please recheck our order before you bring it back, Mr. Arnold. And make sure the candelabra are included," Andy said crisply.

"Young Markham here went and got 'em soon as he discovered the foul-up. Matter of fact, he's done a big chunk of my work already—when I get back, all I have to do is plunk down the flowers and pick up the check." The man shifted his wad of tobacco to the other side of his mouth and favored her with a brown-stained grin as he headed back outside.

Andrea walked through the archway into the sanctuary, which, except for the wide streamers of satin that would mark off the front family pews, had been decorated precisely as her plans specified. "This is a terrific job, Jase. You must have gotten here at the crack of dawn."

"You finished the real work months ago; I just provided the muscle," he said modestly.

She surveyed the effect of the double row of tall candle holders flanking the center aisle, walking over to one that was slightly out of alignment. Jason beat her to it.

"That's too heavy for you," he said, and pushing her gently aside, repositioned the metal ornament himself.

"Are you turning chauvinistic in your old age?" What Andrea intended as a joke came out as irritation.

Her partner stepped back quickly, his troubled amber gaze meeting her eyes for a moment, then dropping to the floor. "No, but you're too stubborn to ask for help, and I just wanted to show that I'm here if you need me."

I do, my friend—I sure as hell do, she thought, overwhelmed by the way her world seemed to be cracking around the edges. As though an unplanned pregnancy were not worry enough, her husband-to-be was exhibiting the classic symptoms of the confirmed workaholic. *If Matt is going to pop off every time there's a leaky toilet at the Regent, we're going to have a very short marriage,* she fumed inwardly, dismissing her earlier intuition that the hotel was not the cause of his apparent distress.

An impatient pat on her arm from behind pulled her from her brown study.

"Can I put on my clothes now?" Jennifer asked.

"Not yet, honey. But we should hang up our things so they won't get wrinkled," Andy said, escorting the teenager through a door on the right that opened into the vestry complex.

"Oh, no! I think I forgot my lipstick," Jenny moaned. By the time they reached the dressing room, she was already digging through her tote bag, scattering her hoard of cosmetics right and left. Barbie popped out in the process. "She wanted to come hear me sing" was the defensive explanation.

At this point Andrea would not have cared if the girl had brought along an entire toy store; at least the doll would keep her occupied. "Why don't you and Barbie stay back here while I help Jason put the bows on the pews? And after you finish playing, you can put on your new heels and practice walking in them," she suggested brightly.

She was much relieved when the teenager readily agreed, and as she reentered the nave, she found her partner already hard at work. Glancing at the rose window behind the altar, she noticed that the jeweled circle of light was dimming at an alarming rate.

"Did you happen to hear the forecast this morning, Jase?" Andy asked with some concern.

"The weatherman on Channel four said clear and warm, with temperature in the low seventies."

The reassuring reply was accompanied by a menacing rumble from outside.

"The guy is almost never right, though. He must base his predictions on his corns instead of radar. I brought a stack of umbrellas just in case," Jason continued. "I hope you have some extra T-pins. I'm running out."

"There are some in the car. I'll go get them," she said, bounding down the aisle toward the vestibule.

The mid-May sky outside had turned mean as a stray alley cat; dirty banks of clouds spitting ominous slivers of lightning now hunkered over the spire of Valley Baptist, and a second snarl of thunder sent Andrea skittering for the station wagon.

In the scant minute it took to retrieve the pins, the storm hit head-on, and sheets of water, interspersed with pellets of hail the size of marbles, pelted the top of the car. She cringed against the seat, eyes squeezed tight against a livid pyrotechnical display.

After ten minutes the rain slackened as suddenly as it had begun, and thinking the worst of it over, Andy left the wagon and sprinted for the church.

Her assessment was wrong. As she reached the steps, she was nearly blown over by the reviving wind, and the second onslaught of the deluge sent her staggering into the vestibule, dripping wet.

"Jason?" The hollow echo of her voice mocked her from the inside of the now gloomy nave; the electricity had gone out. "Oh, my gosh—Jenny must be scared to death," she mumbled, making her way toward the vestry.

The hallway was pitch-black. Andrea scrambled for the closest candelabrum and snatched down one of its wax tapers. She was halfway back to the door before she realized she didn't have a match.

"Damn it; this is all I need," she said furiously, snapping the useless candle in two. Throwing the pieces aside, she promptly burst into tears.

"Take it easy, Andy," Jason said, emerging from the vestry with a flashlight. He set the thermos he was carrying in a pew and hurried to meet her.

"I've got to see about Jenny," she sobbed, brushing past him.

Her partner caught her arm. "I gave her my extra flashlight and a cup of cocoa, and she's busy with Barbie. Are you okay?"

Maintaining the illusion that everything was perfectly normal would have required the coolness and steely nerve of a master magician, and Andrea had just run short of both qualities. "No, I'm not," she wailed, burying her face in the comfort of his chest.

Jason sat her down in a pew, silently patting her shaking shoulders until the storm within subsided.

"Thanks—I needed that," she sniffled after a while. The weight of the secret pressed down, now too much to hold alone. "I'm pregnant, Jase," she added miserably.

"I guessed you might be, and I was getting pretty tired of playing dumb." He fished a handkerchief from his pocket and dabbed at her cheeks.

"You're the first person I've told," Andrea said, fixing her gaze firmly on the rack of hymnals in front of her. "I don't know how I'm going to break the news to Matt. We decided not to have children."

Jason glanced at her obliquely, the expression on his caramel face startled. "Well, you'd better call another board meeting—somebody backed out on the deal," he commented dryly. "I don't see why you're worried, though. As much as Matt loves you, he'll be tickled pink."

Recalling the stony determination in her lover's eyes when he told her that having their own child would be totally irresponsible, Andrea shivered. "Take my word for it—he won't be happy. The last thing Matthew wants is a baby. You won't tell him, will you?"

Jason looked faintly insulted. "Of course not, but he has to know sooner or later. Today is as good a time as any, don't you think?"

"Matt is leaving to handle some emergency in Atlanta right after Nancy's wedding, and he'll have enough on his mind without worrying about me and the baby. I'll tell him when he gets back, though," she hedged.

"Bull—you're more important than the Regent. He'd cancel that trip in a minute if he knew how upset you were," Jason quickly asserted. His long face relaxed into a grin, and he reached over to squeeze her hand. "For what it's worth, I think Peewee is one lucky little dude to be getting you for a mother. Don't sweat it, Andy—things are going to work out just fine."

As if to substantiate his prediction, the lights in the ceiling came back on, and tentative rays of sunshine explored the panes of the stained-glass windows on the east side of the church.

"Y'all ready? Your flowers are out in the truck," Arnold called from the vestibule.

"Be right there with your check," Andrea answered, smoothing her hair and tucking the still-damp blouse more securely into the waistband of her jeans. But as she started down the aisle, Jason's hand restrained her.

"I'll take care of it. You go change and get Jenny ready. The bridal party will be here soon," he reminded her.

She glanced at her watch; it was already a quarter to twelve. "Time flies when you're having fun." With a ragged smile, she stood on tiptoe to kiss Jason's cheek, then headed for the vestry.

As they hastily dressed for the wedding, Jennifer was by turns subdued and intensely excited. Dealing with the mood swings was taxing Andrea's already limited patience and gobbling up a large chunk of precious time in the bargain.

"Are you catching a cold? The end of your nose is kind of red," the teenager observed, wriggling as Andy applied light touches of cosmetics to her face.

"I don't think so."

"Maybe you've got stomach flu again. Did you eat all of your breakfast this morning?"

Andy could now hear the muffled voices of the bridal party in the next room, and it was all she could do to keep her exasperation under control.

"If you don't hold still, I'll smudge your eye shadow and you'll look like a raccoon," she commented testily.

"I'm glad you're gonna be my sister," the teenager said, hugging her tightly.

She gently loosened the girl's grip and smoothed her golden hair. "I am, too. There, now you're absolutely gorgeous. And don't be so nervous about your solo. You'll be as wonderful as ever," she said absently.

"I'm not worried about singing." The blue eyes scanned Andy's face anxiously. "How do you feel?"

A few preliminary chords from the pipe organ outside caught her attention; the prenuptial recital was about to begin. "Terrific. Hurry up and put on your shoes. It's almost show time."

As they walked out into the vestry hallway, Andy paused beside the door to the other dressing room. "Jenny, you know where the choir room is, don't you?"

"Uh-huh."

"I want you to wait for me there. As soon as I've checked on Nancy, we'll go over all the things we practiced last week."

Jennifer's face clouded. "I know that stuff already."

"Well, it won't hurt to run through it one last time," she persisted. "Okay, when the organist finishes playing 'Sinfonia,' you will—"

"You're acting like I'm your baby," the teenager interrupted stubbornly.

Andrea glanced at her quizzically. Something in the accusation was odd, but since there wasn't time to identify it, she kissed the girl's cheek in apology. "I didn't mean to. You're my friend, and the best professional soloist this side of Richmond."

Smiling, her future sister-in-law ventured cautiously down the hallway by herself, teetering only slightly on the unaccustomed high heels. "Don't worry anymore; I can take care of everything," she called back over her shoulder.

Andrea watched Jennifer fondly, then, remembering her waiting clients, opened the door.

"It's a cliché, but you're radiant, Nancy," she said after an inspection of the serene bride and her bevy of pastel-clad attendants.

"I wouldn't be if you hadn't talked me out of my jitters," Nancy replied. "You look pretty good yourself, kiddo."

"Are you using some new beauty soap, Andy? Your skin is simply marvelous these days," the maid of honor interjected, adjusting a fold of her skirt. "By the way, I heard you had a virus—how are you feeling now?"

"Very well, thank you," she answered, trying to refrain from gritting her teeth. *That question is rapidly growing old—even Jenny is getting in on the act,* she mused irritably.

The thought preceded a creeping chill. Hadn't Matt's sister been a shade too preoccupied with the subject of her health? *If she overheard my conversation with Jason, I'm in big trouble,* a horrified Andrea told herself.

"Do you want to sit down? You're as pale as a ghost," Nancy's mother said, patting her arm.

"E-excuse me. I have to go c-call the caterer," she stammered, backing out the door.

In the hallway it was all Andy could do to keep from running. Her fiancé would arrive any minute, and she had to get to Jenny before he did.

But when she reached the sanctuary, her footsteps slowed. There was no longer any reason to hurry; she caught a glimpse of a tall, familiar figure striding down the far aisle toward the choir room.

A weird numbness stole over her. Andrea knew she must have instructed her feet to follow Matthew, because they obeyed the command, but she was not aware of the floor beneath her. The strange detachment carried her at a leisurely pace through the nave, allowing her to nod and smile at the rapidly assembling citizens of Laurel Valley as though she were running for office.

The scene in the stuffy chamber at the side of the altar brought her back to reality in a hurry.

"Why aren't you talking to me?" a concerned Matthew was asking his sister.

Jenny's mouth pressed into a thin line, and she turned away without answering.

He was obviously relieved as Andy joined them. "I've never seen her this nervous. It might be a good idea for you to cancel the solo," he said in a low voice.

Jennifer whirled to face them. "I'm gonna sing, and you can't stop me, Bubba."

The expression on Matt's face was total confusion. "You're angry with me, aren't you?"

His sister nodded stiffly.

"But why?"

Again there was no answer.

"Do you know what the problem is, Andy?" he asked as the final measures of the preliminary recital drifted in from the nave.

"I think so," she said dully, almost certain the teenager's displeasure stemmed from having heard her say Matthew would not want his child. But before she could enlighten him, Jason stuck his head through the doorway.

"Five minutes till curtain time, folks. Sara is saving you seats, but you had better get a move on—it's getting crowded out there," he informed them.

Jennifer held out a shaking hand to Andrea. "I'm scared. Will you come with me?"

She realized that the teenager was attempting to give her a reprieve and loved her all the more for the gallant gesture, but she could not let her problems drive a wedge between brother and sister. "You don't need me, Jenny, because you're a real pro. Bubba and I will straighten everything out, I promise you. Please give him a hug before you go, though. He looks as if he could use one."

Jennifer gladly complied. "I'll stop being mad at you, but you had better not yell at Andy," she said, leaving for the choir loft.

The expression on Matthew's face was the epitome of bewilderment as he and Andrea went into the sanctuary. "What the devil was that all about?" he asked in a low tone after they took their places.

She ventured a sidewise glance at the other occupants of the pew. This was hardly the setting for an in-depth discussion of her condition. "Tell you later. What is the big emergency in Atlanta?" she whispered.

The triumphant notes of the processional obviated an immediate explanation. As the time for his sister's rendition of "Oh, Promise Me" drew near, Matthew's hand sought and found Andrea's.

"Jenny will do beautifully," she whispered.

But she heard very little of the perfect solo; she was too occupied with the steady pressure of Matt's fingers and the solid reassurance of his presence. *A lifetime isn't long enough—I'll love this man forever,* she told herself, bemused by the endearing way his lips silently followed the progress of the song and the tension in his shoulders telegraphed a message of support toward the choir loft.

Her mind's eye allowed her the future vision of the two of them on the sidelines, whooping and thumping each other's back as a miniature replica of Matthew ran for a sandlot touchdown.

"You're a genius at this wedding business, sweet. Everything went like clockwork," he leaned over to crow.

Andy glanced around in confusion, startled to find herself on her feet and the newly married couple headed for the vestibule.

Matthew quickly checked his watch. "I don't have too much time left. A lot of folks will probably want to congratulate Jenny, so let's get to her before the mob. Afterward, I'd like you to walk me to the car so we can have a few minutes alone," he said, ushering her toward the front of the church.

They did manage to beat the crowd; except for a jubilant Jason, Jenny was alone.

"This is a very special day for me—you were magnificent, pumpkin," Matt said, whirling his sister around in a bear hug. "When I get back, I'm taking my two ladies out for a big celebration!"

"I'm so glad Andy told you. I just knew you'd be happy about our baby," Jenny said, clasping her arms tightly about his shoulders.

"Our what?" Matthew returned his sister to her feet so abruptly that she almost lost her balance. Catching her arms, he stared down at her intently.

"Our baby, silly. The one Andy is gonna have when she gets all fat," Jenny said playfully. The smile on her face faded under the pressure of his incredulous eyes.

Jason's "Oops" was barely audible. He discreetly backed out of the room, closing the door behind him.

Matt's mouth moved a few times but produced no sound.

Andrea slipped one arm about Jennifer's waist, as much to steady herself as to soothe the ruffled teenager.

"Jenny's right, Matt. I am pregnant. As close as I can figure it, our baby is due in mid-January," she said quietly.

Disbelief, followed in rapid succession by confusion and panic, flickered over Matthew's face. "You want a child so much you might have fooled yourself into believing it. Things like that happen all the time," he said desperately.

She shook her head, a hidden well of inner strength allowing her to meet the flinty chill in his eyes. "I'm almost positive. I hadn't intended for you to find out this way, but I'm glad you know now. Can we go somewhere and talk?"

"What is there to say?" he asked numbly, dropping his gaze to his watch. "If I don't leave now, I'll miss my plane."

"Isn't this more important than the hotel?" Keeping her voice calm and level was hard work, but she managed. "Please, Matt—don't go."

His arms were at his sides, fists clenched tightly. He glanced at Jennifer, then shaking his head as though discarding an impossible thought, returned his gaze to Andrea. "You simply don't understand. I have to. I'm staying at the Atlanta Regent, and I'll call you the first chance I get," he said curtly, moving toward the door.

"Wait—I'll walk you to the car. I want to know about your trip," she pleaded.

"You have enough to worry about as it is. I don't want to add my problems to the list." Without another word, he spun on his heel and left.

"Bubba didn't even say goodbye to me," Jennifer quavered.

"He's just surprised, that's all. When he gets a chance to think it through, I'm sure he'll call to tell us both how happy he is," Andy replied with much more certainly that she felt.

"I'm sorry I told on you. I'm never gonna e-vas-drop again as long as I live." Jenny's eyes were shaded with remorse.

"You mustn't blame yourself, honey. I'm the one who let you down. If I had shared the secret with you and Bubba right away, none of this would have happened." She hugged the teenager and, taking her hand, pulled her toward the nave. "I'm sure everyone is waiting to tell you how wonderful your performance was. Ready to take your bows?"

"No, I want to go home now" was the doleful reply.

Blessedly, Ida Pickering was in the vanguard of the well-wishers, and after hearing an extremely minimal explanation of the situation, quickly agreed to take charge of Jennifer.

"I'll come over this evening, Mrs. P.," Andrea promised.

"Don't even think of it; you need peace and quiet," the housekeeper drew her aside to say. "Jenny and I have a few recipes that'll keep us busy till Jane Fonda time."

Getting through the reception was the worst agony Andrea had ever endured. Every ounce of her fortitude went into the cheerful mask she donned, and by the time the last details were seen to, there was nothing left but utter exhaustion. She didn't even attempt to argue when Jason insisted on driving her home.

"Sara and I are going over to Mom's house tonight to pig out on strawberry pie. Why don't you come with us?" he asked as he parked the car in front of the apartment on Petunia Lane.

"Thanks, but I don't want to miss Matt's call," Andrea said wearily, reaching for the door handle.

"I could come up and wait with you," her partner offered.

"I'd be lousy company. I'm going to take a hot bath and then drown my troubles in a glass of milk." She grimaced in wry distaste. "You have no idea how I detest that stuff. Peewee damned well better appreciate the changes I'm going through for him!"

"We'll have a heart-to-heart talk—soon as he's housebroken, that is. Uncle Jase doesn't do diapers," he said with a comical shudder.

When Andrea laughed, he reached over to rumple her hair. "That's what I wanted to hear. Now I know my partner is going to be all right."

"I always dreamed of having a brother. Thank you for making it come true, Uncle Jase," she said as she climbed out, scarcely able to see the sidewalk for a sudden blur of tears.

The hot bath she had promised herself was shortened to a hasty shower, and dinner turned into a sandwich eaten within easy reach of a phone that adamantly refused to ring. At nine o'clock Andy finally got up from the ladder-back kitchen chair and wandered into the bedroom. Pummeling the obstinate pillows into submission, she lay down and closed her eyes against the relentless advance of the clock.

"This is stupid!" She popped up, snatching the telephone from the nightstand. Once she had obtained the Atlanta Regent number from long-distance information, she stared at it for a long moment. Why should she make the first move—hadn't he already indicated they had little to talk about?

"You might not, buster, but I sure as hell do. For starters, the next time you walk out on me like that, you needn't bother coming back." With each stab at the push-button digits she thought of a new facet of his insensitivity to bring to his attention.

"Would you please ring Matthew Donaldson's room?" she asked after the hotel operator's honeysuckle greeting.

There was a pause, then, "Mr. Donaldson's room is reserved, but he hasn't checked in yet. Would you like to leave a message?"

Andy frowned. The flight was less than two hours, and even if the traffic had been extremely heavy, Matt should have arrived at the Regent by early evening. Perhaps the problem had required his immediate attention, and he hadn't had time to go to his room. She hesitated, not relishing the thought of interrupting his work but less willing to let another minute go by without talking to him. "No, but please connect me with the manager's office."

She hung up a few minutes later, thoroughly baffled; the hotel administration had no indication that their regional director was, or would be, in town.

Why else would he go to Atlanta? she asked herself numbly. Her mind was too confused and exhausted to produce a rational answer. Turning off the light, she fell into a restless sleep.

Chapter Fourteen

For all intents and purposes, Matthew Donaldson had disappeared from the face of the earth; he still had not checked into the Regent by the next afternoon and, inexplicably, no one in Laurel Valley had heard from him.

"I even called all the hospitals in Atlanta to make sure he hadn't been in an accident. There is nothing else I can do, Jase," Andrea told her partner grimly when he stopped by her apartment to cheer her up. "I knew he wouldn't be overjoyed about the baby, but I sure as hell didn't think he'd walk out on us."

"Matt isn't that kind of guy, and if you weren't under so much stress, you would be the first to realize it," Jason defended. "He planned the trip before he knew about Peewee, and he must have had a very good reason not to cancel."

"For instance?"

He dropped his gaze to the cola in his hand, absently tracing circles in the condensation on the side of the can.

"I couldn't think of one, either." Her tone was bitter, and her fingers wandered to the little gold frog dangling from the chain around her neck. "The fairy tale was nice while it lasted, but this time there isn't going to be a happily ever after."

Jason set his drink on the coffee table, running a hand over his close-cropped hair in obvious frustration. "Shouldn't you at least wait until Matt comes back before you write him out of the script? So what if the guy panicked a little? I believe he'll eventually do the right thing."

"What—marry poor, pregnant Andy so her baby will have a name? No, thank you! My parents already did that bit, and I refuse to repeat the family pattern," she said fiercely.

"But you love Matt," Jason protested.

"That's why I won't trap him in a marriage with a child he doesn't want. I would rather lose him now than have him come to hate me," Andrea said, hurt slamming into her chest with the force of a heavyweight's fist. Rising from the couch, she strode to the hall closet and pulled a small suitcase from the top shelf. "If I stay in this apartment one more hour, I'll be certifiable. Jase, would you mind taking over the shop? I have to get away."

Her partner's brows shot up in alarm. "It's raining pitchforks outside. You certainly can't leave now."

"Just try and stop me."

Jason followed her helplessly to the bedroom, his amber eyes bleak as he leaned against the door frame, watching her throw a haphazard assortment into the bag. "Where will you go?"

"As far as my emergency fund will take me," Andy answered. Reaching for her jewelry box, she dumped its contents out on the bed and fished a wad of bills from a compartment in the bottom.

In the process, a metal object skidded across the coverlet and fell to the floor; Jason retrieved it, morosely handing it back.

She took it, identifying it as the key Henrietta had entrusted to her on the day of the wedding.

"Never can tell when you might need to get away from it all," she recalled her elderly friend saying.

Andrea clasped the key so tightly the serrations in its blade bit deeply into the palm of her hand. If she had to say goodbye to Matthew, where better to do it than the place where they first made love?

Jason's voice snapped her back to the present.

"Okay, I can halfway understand you feeling sorry for yourself, but have you stopped to consider how much Jenny needs you? She's as worried about Matt as you are."

The shot hit its intended target, but Andy could not let the wound stop her. "Mrs. Pickering is going to take her to the Ark to stay with her friend Melissa tonight—that will keep her mind off her brother. And he might have left me, but he's certainly not going to desert Jenny. When he returns from Atlanta, he can explain to her that things simply didn't work out."

Jason wore an expression of defeat. "Are you coming back?"

"I suppose I'll have to—eventually. But I can't think about it right now. Do me a favor, will you?"

Andrea twisted the ring from her left hand. "Return this for me," she finished, depositing the diamond in Jason's hand.

He nodded glumly, then fished the wallet from his back pocket. "I don't have but twenty-six bucks on me, but I want you to take it. If you need more, just call." Lowering his gaze, he traced the pattern on the bedroom carpet with the toe of his sneaker, adding softly, "You're the best friend I've got. Not having a partner around to bug me is going to hurt like hell."

She hugged him tightly. "Partners come and go, but sisters have a lifetime guarantee. If Peewee is a boy, I'll name him after his uncle."

"I appreciate the thought, but my middle name is Sylvester. You can't stick the poor kid with a handle like that." He picked up the suitcase, and as they left the apartment, he asked, "Are you sure you want to do this?"

"No, but I don't see that I have much choice," she answered softly.

Knowing full well that Jason would try to stop her, Andrea waited until he was out of sight of Petunia Lane before she switched her bag from the sleek vehicle Matthew had given her to her old heap.

All I want from him is already with me, she mused, resting her head wearily against the steering wheel while waiting for the engine to warm up. But an afterthought made her open the door and dash back through the rain to the other car.

"No use letting this go to waste," she muttered grimly, retrieving the box that contained Wild Willie's bonus infant seat.

Five miles out of Laurel Valley, she began to regret her hasty decision to leave the rest of her engagement present behind; the windshield wipers on the old car were hardly a match for the steady downpour that glazed the pavement of Route 60 east, and the engine wheezed as though it were in the terminal stages of emphysema.

"C'mon baby—you can do it," she urged, slowing the ailing machine to a bare crawl after a particularly ominous cough.

It took a half hour to reach an exit that was twelve miles away, and the owner of the filling station where she stopped fairly snorted when she asked him to fix the problem.

"Lady, a mechanic ain't gonna do you much good. What you really need is a priest," he said, shaking his head dubiously at the mess under the hood. "Go in the office and get yourself a cup of coffee. This could take a while."

The mixed odors of gasoline, new rubber tires and stale tobacco permeated the interior of the cluttered space into which Andrea wandered, and the muddy brew she poured was roughly the strength of battery acid, but the heat coming through the Styrofoam cup did comfort her shaking fingers.

After one cautious sip she discarded the cup. As she waited, a comment she had made earlier to Jason came back to mock her. The assertion that sisters come with a lifetime guarantee sounded very noble, but if she really meant it, why was she running out on Jennifer without so much as a goodbye? Thinking back, it was hard to recall a single time she had ever told the teenager how much their relationship meant to her.

"I owe her at least that," she muttered ruefully, digging into her purse to find a handful of change for the pay phone in the corner.

"Donaldsons' re-zi-dents," Jenny chirped breathlessly after the fifth ring.

"Hi, pumpkin, how's it going?"

"Fine. Melissa is staying over here tonight, and I'm teaching her my exercises. Mrs. P.'s making rice pudding with raisins—will you come have supper with us, Andy?"

"I can't, but eat an extra helping for me." She swallowed to rid her throat of its sudden thickness. "Has your brother called yet?"

"Uh-huh, but me and Melissa were out for a walk. He told Mrs. Pickering he wasn't quite ready to come back yet. You want to speak to her?"

What could the housekeeper possibly say that she wanted to hear? "No, I called to talk with you. I love you very much, Jenny. No matter what happens, I always will."

"You sound funny, Andy. Are you crying?"

"No," she lied.

There was a hesitation at the other end, then, "You and Bubba and me and the baby aren't going to be a four, are we?" Jennifer said slowly.

"Sometimes things just won't work out the way we want them to, honey. I have to go away for a while, but I'll come back to visit you." Andrea grasped the receiver so tightly that her knuckles showed white. "Don't be angry with Bubba, because this isn't his fault. I want you to love him and take very good care of him."

"I will, but who's gonna take care of you and our baby?"

The poignant question roused the doubts that had slumbered fitfully at the edge of her consciousness for the past few days. What kind of future could she hope to give her child if she were alone, particularly if it were handicapped? And even if the baby were perfectly normal, it still would be robbed of the nurturing a loving father could give. "Don't worry—we'll both be fine," she faltered.

"Bubba is gonna be real sad 'cause you aren't here. How can I make him feel better?"

"T-tell him..." The words did not seem to want to come out, but Andrea forced them. "Just say that I'll always remember the daffodils."

THE MECHANIC'S SKILL and a few fervent prayers from its driver coaxed the temperamental vehicle along the road to Gloucester. Since Andrea had been asleep for most of her only other trip to the small tidewater town, the country lane was totally unfamiliar, and the map beside her on the seat offered scant assistance.

As evening further deepened the gloom of the cloud-ladened sky, the journey assumed a frighteningly surrealistic aspect. Andy tapped the glass covering at the gas gauge worriedly, hoping to dislodge the needle from its precarious position next to the E on the dial.

"We must have taken a detour through the *Twilight Zone*, Peewee. With our luck, there'll be a couple of scaly, purple hitchhikers around the next turn," she grimly informed the tiny passenger she carried inside.

The one-way conversation engendered a sense of peace that, though fleeting and fragile as a whisper, was nonetheless real, and the ache of loneliness for Matthew became more bearable when she reminded herself that part of him was still with her.

A copse of pine dead-ended the road ahead, forcing a quick decision. "No use turning back now, kid. Let's hang a right and see where it leads."

It was a fortunate choice. Less than a mile down the rural byway, the welcoming lights of Della's Dew Drop Inn shone through the trees. The mental vision of a steaming plate of Della Shoffner's fluffy biscuits started an impatient tingle in Andrea's salivary glands, and she was pleasantly surprised to identify the sudden gnawing in her stomach as hunger; it seemed like ages since she had been enthusiastic about food.

"Well, this is an unexpected pleasure. How are things in Laurel Valley?" the café owner said, smiling as a bedraggled Andy wandered in to take a stool at the counter.

"Soggy. It's been raining for two days," she answered, focusing on a neutral topic to prevent any discussion of why she was there alone.

The ploy apparently worked; Mrs. Shoffner offered a running commentary on the vicissitudes of the weather while she swabbed the Formica surface in front of her lone customer.

To avoid the unspoken question on the other woman's face, Andy glanced around the restaurant. She immediately regretted the action; memories of the last time she occupied the booth by the window were so compelling that Matthew became an almost tangible presence.

"The special tonight is meat loaf and mashed potatoes. Would you like to try it?" Della asked.

Andrea's appetite had mysteriously vanished again. "I'll just have a chicken salad sandwich and a cup of coffee," she ordered. Then, with a wry grimace, she hastily amended, "Better make that a glass of milk instead."

Except for the slight elevation of one eyebrow, Mrs. Shoffner's face was a noncommittal mask, and she was quiet as she prepared the food with spare, efficient motions.

"Is the filling station down the road still open? I'm kind of low on gas, and I don't want to run out before I get to the cabin," Andrea said, nibbling fitfully at a wedge of bread.

Della shook her head. "If you can wait fifteen minutes till I close up, I'll drop you by Gilly's place. You can give me your keys, and tomorrow morning my nephew will gas up your car and run it over."

"That's very kind, but I wouldn't want to put you to any trouble," Andy protested.

"No trouble at all. I'm glad to do it."

The café owner disappeared into the kitchen, returning a few moments later with a brown paper sack. "Finish your milk and we'll be on our way," she said, whisking the plate with its half-eaten sandwich into the sink behind the counter.

Andy pushed the full glass aside. "I've had enough, thank you."

Della returned it to its original position. "I don't want to see a drop left," she said, the twinkle in the depths of her eyes mitigating the severity of her tone.

Andrea meekly obeyed.

She was glad that Mrs. Shoffner didn't seem inclined to talk on the short drive to the cabin; the companionable silence was far more comforting than words. After the café owner pulled to a stop in Gilly's driveway, she reached in the back seat for the brown bag.

"Just a few things for breakfast in the morning. Stir a couple of teaspoons of the chocolate syrup in your milk to kill the taste," she said with a grin.

"I don't know how I can ever repay your kindness."

"You don't have to—just pass it along."

As Andrea prepared to get out of the car, Della's hand restrained her. "Whatever it is, talk to Matthew about it, honey. When two people are really in love, there's no problem too big for them to handle together."

"I-I don't know where he is."

"That makes the two of you even. He has no idea you're here, does he?" Della said.

"He probably doesn't care one way or the other."

"Nonsense. I give Matthew a day—two, at most—before he comes to take you home," the café owner told her with a confident smile. "On your way out, be sure to stop by my place so I can say 'I told you so.'"

The assurance followed Andrea into the cabin, but as she lit a fire to knock the dank chill off the air in the living room, her doubts returned, and she stifled an impulse to try one last time to contact Matthew. The mental wounds she had already sustained were critical—why subject herself to more pain? Huddling in the recliner by the mantel, she clasped her arms across her abdomen and rocked gently back and forth, the halting lullaby on her lips soon giving way to sobs.

WHEN THE HUMAN SPIRIT can bear no more grief, it will either break or begin the process of healing. Andrea Kirkland's soul belonged to the latter category. On the fourth morning of her respite at Gilly's place, she opened her eyes, gazing at the fresh day beyond the bedroom window with a strange sense of calm.

"Let's see—I can either lie here till noon and cry or get up and fix some breakfast," she mused dispassionately.

Since her well of tears was by now bone-dry and her stomach growled ominously, she swung her legs over the side of the bed and, wriggling her feet into a pair of Gilly's outsized slippers, flapped out into the kitchen.

In the middle of cracking the last of the half-dozen eggs Della had so thoughtfully provided, it occurred to Andy that her meager funds were running out and she could no longer drift along without a plan. As much as she hated the idea, she would soon have to return to Laurel Valley to dispose of her business and close up the apartment.

The prospect of facing Matthew was still too painful to deal with, so she tiptoed around it and went on to the rest of her life. Having the baby in Cincinnati where she would be near Rosa Mascari seemed as good an option as any, and perhaps she and her parents could work through their difficulties.

"We're going to need all the family we can scrape together, Peewee," she said with a catch in her voice.

Confronting the future was proving more formidable than she expected. Rising wearily to discard the barely touched remains of her breakfast, she blocked out all thoughts and concentrated on simple physical tasks. In an hour or so, not a speck of dust remained on any surface in Gilly's cabin, and Andy's hair was freshly washed and shining. Donning jeans and the last clean T-shirt in her bag, she dumped her clothes in the washer on the back porch and wandered out into the yard.

The air was filled with the scent of the roses blooming beside the stockade fence. Andrea drew in huge gulps of it, letting the earthy sounds of busy insects fill her ears and a warm May wind blow away the shadows in her mind. Making a wide circle to avoid Henrietta's gazebo and the grassy knoll that held so many memories, she headed for Mobjack Bay.

Her pace quickened as she reached the shore, and before she knew it, she was running to release the pent-up energy inside, sneakers thudding against the sandy soil as though Satan himself were in hot pursuit.

It probably wasn't the devil, but Andy could hear someone coming up from behind—fast. She realized that she was in the middle of nowhere, with not a soul within five miles to help her. Instincts honed to a fine edge in New York took over, and without looking back, she sprinted desperately down the beach, ignoring the urgent "Wait, don't run from me!" her would-be assailant shouted out as he shortened the distance between them.

Sparkles of light danced in front of her eyes, and she staggered, knowing that she could not last much longer. But she was determined not to make it easy for the man. As a pair of muscular arms encircled her waist, she spun, fighting back with the ferocity of a she-lion protecting her young.

"Stop it before you hurt the baby," Matthew panted, clasping her wrists.

The air whooshed out of her lungs, and she fell against him weakly. "What the ... hell do ... you care?" she gasped. All things considered, she would have rather taken her chances with a mugger.

"Are you okay?"

Andrea could not tell whether concern or exertion roughened his voice, but it did not seem to matter much. When she finally caught her breath, she tried to pull back. "I'll be fine as soon as you let me go," she answered angrily.

Matt would not comply. In fact, he held her closer. "You don't know how grateful I am that you're safe. I went all the way to Cincinnati looking for you."

"How exciting for you. And did you and my parents have a nice chat about my interesting condition?" Some of the bitterness in the question was muffled as he pressed her head tenderly against his chest.

"Yep. And after your dad put away his shotgun, we got to know each other fairly well. I like the guy." He frowned down at her. "I've been worried to death about you, you little idiot. Why did you run off without telling anyone where you were going?"

She glared at him. "You've got a hell of a lot of nerve. You're the one who waltzed off to Atlanta and disappeared for two days!"

"You have a point." He loosened his hold on her and, as she backed away, looked at her levelly. "But at least I had a good reason. I went to see my father."

That at least explained why Matt had been reluctant to discuss the trip in Jennifer's presence, but as far as Andrea was concerned, it was a very lame excuse for his behavior. "How touching. And how was the big reunion—did he give you some pointers on avoiding responsibility?"

"He wasn't in shape to say much of anything until he got out of intensive care" was the unexpected reply.

Had Matthew said William Donaldson just boarded a space shuttle to Mars, Andy could not have been much more shocked.

She gulped. "What's wrong with him?"

"He had a slight heart attack. But the doctors say he'll be as good as new in a couple of months."

"I'm sorry—not that he'll be all right—I'm glad about that, of course. What I meant was . . ." She was babbling but didn't seem to be able to stop herself.

"I know what you meant." Matt shoved his hands in his pockets, an errant breeze ruffling his hair into a dark halo around his forehead. "I'm going to take Jenny down for a visit as soon as possible. You were right, sweet; I should have told her long ago."

The endearment sliced through her confusion, laying bare a cold fury that still lurked beneath. "Your father's illness does let you off the hook, doesn't it? Knowing what a dutiful son you are, I'm not surprised that you couldn't leave Big Bill's bedside for a single minute to get to a phone," she said sarcastically.

Matthew lowered his gaze to the sandy soil. "I should have gotten in touch with you."

Rage diminished, supplanted in part by anguish over what a rough time he must have had. "Then why didn't you? I would have been on the next plane to Atlanta. You needn't have gone through all that alone."

Matthew avoided her troubled eyes. "That's why I didn't call. I told you before I left—you had enough problems without taking on mine."

"Baloney! Why can't you just admit the truth? You were hoping that if you ignored my pregnancy long enough, it would go away. Well, you got your wish—my baby and I won't be around to inconvenience you much longer," she said stiffly, starting back up the beach at a brisk clip.

Matt caught up with her, reaching for her hand. "Please try to understand. When I was in Atlanta, I was so confused by my feelings for Dad. I thought I hated him, but I don't."

She jerked her arm away, walking even faster. "I could have told you that. Why even bring that up now? It has absolutely nothing to do with me or the baby."

"It has everything to do with you and the baby. I always knew Dad was a very strong man—a lot tougher than me, in fact—and if he could break under the strain of having a handicapped child, what chance did I have? I was afraid that I might fail you, and I didn't want to take the risk of losing your respect." His dark eyes begged for her understanding.

Andy avoided his gaze and continued walking, but at a slower pace. "You don't know me at all, do you? I never asked you to be invincible—all I ever wanted from you was your love.''

"I didn't think that would be enough. I always assumed that my parents had a solid relationship—neither of them showed their emotions very easily, and on the surface everything was fine. But I found out that having Jennifer was a last-ditch attempt to hold together something that had already gone sour. When she was born handicapped, it all blew apart.''

"I'm sorry you got twisted up in your parents' bad marriage, but it still doesn't change things. I intend to leave Laurel Valley as soon as I settle my business affairs.''

His eyes glinted dangerously. "Just like that, huh? I waited a long time for you to decide to take a chance on a future with me. Don't you think I deserve more than a few days to get over my hang-ups?''

Andrea stopped beneath the willow at the edge of the shore and, resting her head against the rough bark, said, "I love you, Matt, but I love this child, too. And I can't go through eight more months of pregnancy with the worry that you won't be able to accept my baby if he isn't normal.''

"Our baby," he corrected. "Peewee is half mine, you know.''

His use of the diminutive was both unexpected and touching. "How did you know his nickname?''

"If I thought it would help my case, I'd say I love you so much I can read your mind, but I'd better stick with the truth. Jason told me," Matt admitted, grinning crookedly. He reached for her, gathering her to him as though she were made of porcelain.

She did not resist.

"Since you have sole custody of Peewee for the moment, there's not much I can do if you want to take her away from me, but you can't stop me from giving her the present I brought back from Atlanta," Matt said softly, leading Andrea toward Henrietta's gazebo.

As they neared the hexagonal structure, Andrea saw red roses—dozens of them—spilling across the railings in bright confusion.

"I wanted to bring you daffodils, but they're out of season now. Jenny gave me your message." He stopped walking long enough to brush her mouth lightly with his lips.

"Is that how you found me?"

"It was a good clue. I still wasn't sure you would be here until Della Shoffner called yesterday. She told me if I didn't get my butt to Gloucester by nine o'clock this morning I'd be in hot grease up to my eyeballs."

Andrea smiled tremulously. "You're late. It's almost eleven."

"I've been sitting here since eight-thirty waiting for you to wake up. I'm already in enough trouble without getting bawled out for disturbing your beauty rest," he said ruefully, pulling her into the gazebo.

Completely surrounded by flowers, Wild Willie's infant seat was propped on the bench, and strapped into it was one of the scruffiest, most pathetic-looking teddy bears Andrea had ever encountered. One ear was hanging by a thread, and a bit of gray fluff showed through the bursting seam of a leg, but its stitched-on smile was still jaunty, and the baby-sized UCLA Bruins sweatshirt it wore was brand new.

"This is No-Doz. When I was a kid, I slept with him because he was always awake to watch out for the monsters behind the closet door," Matthew explained, unbuckling the stuffed animal from its perch and handing it to her. "Dad kept him all these years—said it reminded him of how much he had lost."

She returned the unblinking gaze, then hugged the bear to her, a sudden spate of tears dampening her cheeks.

"When the baby is born, will you give it to her? I want her to feel safe when she goes to sleep." Matt's voice was wistful.

Andy shook her head and returned No-Doz to its rightful owner. "Peewee will feel safer if his father's there to tuck him in at night. You give it to him."

If the teddy bear could have talked, he most surely would have offered a few irate words of protest over being squeezed so tightly between them. And the embrace they shared would have been a candidate for the *Guiness Book of Records*, had anyone been around to clock it.

Swooping Andrea from her feet, Matthew carried her to the hill above the gazebo.

"Peewee will be as beautiful as her mother," he said kissing her eyelids as he laid her gently on the grassy slope and settled down beside her.

Andy wrinkled her nose. "Suppose she inherits her father's shoulders?"

"Well, at least we won't have to save up for her wedding." He sighed, then brightening, added, "But our daughter could be the first female quarterback in Redskins' history."

"It's a moot point, because Peewee is definitely a boy," she told him firmly; then her teasing smile faded. "I don't really care. I just hope our baby's—"

Matthew's lips stopped the wish before she could finish voicing it, and though his dark eyes were now shadowed, his fingers were gentle as he caressed the curve of her waist. "Whatever happens, we'll face it together, sweet. Peewee is a gift, and even though we might not be able to guarantee her perfect life, at least our daughter will have two parents who love her—and each other."

"Son," Andrea corrected.

They both smiled.

Then cried a little.

And then they made love.

Epilogue

In some ways things had changed a lot in five years: Jason and Sara Markham had moved to the West Coast and were now busily expanding Weddings Unlimited to every nook and cranny of California, where the latest franchise would open in Burbank in time for the June matrimony boom. And, intent on making up all the time they had missed, the Gills had hardly set foot in Virginia since their honeymoon trip to Europe. Their last letter home had included a snapshot of Henrietta in front of the Pyramid of Cheops, smiling primly at the camera from her perch atop a camel.

The grapevine was still as active as ever, though, and the current scandal that rocked the sleepy town revolved around Wild Willie MacDougal's landslide victory to the office of mayor. After the election, Winona Bellamy had tossed convention and her husband aside to run off with a retired tobacco auctioneer, and Agnes-Avant-Your-Landlady was now doing her very best to make the former Hizzoner forget his double loss.

But in all the ways that really counted, Laurel Valley was exactly the same. One of the main social events was still the Oratorio Society's yuletide pageant, and on the afternoon of Christmas Eve, everyone in town—including the Donaldsons over on Beech Avenue—were getting ready for it.

"Peewee, that halo belongs on your head, not around your neck. Now, will you hold still so I can get these wings straight?"

Andrea demanded, wondering why her son was so uncharacteristically out of sorts.

"I'm not going to be Peewee anymore 'cause that's a baby name. I'm Matthew Donaldson, just like my daddy," the child announced, folding chubby arms across his chest.

She smiled, unable to refute the assertion; the only trait he had inherited from his mother was a pair of gray eyes, which at the moment happened to be stormy.

"And I'm not no angel, neither!" her son said, shaking his dark curls adamantly.

"Ain't that the truth." Matt came into the living room with a plate of cookies in one hand, and a load of serious-looking camera equipment in the other. Setting his burdens on the coffee table, he grinned and knelt to tip the tinfoil-wrapped circle of cardboard to a rakish angle over his son's eyebrow. "Your halo is not the only thing that's bent out of shape. What are you so mad about, my man?"

"Me and Lisa was playing superheroes, but Gran wouldn't let us alone. She's upstairs now trying to teach Lisa how to knit. I'll be glad when Gran goes back to Sinz-natty—she kisses too much," his heir informed him with a scowl.

Andy pruned her mouth to keep from laughing and telegraphed a silent message of sympathy through the ceiling to their eight-year-old adopted daughter. Margaret Kirkland may not have been enthralled with motherhood, but she had taken to grandparenting with a vengeance.

"You're lucky. My Aunt Luvenia used to kiss me *and* pinch my jaws," Matt confided with a playful demonstration. "Would a cookie make you forget your troubles?"

Peewee's fingers hovered hesitantly over the assortment on the plate. "Which ones did Mommy make?" he asked almost fearfully.

"Mrs. Pickering baked the gingerbread clowns, and I did all the rest," Andrea said, pursing her lips.

Matthew Junior carefully picked off the last gingerbread man and plopped down on the couch, munching contentedly on a leg.

"When are Jenny and What's-His-Face supposed to get here?" Matt asked, his voice a touch glum as he hauled a tripod out of the closet and started setting up a spotlight to illuminate the area beside the Christmas tree.

Lately Jennifer had been dating David Chatham, one of her neighbors in the independent-living complex where she had resided for the past year, and her brother was doing his best to ignore the growing closeness of the relationship.

"Big Bill and Pop went to pick them up ten minutes ago. Can the What's-His-Face stuff—his name is David, and I have the feeling he is going to be your brother-in-law one of these days," Andy said reprovingly.

Matt's grin was sheepish as he walked over and drew his wife into his arms. "I promise I'll behave. David is a nice guy, and if Jenny's happy with him, so am I," he said, pushing aside the weight of her hair to nibble her neck.

"Yuck," Peewee commented, watching the caress with a disgusted grimace.

"There's my other little angel," Andrea's mother cooed as, with a long-suffering Lisa firmly in tow, she descended the stairs and made a beeline for the couch. When she was comfortably ensconced with a grandchild on either side, she beamed at her son-in-law. "You're setting up to take pictures, aren't you?"

"You bet. This is the first time the whole family has gotten together for Christmas, and we have to have a portrait to commemorate the occasion," Matt answered, sending his wife a sunshine-and-daffodil smile that speeded the pace of her heart considerably.

"When you have them developed, would you send us two copies? I'd like to give one to Rosa Mascari. You remember her, don't you, Andy?"

"Of course, Mother. What a wonderful idea."

"She and Tony have been lonely since the children all left, so Henry and I try to keep them busy. Rosa's showing me how to make cannoli, and I'm teaching her bridge." Margaret's gray eyes held a hint of wistfulness as she added, "It's too bad we wasted so much time before we got to be friends. She's one of a kind."

"So are you, Mother," Andrea said softly. "I'm glad you and Pop could come this year."

Margaret seemed uncomfortable with the compliment, but it was obvious that she was pleased. Flushing, she changed the subject. "My baby's hearing aids still aren't working properly, Andy. I mentioned it the day after Henry and I got here, but apparently you haven't seen fit to do anything about it."

"I'll check right now." Andrea sighed, beckoning for Lisa to come to her.

Eschewing her spot on the couch with a relieved grin, the lovely little girl obeyed, bouncing over to her mother with an energy that set her mop of red curls dancing.

Please don't snitch on me, Mommy. It was the only way I could shut Gran up. Lisa's blue eyes were pleading and the silent motions of her lips were accompanied by rapid gestures of her small fingers signing the urgent request.

Andrea struggled to keep a straight face as she inspected the equipment that augmented her daughter's severely limited hearing, a congenital handicap. The tiny switch was set in the Off position. "Hmm, your batteries are shot, Peaches. We'll get a fresh set next week."

"Henry and I are leaving day after tomorrow—how will I be able to communicate with my darling girl? Can't you get them today?" Gran's tone was anguished.

Matt entered the conspiracy. "We buy the batteries at a shop in Richmond, Margaret. But Lisa and Peewee would be happy to start teaching you sign language. Show your grandmother how it's done, kids."

More than hand signals flowed between the two children as they stood up to comply. Peewee had been a year old when Lisa became a Donaldson, and from the first moment he laid eyes on her, he had been her willing slave. His big sister was no less enthralled with Matthew Junior, and the bond between them could not have been stronger if it were one of blood and bone.

After a rapid exchange, the two of them started to giggle. Matt added a hearty guffaw, but Andrea's reaction to the silent conversation was an indignant "Hhumph!"

"What did Lisa say, Peewee?" Margaret asked eagerly.

With a cherubic smile that belied the deviltry in his gray eyes, Matthew Junior kissed his grandmother's cheek, then, gingerly lifting the plate from the coffee table, set it carefully in her lap. "She told me to give you one of Mommy's cookies."

Harlequin Romance ®

Delightful

Affectionate

Romantic

Emotional

Tender

Original

Daring

Riveting

Enchanting

Adventurous

Moving

Harlequin Romance—the
series that has it all!

HROM-G

HARLEQUIN 🌸 PRESENTS®

HARLEQUIN PRESENTS
men you won't be able to resist falling in love with...

HARLEQUIN PRESENTS
women who have feelings just like your own...

HARLEQUIN PRESENTS
powerful passion in exotic international settings...

HARLEQUIN PRESENTS
intense, dramatic stories that will keep you turning
to the very last page...

HARLEQUIN PRESENTS
The world's bestselling romance series!

Bette Midler
and
Harry Kipper

When Bette Midler and Harry Kipper first met,
Kipper didn't even know who Midler was. Later, in a
Los Angeles club, sparks started to fly. After seeing
each other full-time for about two months, Kipper
proposed, and they left by car that evening for
Las Vegas. They arrived about two in the morning
and were married in The Candlelight Wedding Chapel
by a minister who moonlighted as an
Elvis impersonator.

In her biography, titled *Bette*, she said, "For the first
couple of weeks after we got married it was 'Uh-oh,
what did we do?' There were some rough spots, but
we didn't stop talking; we did our compromising.
Fortunately, we liked what we got to know. Since I got
married, I say thank you every night to God or
whoever it is who's listening up there."

B-BETTE